April,

SMART *and* SEXY

So great to meet you!
Jill Shalvis

SMART *and* SEXY

JILL SHALVIS

KENSINGTON PUBLISHING CORP.
http://www.kensingtonbooks.com

BRAVA BOOKS are published by

Kensington Publishing Corp.
850 Third Avenue
New York, NY 10022

All Kensington titles, imprints and distributed lines are available at special quantity discounts for bulk purchases for sales promotion, premiums, fund-raising, educational or institutional use.

Special book excerpts or customized printings can also be created to fit specific needs. For details, write or phone the office of the Kensington Special Sales Manager: Kensington Publishing Corp., 850 Third Avenue, New York, NY 10022. Attn. Special Sales Department. Phone: 1-800-221-2647.

Brava and the B logo Reg. U.S. Pat. & TM Off.

ISBN-13: 978-0-7582-1445-4
ISBN-10: 0-7582-1445-6

First Kensington Trade Paperback Printing: April 2007
10 9 8 7 6 5 4 3 2 1

Printed in the United States of America

SMART *and* SEXY

Chapter 1

Noah Fisher needed a double-diamond ski slope, a hot ski-bunny babe, and a beer, and not necessarily in that order.

Mammoth Mountain, here he came.

He studied the gauges in front of him, then stroked the dash of his favorite Piper. "Don't worry, baby. The weather's going to hold for us."

Hopefully.

He put on his headset, then took a moment to lean back and draw in a deep breath. His first flight in six months. Man, he was ready to get into the sky, heading for that desperately needed R&R.

R&R, and hopefully that ski bunny . . .

With that in mind, he okayed his takeoff and began to taxi down the runway, the scent of the burrito Maddie had left for him on the copilot's seat making his mouth water. Within five minutes, he was ten thousand feet and counting as he headed toward his utter freedom.

God, he loved, *loved*, being up here. Here there were no distractions, no memories, nothing but a spattering of cotton-ball clouds and azure sky as far as he could see.

Just what the doctor had ordered.

He checked the instruments and then the horizon. Ah, yeah,

conditions were good. The Piper was doing her thing, as always. She was a classic, though not necessarily a beauty, which meant that most of their customers wouldn't have given her a second look.

Their loss.

She flew like a dream. He could fix her up real pretty, he knew, and then everyone would be clamoring for her, but he didn't feel the need to share her.

As he leveled out, he grabbed a stowed-away chocolate bar to munch on before the burrito. He'd always eaten his dessert first, because hell, once upon a time, he hadn't known when and where his next meal would come from. Chewing, he began to picture the weekend ahead: the slopes, the wind in his face, powdery snow up to his knees as he plowed straight down the mountain, his hair blown back by his own speed. . . .

Then he pictured the sexy ski bunnies waiting in the warm lodge afterward, and one of those rare but genuine smiles tugged at his mouth.

Yeah, a sexy ski bunny—or two—was key to this whole event. She'd be an expert in erotic massage, of course, and ready, willing, and able to do . . . well, pretty much whatever came to mind.

And plenty did.

At the thought, he actually smiled again.

Yes sirree, his muscles were getting quite the workout today, after six long months of neglect. Thanks to his crash, it'd been a long time since he'd fantasized about women, or even craved sex at all—

A rustle sounded from behind Noah, startling the shit out of him, but before he could react, something jammed into his shoulder, something that unbelievably felt an awful lot like a—

Gun?

"Keep flying," said a ragged voice. "Just keep flying."

Holy shit. Noah craned his neck. The soft, fuzzy blanket he kept on the backseat was on the floor now. She'd been hiding beneath it, and yeah, the person behind him was most definitely a she. Once upon a time, he'd been considered an expert on the species, and despite her gruff, uneven tones, her voice shimmered with nerves.

Female nerves.

Unbelievably, he'd just been hijacked by a nervous woman with a gun. He tried to get a good look at her, but the gun shifted to his jaw, shoving his head forward before he could take in more than a big, bulky sweater with a hood down low over her face—

"Don't turn around," she demanded. "Just keep us in the air."

He could. He'd been a pilot ever since the day he'd been old enough, flying on a daily basis, either for a job or on a whim, into a storm or with one on his ass, without much thought.

He was giving it plenty of thought now. "Hell, no." His fingers tightened on the yoke. *Goddamnit.* "What the fuck is this?"

"You're flying me to Mammoth Mountain."

"Hell, no, I'm not."

"Yes, you are. You have no choice." Then she let out a disparaging, desperate sound and softened her voice. "Look, just get us there, okay? Get us there and everything will be all right."

Yeah, except that she didn't sound as if she believed that line of crap, and he sure as hell didn't believe it either. Worse, he suddenly had a nasty flashback to another of his flights that had gone bad, six months ago. Only in that one, there'd been no gun, just a hell of a storm in Baja Mexico, where he'd hit a surprise thunderstorm, one with a vicious kick. That time he'd ended up on a side of a mountain in a fiery crash, holding his passenger as she died in his arms. . . .

So really, in comparison, this flight, with a measly gun at his back, should be a piece of cake. Just a day in the life.

Knowing it, he swiped a forearm over his forehead and concentrated on breathing. Maybe she was all talk, no show. Maybe she didn't really know how to use the weapon. Maybe he could talk her out of the insanity that had become his life today. "How did you get in here?"

The gun remained against his shoulder, but not as hard, as if maybe she didn't want to hurt him. "No questions, or I'll—"

"What? *Shoot?*"

She didn't answer.

Yeah, all talk, no show, he decided, and reached over to switch his radio on, then went very still at the feel of the muzzle just beneath his jaw now.

"Don't," she said, sounding more desperate, if that was even possible. "Don't tell anyone I'm here."

Hell if he'd suffer this quietly, and he braced himself for action, but then she added a low, softly uttered, "*Please.*"

Jesus, he felt like such a fool. Who the hell was she? She'd been careful to stay just behind him, just out of range of his peripheral. He could smell her, though, some complicated mixture of exotic flowers and woman, which under very different circumstances he'd find sexy as hell.

But not today, the day that was quickly turning into a living nightmare. He couldn't believe this was happening. Not when he was getting back on the horse. Wasn't that what Shayne and Brody had told him to do, *get back on the horse.*

And he had.

Was.

Hence the ski/fuck-his-brains-out weekend.

What the hell was in Mammoth that was worth hijacking someone? And why was she so desperate to get there? Instinct had him checking the gauges, looking for a place to land.

"No." The gun was an emphasis, back to pressing hard between his shoulder blades. "We're going to Mammoth. Just like you planned."

"I didn't plan for this."

"You have a passenger now, that's all. Everything else is the same."

Yeah, he had a passenger. A shaking, unnerved, freaked-out desperate one.

Give him a thunderstorm in Cabo any day over this. . . .

"There's no need to panic, or do anything rash," she said, and he wondered if she was talking to him—or herself.

"Yeah, well, if you're insisting on coming along, then sit." He jerked his chin toward the copilot seat next to him, because he wanted to see her, wanted to know exactly what he was up against.

"I'm fine right where I am."

Hell if he'd have her at his back with a gun jammed against him for the next hour. "Sit. Down."

As if for emphasis, they hit a pocket of air, and the plane dipped. With a gasp, the woman fell backward into the seat behind him.

Noah smiled grimly. He wasn't stupid, and he hadn't been born yesterday. Actually, he hadn't even been born in this country at all, but in England. He'd ended up here, orphaned as a teen, where he'd proceeded to beg, borrow, and steal his way to his dream.

A life of flying.

And she was not going to take that life away from him.

"You did that on purpose." Her voice was tight and angry. "Don't do anything like that again."

He hadn't done it in the first place, but he could have, and *would* if he got the chance and could manage it without getting his head accidentally shot off, because he really hated it when that happened. "Who the hell are you?"

"Doesn't matter."

"What's in Mammoth?"

"Doesn't matter."

Great. A stubborn female. Who happened to have a gun.

Never a good combination.

He glanced back and wasn't happy to see her standing again, directly behind him so that he still couldn't get a good look at her.

"Don't." Once again she shoved the gun into his back, a situation of which he was quickly tiring. Right before his crash, adrenaline had pumped through him, but it was nothing compared to what flowed through his veins now.

Then he'd been scared, to the bone.

Now he was pissed. To the bone. His radio crackled, and then Shayne's voice filled the cabin. As a team called Sky High Air, they had a fleet of three jets, three Cessnas, two Beechcraft, a Moody, a Piper, and a Cirrus, and access to others via a leasing network, and had just constructed a building to house them all instead of working out of a very expensive leased wing at LAX. It gave them their own hub, a fixed operating base for their picky, finicky clientele, complete with maintenance and concierge services.

Not bad for three punks who'd once been nothing more than sorry-ass teenage delinquents.

"Noah?" Shayne asked via radio. "You there?"

"I have to answer that," he told his hijacker. "Or he'll know something's wrong." Without waiting for her response, he pushed the button on the radio. "Here."

"Just checking in on your inaugural flight."

He was doing fine. Great.

If he forgot about the gun digging into him.

"You okay?" Shayne asked.

Noah hated that his friend even had to ask, but could admit, at least to himself, that the past six months had been just rough enough that Shayne felt he had to. "I'm . . ." He pushed back at the gun. "Hanging in."

His kidnapper remained silent, tense.

"Brody's flying Mrs. Sinclair to Aspen," Shayne said. "At least so she says, but she's had us ready-up four times this past week, only to correct at the last minute. I don't see today being any different."

The idiosyncrasies of the rich and famous didn't bother him any, as long as they paid for it, but just the words "Mrs. Sinclair" made the butterflies in his stomach tap-dance.

Mr. Sinclair had been a forty-year-old trust-fund baby who'd built huge resort complexes in every party town along the West Coast while showing off his much younger trophy wife, Bailey Sinclair, an ex-model, a woman who screamed sophistication and elegance.

Not to mention her *muy caliente* factor.

But her husband had bitten the big one three months ago in a mysterious hunting accident, and they hadn't seen much of the missus since then. She was probably off spending her husband's billions of dollars, and . . . and hell.

Bailey Sinclair was intelligent, and sexy, stubborn as hell—three of Noah's favorite qualities in a woman. She had strawberry blond, wild flyaway hair that framed her face in a way that seemed as if maybe she'd just gotten out of bed and wasn't averse to going back. Her baby blues were deep enough to drown a man, and her mouth . . .

Christ, he'd had entire day-long fantasies about her mouth. Truth was, she was his living secret crush.

It was pathetic, really. Getting weak-kneed over another man's wife.

Even if that man was dead.

But he was a little busy today, so it was probably time to get over Bailey Sinclair.

Cold turkey, pal.

"She's already on board and locked up in her stateroom," Shayne said. "And if the rumors are true—"

"Rumors?"

"That she's selling everything off . . . then she's probably going for one last hurrah. Said she was taking a sleeping pill and just to wake her after arrival."

Noah could picture the sleek honey of a plane on the tarmac. It didn't take much for his imagination to go farther and see the gorgeous, lush stateroom on board, the huge king-sized bed covered in the best of the best silk, and Bailey sprawled on it, her hair streaming across a pillow, her long, willowy body barely wrapped in satin and lace—

Scratch that.

No satin, no lace.

Nothing but Bailey. Yeah, that might help him get over himself real quick.

If he lived through this, that was.

"Be careful," Shayne said.

"I will be, Mom. Thanks."

"*Mom?*"

"Better than old lady," Noah said, checking the horizon, ignoring his "passenger" while Shayne huffed out a low laugh.

"Smart-ass," he muttered, and clicked off.

Yeah, that was him: Noah Fisher, smart-ass. Among other things. And actually, he'd heard them all: selfish bastard, good-for-nothing lout, cocky SOB. . . .

That most of them were completely one-hundred-percent true didn't keep him up at night. Nope, he saved that for the nightmares, of which he now had a new one.

He glanced at his altimeter and airspeed indicator. Everything looked okay. Everything *was* okay, because he'd checked and double-checked over the static-system vents and Pitot tube for foreign bodies, like the bird that had fucked him just before his crash. All was clear right now. Good to know. He would not be crashing tonight.

"Thanks," said the woman at his back, "for not giving me away."

He did some more ignoring, and the silence filled the cockpit. Reaching out beside him, he lifted the brown bag from which came the most heavenly scent on earth—his burrito. *Bless you, Maddie,* he said silently to Sky High's concierge. She always stocked him with his favorite fast food. "Hungry?" he asked his hijacker. He hadn't had a real mother, but he still knew how to mock politeness.

"Just fly."

"Suit yourself." He opened the bag and stuffed a bite into his mouth. His taste buds exploded with pleasure, and to be as annoying as possible, he moaned with it. "You have no idea what you're missing."

"Looks like I'm missing a boatload of calories." She sounded tense enough to shatter. "Can't you fly faster?"

Yes. "No."

"How much longer?"

"As long as it takes." Taking another bite—if he was going to die, it wouldn't be hungry—he checked the instruments, the horizon.

Still no weather between here and there, and he supposed he should be thankful for small favors. "So . . . what's your story?"

She didn't respond. Shocker.

"You rob a bank?" he tried.

Nothing but the disquieting sensation of the gun against his skin.

"Kill someone?"

The silence seemed to thicken, and his gut clenched. Great, she'd killed someone. "Oh, I know," he said conversationally. "Your rich husband has a ski bunny at your Mammoth cabin, and you're going after them."

She choked out a laugh utterly without mirth. "Can you fly without talking?"

He opened his mouth to give a smart-ass reply to that, but the gun at his back pressed into him and shut him up. Yeah, okay, maybe he could fly without talking.

For now.

Chapter 2

Not wanting him to smell the fear and panic swirling around her like a cloak of fog, Bailey Sinclair focused in on the one consolation she had—

He actually believed she held a gun on him.

Good God, she was hijacking the tall, dark, and attitude-ridden Noah Fisher with her fatty Bic pen, and if the enigmatic, rough-edged pilot even caught a sniff of her false bravado, it'd be over. He would wrestle her to the seat or toss her out the window, as she deserved.

At least it'd be over.

No. No destructive thoughts. She had to see this through, *had to*, or she was going to end up in the same situation as her rat fink bastard husband.

Which was six feet under.

For the umpteenth time, she wished Alan weren't already dead, so she could kill him herself.

But someone had beaten her to that game, hadn't they. And now her own life hung in the balance.

Hope you're rotting in hell, Alan.

God. With her free hand, she hugged herself. She'd had bad days before, she reminded herself. Unfortunately, this one was shaping up to be the king of all bad days.

Bad weeks.

Bad months . . .

Actually, she could write the entire year off to a string of rotten luck piled on top of rotten decisions piled on top of the fact that Fate seemed to have it in for her.

She needed a break, just one.

And then suddenly the plane dipped again, and she nearly lost her sweaty grip on her Bic pen. "*What are you doing?*" she cried, flying backward and hitting the seat behind her.

Noah didn't answer, which pretty much did her in. Nerves already scraped raw, she desperately needed some answers, and he was going to give them to her, damn it.

Scrambling back up, she tightened her hold on the pen and jammed it hard into the muscle of his shoulder. "Answer me!"

Rolling his shoulder, he pushed back at her.

Damn it, didn't he realize? She had a *gun*.

Okay, she didn't, really, but he thought she did! Why wasn't he cowering? Begging for mercy?

She wanted to do both. She wanted to drop to the floor and roll into a ball and do something distinctly juvenile, like burst into tears.

Instead she locked her knees and thrust up her chin, reminding herself she was in charge at the moment. "Tell me what's happening."

"Weather pockets."

"What does that mean?"

"We've hit a few weather pockets," he said very slowly, as if speaking to an idiot.

"Is that bad?"

"Depends on how good a flyer you are."

"How good a flyer are you?" she asked a little weakly.

He let out a low, mirthless laugh. "Little late to be asking that."

She was just behind him, and off to the side enough to catch him in profile. And he had quite the profile. His dark hair hadn't seen a comb today, maybe not yesterday either, and yet the untamed waves would most definitely call to a woman's fingers. She knew this because they called to hers.

His striking face gave nothing away as he spoke: no alarm, no worry, no inflection at all. He was good at that, at being calm.

She knew this because he'd flown her places before, many times; he just didn't know it. She'd always admired his calm strength, his smooth, easy demeanor, and that low, husky voice with the whisper of England in it.

He handled the controls like the pro he was. The material of his shirt strained over shoulders wide enough to block her view of the horizon, and she knew without looking that his chest was broad, his stomach enticingly flat, because one time last summer she'd seen him on the tarmac stripping out of a dirty shirt, shrugging into a new one. His arms had been corded with long, steely muscles, his fingers also long and undoubtedly callused and work-roughened from all the mechanic work he often did on his plane for the joy of it.

"Thunderstorm, gathering early," he said, working the controls as the plane dipped once more, pitching as violently as her stomach.

"Ohmigod," she whispered, gripping the back of his seat.

Another dip.

She gritted her teeth and did her best not to reveal her fear. "Can't you avoid this?"

"Sure."

His voice came perfectly calm, perfectly collected, with just that curious and intoxicating hint of British in it. "I'll just call mother nature and tell her to knock it off."

In another place and time, she'd be fascinated by the sheer strength and control he was exhibiting under what had to be enormous pressure.

But right now it was all she could do not to throw herself down and give up, give in.

Let them have her.

No. No, she wasn't dead yet, damn it. She opened her mouth, but when the plane shuddered, so did she.

Oh, God.

"Are we going to crash?" she whispered.

He didn't answer, and if she'd thought her stomach had pitched before, it was nothing to the sommersault it did now in the face of his silence. "Hello?"

When he didn't answer, she sucked in a breath and nudged him with her "gun."

"Do you want me to chat, or keep us in the air?" he asked in such perfect politeness that it actually took her a moment to process the words.

"Air," she managed, nodding even though he couldn't see her. "Keep us in the air."

With a gruff nod, he did as she'd asked.

She just hoped he intended to keep doing it.

"I need to use the radio," he said after a few moments, and without waiting for her to okay that, he checked in with someone via his headset and got the weather update. She stood there on pins and needles, the pen in his shoulder, terrified he'd give her away this time.

He could have, and there was nothing she could do. She knew how close he was to the two men he ran Sky High Air with—Brody and Shayne. Hell, he could probably give her away to either of them without her even knowing it, or maybe he already had.

If so, she was as good as dead.

Chapter 3

Keeping herself standing still in that plane while Noah spoke into his headset was the hardest thing Bailey had ever done.

Any second now, he'd give her away.

But he didn't. He simply finished his radio conversation and then went back to flying.

"Thanks," she said, letting out a long breath.

He didn't speak.

"I really appreciate it." He could have no idea how much; no one did. Because no one could keep her safe. "I promise you, Noah. I don't want to hurt you."

More of his loaded nothing. It was like an art form with him, not talking unless absolutely necessary, remaining cool, calm, and collected under any circumstance, a talent she could learn from. "I just need to get to Mammoth," she said softly.

"Yes, the skiing is great this time of year."

Heavy sarcasm. Well, she couldn't blame him. Noah Fisher wasn't the kind of man who took well to being made helpless. In fact, he was the least helpless man she knew, not that she really knew him at all. . . .

On the occasions he'd piloted for her and Alan, or her younger brother Kenny, who'd worked for Alan, Noah had always been perfectly professional. Perfectly professional, and perfectly magnificent in his pilot duds, with his crisp white shirt and dark blue uniform trousers—which nicely covered his mile-long legs and firm butt.

Yes, she'd looked.

She hadn't been able to help herself; he was almost ridiculously gorgeous. And she wasn't the only one who thought so. The numerous times she'd been at Sky High Air, any and all other females around were usually doing their best to get his attention.

Interesting enough, he never seemed to notice.

He was noticing her now, and wasn't that just the irony of the whole thing. He had no idea who she was, but when—if—he found out, he was going to be all the more furious.

He'd call 9-1-1.

She couldn't let that happen. If she went to jail for this, they'd find her there. They'd promised. She let out another long, pent-up breath, purposely thinking about something else.

Noah.

He wore one of his long-sleeved, white button-downs with the Sky High Air patch on his pec. A very nice pec. A pec worthy of the rest of him. But it was his face that always captured her and held tight. His dark, wavy hair was thick, curling past his collar, nearly to his broad shoulders. And as usual, a tumble of it fell over his strong forehead and into his mesmerizing eyes, which were a clear, deep jade and always full of secrets.

Unlike her, he didn't wear his heart on his sleeve. She never had any idea what he was thinking. But she knew what *she* was thinking. She was thinking she had no business noticing that he induced drool tendencies in every woman he passed, or that his eyes, that dreamy shade of green, inspired thoughts a married woman had no right thinking. . . .

Except that she was no longer married. Nope, her husband had died.

Correction—gotten himself killed by his own greed, because Alan Sinclair had never met a gamble he could walk away from, including Bailey. This had been a well-hidden fact that she'd learned about upon Alan's death, when her own father had come clean.

Alan had dated her on a bet.

That shouldn't have hurt. Of course he'd dated her on a bet, because why in the world would a man as wealthy, as cool and sophisticated and elegant, as he'd been, be interested in her for any reason other than her father's money?

But in the end, the laugh had been on Alan, hadn't it? Because her father's "wealth" had all been an illusion, and Alan had fallen for that illusion—hook, line, and sinker.

But the deal had been made. He'd married her and forgiven her father's debt. He'd even given her brother a job when Kenny hadn't been able to find a direction for himself.

She'd been sheltered from the details, and as a model at the time, traveling a lot, she'd also been fairly clueless. But Alan had always been kind and sweet to her, and after a lifetime of living with her volatile, quick-tempered father, that kindness and sweetness had gone a long way with her.

Very long.

She'd given up modeling to stay in the States to be near her husband, unhappily surprised to realize that *he* traveled incessantly as well. So she'd gone back to school to pass the time and had found her passion—teaching.

Yes, Alan had been slightly distant during the two years they'd been married, and gone much of that, and yes, he'd held a lot of himself back, including almost all of his business dealings, but she'd told herself that a husband and wife didn't share everything.

Her parents certainly hadn't.

Besides, she had her life, teaching second grade, and that was enough for her. She'd been happy.

Or so she'd thought.

But then Alan had left for a hunting trip, first giving her a rare hug, looking her deeply in the eyes. "Whatever you need after I'm gone," he'd said. "I've kept it all safe, Precious."

She never saw him again.

After his death, she'd sat in his attorney's office, shocked to the core to find her father hadn't been the only illusionist.

Nope, when Alan's will had been read, it had turned out he was flat broke, and worse, owed his investors big-time.

Which had been especially bad news for Bailey, because now she was about to be flat dead if she didn't come up with some serious dough for them.

They'd come to her, late two nights ago, and had demanded the money, prepared to kill her if she couldn't provide it. So she'd lied, said she could get it but she needed time.

They'd bought that.

Now if she didn't come up with the money, they were going to take it out of her skin, and with the scare they'd given her, when they'd broken into what she'd thought was the impenetrable fortress of their Burbank Hills house, she believed every word.

Especially since they hadn't been nameless strangers, but some of Alan's longtime friends, his "investors," led by the smooth, elegant Stephen Stonehelm.

At first she couldn't believe that Stephen, whom she'd entertained and socialized with on numerous occasions, was going to seriously turn on her.

But he had, with ice-cold eyes and a colder voice, making it clear that if she told anyone, especially the police, then she, along with Kenny and her students, would start appearing as dead as Alan.

It was simple, really—pay them back or die.

Slowly, painfully.

And yet she couldn't pay back what she didn't have. She'd called Kenny, terrified for his safety. Since Alan's death, he'd been moving around, working carpentry here and there, not sticking in any one spot.

Bailey had said nothing about how much she missed him because he seemed content with his new direction or lack thereof. But now she was worried that wherever he was, he wasn't far enough away.

"Get out of town," he'd said urgently when she'd told him what had happened. "Get out of town and stay out until this thing blows over. I'll come back and—"

"No. That's what I wanted to tell you." Terror had filled her at the thought of him being anywhere near Alan's thugs. "You've got to stay away. Please, Kenny. I can't lose you, too."

"Bailey—"

"I'll go," she'd promised him rashly, knowing that was the only way to guarantee he stay gone. "I'll go if you promise to stay far away."

"Check in with me," he'd demanded. "Text me if you can't call, let me know where you are."

"I'll be fine."

"Promise. Promise me, Bail."

She'd made that promise, and they'd been in touch by text messages at least every other day.

Small comfort.

She'd called into work for a substitute teacher, saying she had a horrible flu and needed at least a week off. No way was she going to endanger the children she'd come to love and care about as her own.

That had turned out to be a good decision, because now she had the feeling that she was being followed—everywhere she went she experienced an itch between her shoulder blades.

They were watching her, waiting for her to find the money.

She needed to get on that.

She'd thought long and hard. If Alan had stashed money—and he'd been just tight enough to do something like that—

then where? Their house was too obvious; plus it was now up for sale, and every inch of it had been gone over, cleaned, redone. It had to be at one of his resorts. All had been sold except the ones in Mammoth, Catalina, and Cabo.

Kenny agreed that it was entirely likely that the money was in one of those last places. She'd started with Mammoth simply because when she'd gotten to Sky High Air, that was where Noah had been going.

She'd put out word that she was going to Aspen to throw the thugs off her tail and had hitched a ride with him.

So to speak.

Noah kept his gaze straight ahead, dividing his concentration between the horizon and his controls, flicking switches, doing whatever it was he was doing to keep them in the air.

"The sooner we're there," she told him, "the sooner you're free of me."

"How did you know my name?"

"I—I don't."

"Liar," he said very softly. "You called me by name a few minutes ago." Apparently no longer afraid of her, or caring that she had her "weapon" pressed against him, he turned his head and looked right at her.

And she let him.

Maybe it was exhaustion, or the fact that her head hurt from all that was racing through it. Or maybe she simply couldn't make room for one more fear—that being that he would let them crash.

He wouldn't. He loved living too much.

She was banking on that.

His gaze traveled from the hood low over her face, to her jeans, to her boots and back, before he looked at the horizon again, jaw tight.

She knew why. He'd looked, but he still couldn't ID her. That was what happened when she wasn't all vamped up; she was a nobody. If she lived through this mess, she was going to love being a nobody. She'd spend the rest of her days happily being a nobody.

"You might as well have a seat," he said, gesturing to the spot at his right. "Now that I can identify you to the authorities."

"Now who's the liar?"

He swore, and kept flying. "You're not going to get away with this."

"I have to."

He glanced over at her, utterly bewildered and baffled. "Why? Why do you have to do this?"

"It's complicated." The understatement of the century.

"You're late for a manicure?"

"You wouldn't believe me if I told you," she said grimly.

"Try me."

She stared at him, wishing she could. Wishing a lot of things . . .

"I know. You've got a hot date on the slopes."

"No, that's you." She knew he planned to ski his brains out, then hopefully screw his brains out. That the thought had given her an odd ping didn't matter. What he did after he got her to Mammoth didn't concern her.

"At least it's not a date with the cops," he said. "You've committed quite a few felonies today, Ms. Hijacker."

She'd wondered, several times today alone, if being dead would be easier than being in prison. But despite appearances, she'd never taken the easy way out in her life.

Inside her pocket, her cell vibrated, signaling an incoming text message. She pulled it out and read Kenny's message: *R U in Aspen yet? K*

She swallowed the lump of fear. He was still safe. *Safe*, she repeated to herself, and that was all that mattered. For now, at least, they were both safe.

Inhaling a deep breath, she thumbed a *yes* in answer, because she needed the world to think she was in Aspen. Carefree.

She hoped to God that Kenny was carefree on an island somewhere soaking up the sun, free of trouble.

She didn't want *her* trouble landing on his head.

Unfortunately, Kenny attracted trouble like a moth to flame. He always had. He'd probably gotten that special gift from their father, she thought with some bitterness.

Thanks, Dad.

Ironically enough, Kenny had stayed trouble-free while working for Alan, but now he was directionless again, and that terrified her. But that was a worry for another day.

Say if she lived.

"Please," she begged Noah, forgetting for a moment that she was supposed to be in charge. "Please, just do this. Just get me to Mammoth."

"And then . . . ?"

And then, she would hopefully find the money, hand it over to the bad guys, and go back to teaching second grade, go back to her quiet, sweet little world where bad things didn't happen to good people.

He was waiting for an answer, so she swallowed hard. "And then you'll land and let me go."

"And you'll what, ride off into the sunset?"

"You'll never hear from me again, I swear. No need to turn me in."

"Other than the whole kidnapping thing."

"You were going to Mammoth anyway," she pointed out.

He looked at her, his green, green eyes utterly unfathomable, cool, and assessing, his mouth in a tight line of unforgiving grimness. "Just for curiosity's sake, why don't you tell me what else I'd be turning you in for? You know, besides hijacking and assault with a deadly weapon."

Deadly weapon, with a fat Bic pen.

He was going to be royally pissed if he ever figured out that her gun was nothing but blue ink and plastic. At the thought, a half-manic giggle bubbled up, but she managed to swallow it. God, she was so tired, exhausted really, and she gave in to her trembling legs, sinking into the seat next to him.

Noah was watching her, his aviator sunglasses shoved to the top of his head, which kept his hair out of his eyes.

His oddly mesmerizing eyes.

Yeah, she was losing it if she was noticing his eyes. She'd had enough of men. In fact, if she lived, she never wanted another man again.

Never. Ever.

The sheer, bone-deep exhaustion weighed her down. Staying alive was damn hard work. Too hard, and for a second, just a second, she let her head fall back to the seat. The movement had her hood slipping off. She jerked upright immediately, but it was too late.

He'd seen.

"*Jesus Christ.*" His eyes widened in recognition and shock, but his attention was jerked forward when the plane bobbed and dipped. He spent a moment dealing with keeping the plane steady in the sudden turbulence.

But what was lethally turbulent was her stomach.

"*Bailey Sinclair.*" He shook his head, his body tense as he continued to handle the plane, his legs working the rudders on the floor, his arms taut on the steering wheel, or whatever it was called on a plane, his entire body piloting while his eyes remained focused on her. "What the fuck sort of game is this?"

She drew a deep breath. "No game," she said quietly. "I swear to you, this is no game."

He took a moment to run his gaze over her features. "Goddamnit." His jaw tightened. "I don't get this. Start at the beginning."

"I need a ride to Mammoth."

"Earlier than that."

Right. Yet another bubble of hysterical laughter tickled her throat, but she held it back because she was afraid that once she started, she'd never stop, and then she'd probably cry, and then . . . well, she didn't have time for any pity.

Hadn't in a good long time.

"This is where you talk," he prompted.

He had his sleeves shoved up, his forearms corded with strength, his hands working the controls like a pro. He wasn't a man who did anything halfway. He knew his way around a plane, the way she imagined he knew his way around anything he set his mind to. He was sharp, intelligent, and street rough.

If anyone in her world could possibly hear her problems and help her figure them out, it was this man.

But still, she hesitated. Yes, telling him would release a burden, and maybe, just maybe, get her some desperately needed help.

Good plan.

Except it could also kill him.

Bad plan.

No way was she going to jeopardize another person.

She was unequipped to deal with this. She'd grown up in a quiet, affluent neighborhood and had gone to a small, private college before marrying Alan and moving to yet a different quiet, affluent neighborhood.

She was so out of her league. She had no idea what to do. She knew she needed to tell Noah just enough to ensure he wouldn't turn her in, but not enough to get him involved.

Was that even possible?

Looking into his stormy eyes, she had to wonder if she could get anything past this man, especially a lie. "It's not important for you to know the details."

He swore again.

"Just get me there," she said. "You'll never see me again, I promise."

He didn't say anything to that.

Good sign. Or so she told herself, and a ridiculous amount of an emotion she nearly didn't recognize burgeoned through her veins.

Hope. He was going to do this, and he'd be okay.

Then he looked at her. If she'd been standing, she'd have staggered back.

Jaw tight, eyes flashing fury and a promised retribution that made her swallow hard as a little frisson of alarm buzzed through her, he said, "I won't make this easy for you. That's *my* promise."

Chapter 4

Noah still couldn't quite believe his eyes, but she sat there in the flesh, wild strawberry blond hair rioting around her proud, terrified, nervous-as-hell face.

Bailey Sinclair's face.

He should know; he'd stared at her often enough. Those aristocratic cheekbones, the fantasy mouth, the eyes that said she was so much, much more than a model and sex kitten wife of a playboy. The baggy, oversized sweatshirt and jeans had thrown him, but still, he kicked himself for not realizing.

The odd thing was, he had known. Somehow, deep down, some hidden away part of him *had* recognized her, which really got him.

Women didn't get under his skin. In fact, not much did. Until six months ago, he'd been Sky High Air's most requested pilot for a very good reason—he'd traveled far and wide all his life and exuded those experiences he'd had in every step he took. He'd never settled down, never called one particular place home, and had never wanted to.

Until the crash.

Yeah, that had changed things. He just hadn't quite figured out how, or what to do with it yet.

"Noah," Bailey said, clearly shaken. "Just get me to Mammoth. That's all I'm asking."

"You can't force me to fly you there—"

"*But you were going anyway!*"

He stared at her, then let out a laugh of pure disbelief. She really believed that line of crap. "Is this going to be your defense? Because honestly, Princess, insanity might be a better plea."

She stared right back, then seemed to sag in on herself. "I'm sorry," she whispered, those lush lips trembling as she spoke to him. "I'm so sorry, Noah, about all of it. It's just that I need everyone to think I'm on that other flight, to Aspen. I was going to secretly drive to Mammoth, but I couldn't get cash, and I couldn't use a credit card, and even if I had, it could have been traced, and I needed to hurry . . . *God.*" She rubbed her temples, and then something happened that was like a punch to his gut.

Her eyes filled.

Christ, not the waterworks. He'd always been helpless against the waterworks. Helpless and clueless, two of his least favorite things to be. And that this was Bailey, his secret fantasy woman, didn't help. He had visions of pulling her close, and not all for comfort.

Idiot.

Seriously, he was a complete idiot to be letting his thoughts go there. He could rush her now, he knew, in her moment of weakness. He could take the gun out of her sweatshirt pocket and overtake her—and probably not crash while he was at it.

Yet something held him back. He wanted to say it had nothing, nothing at all to do with the fact that she'd always made him uncomfortably hot, but he couldn't because it was more than that, way more than the *caliente* factor of Bailey Sinclair's outer package.

Her eyes were wide, her pupils dilated so that he could

hardly see a ring of that sky blue around the black. Her breathing was coming in short little pants, her full lips trembling slightly. Her skin was flushed. Dewy. Damp.

It could have aroused him.

Okay, it *did* arouse him, but she was clearly stressed to the point of shattering, and then the coup de grace—the utter abject terror in her eyes.

Someone had either laid their hands on her or had threatened to.

He hated that. Hated that she was genuinely terrified, and utterly sincere in her urgency.

And in spite of himself, every protective instinct reared its hasty, impulsive head.

Christ. Curiosity had killed the cat, and it just might kill him yet. "Keep talking," he said against his better judgment, doing his best to keep the plane steady and smooth in the gathering thunderstorm that had arrived early.

Shit, what a day.

She swallowed hard, moistened her dry lips with her tongue. Noah told himself not to notice. *Ordered* himself not to notice.

"It's about . . . my finances," she said.

She'd had a rich husband who'd probably left her billions. What could she possibly have to worry about? "What's the matter, the trust fund interest rate go down and you have to give up sushi?"

"It's gone."

"The sushi?"

"The trust fund."

Uh huh. "What happened?"

"My thieving, lying, conniving bastard of a husband happened."

Okay, this part was new. Noah hadn't known Alan from Dick, but the guy had always seemed friendly and charismatic, drawing people to him like bees to honey. "You're saying that Alan was some sort of a thieving, lying, conniving bastard?"

"Yes. Before he got himself dead and buried."

Domestic trouble? The thought made his stomach clench, but Alan had been gone for months. "What does this have to do with Mammoth?"

At that, she rolled her lips together and broke eye contact.

Ah, hell. In his experience, that meant one thing. She was going to start lying. Or maybe just omitting, but neither appealed.

"I have to get something from his resort there," she said, still not looking at him.

Definitely omitting. "Something? Or someone?"

"Like who?" she asked.

"I don't know, you tell me."

"No, it's a something, and, um . . ." More looking away. "I have to get it quickly. Like yesterday quickly."

"As in hijack-a-pilot quickly?"

"I didn't hijack you," she said with a primness that made him want to laugh—if there'd been anything remotely funny about this situation. "You were going anyway," she said in the same old refrain.

He slid her a long glance.

She broke eye contact again.

"Okay," he said, deciding to bite. "So what is this 'something' you have to get quickly?"

She put her nose to the window. "Are we almost there?"

"Done talking, are we?" he asked dryly.

She didn't answer.

Yeah, apparently, she was done talking. She'd definitely omitted plenty, leaving out a whole bunch of her story, including how the hell she'd gotten herself roughed up and by whom.

Not his problem, he reminded himself, even if just looking

at her invoked Superman tendencies. He was going to Mammoth for some desperately needed R&R.

And a ski bunny.

Nothing else, including saving damsels in distress.

With that thought, he began landing preparations, calling in for confirmation. He reduced power and lowered the flaps, controlling the nose, maintaining altitude, but in yet another unwelcome turn of events, the landing gear didn't lower.

Un-fucking-believable. He flicked the switch again, prepared to adjust the trim at the drag to stabilize the nose again, but nope, the landing gear definitely did not lower. "*Shit.*"

"What?" she asked.

He looked into her lovely, terrified face. How to tell her they might be landing on their belly? Well, truthfully, it wasn't the worst thing that had happened to him. "Come here."

"Why?" asked his suspicious little hijacker.

There was no sugarcoating the insanity. "We have a little problem."

"That's an oxymoron when you're in the air."

He let out a mirthless laugh. "Yeah. Listen, the landing gear didn't lower."

Her mouth fell open.

"I need you to fly the plane while I go crank it down manually." Crank, kick . . . whatever it took.

The color drained completely out of her face. "Ohmigod. Without the landing gear, we can't land. Right?"

"Sure we can; we just do it on our belly. Not nearly as smooth, though, trust me."

She swallowed hard. "That's nowhere close to a little problem."

"Compared to falling out of the sky, it is. Get over here, Princess."

"Can you really fix it?"

"Yeah. I've seen a guy do it once or twice."

"Omigod!"

"I'm kidding! Yes, I can fix it. If you get over here."

"Noah—"

The plane shuddered. More turbulence. *Perfect.* "Now, goddamnit." To help her along, he snagged a fistful of the front of her sweatshirt and yanked. With a gasp, she flew toward him, and something slid out of her front pocket, clattering on the floor.

A large, fat pen.

A pen that probably, if shoved up against him, would feel like a gun. He stared down at the thing until it rolled beneath the seat. "You're kidding me."

The truth was written all over her face. "I—"

"You're fucking kidding me." He couldn't believe it, didn't want to believe it. "A pen? You held me up with a pen?"

"I'm sorry," she whispered, then gasped again when with another tug, he had her on his lap.

He really hated to waste the sensation of her curvy bod against his, but now was not the time to enjoy the fact that her ass was snug to his crotch.

And then there were two other things—her full, soft breasts mashed against his forearm that he had tight around her front.

She rectified that right quick by jerking free, but her hair was in his face, smelling like his own little corner of heaven. It was also in his mouth, stabbing into his eyes . . . and though he was flying a plane and still struggling with not strangling her, unbelievably he was fully aroused, desire pumping through him right along with the adrenaline, and he took a second to notice how sweet she fit against him.

Then she began to fight in earnest and managed to knee his inner thigh, uncomfortably close to his goods. "*Hold still,*" he ground out, tightening the arm he had around her middle.

Wriggling to free herself, she continued to grind her ass into his crotch, making him see stars, and not from pain. "*Sit still,*" he repeated in her ear, running his hands down her arms, grasping her hands to set them to the yoke. "Hold here."

She looked out the windshield, saw the setting sun, the storm gathering in huge, black billowy clouds just beyond them, and gulped. "Oh, no. I can't—"

"You held me up with a pen. You can do this." He slid out from beneath her, but not before his legs and arms entangled with hers. Her chest pressed into his forearm, and when he pulled, her breast slid along his skin, nearly right into his palm. For a flash in time, he actually stopped breathing. By the time he managed to scrape her off his lap, his nostrils were filled with her scent, his eyes had crossed with lust, and his body was twitching.

He'd gone over six months without sex, during which time he hadn't even thought about it.

Well, other than the rhetorical ski bunny thing . . .

But he'd been with Bailey Sinclair for what, an hour tops, and suddenly sex was all he could think about. *Distance.* He needed some serious distance.

"Noah—"

"Look, we need the landing gear." He stood over her, guiding her hands with his on the yoke. Hers were small, and icy cold, and he refused to care. "I've done it the other way, without, and trust me, Princess, you don't want to go that route."

"Ohmigod."

"Okay, I'm going to let go."

"*Ohmigod.*"

"Keep your eyes on the horizon. And here." He tapped the altimeter. "Keep that steady. Call me if anything moves."

She had a death grip on the yoke and didn't take her eyes off the horizon. "Hurry," she whispered.

Yeah. Excellent idea. He rushed to the back of the plane, pushing aside the blanket, the duffle bags. He opened the hatch, lowered himself to his belly, and stretched for the hand crank.

The plane jerked, flinging him hard against the hatch door.

"Noah!" she yelled from the pilot's seat.

"Just an air pocket." He hoped. "Hold her as steady as you can!" He swiped the lip he'd just bitten. His fingers came away bloody.

Not as bloody as you'll be if you don't get the landing gear down, came his macabre thought.

It took everything he had to reach the crank with the plane being tossed around, but he did reach it and, with sheer force of will, managed to manually lower the landing gear. Brand, spanking new, and it had stuck, which he'd raise holy hell about later, when his toes were on the ground. "You okay?" he yelled, pushing to his feet, rushing back to the front.

"Peachy," she snapped.

A reluctant smile crossed his face. She had guts, he'd give her that.

The plane dipped violently, and she let out a squeak. "*Noah!*"

"Right here." At her side now, he nudged her stiff form. "Lean forward."

When she did, he slid in behind her. His legs stretched along the outside of hers, and so did his arms.

Turning her head, she met his gaze, and looking into her baby blues felt like a one-two punch. It literally took his breath. For a moment he couldn't even think.

"Did you get it?" she whispered.

A boner? Yeah.

"The landing gear. Did you get it?"

Right. The landing gear. "Yes," he said, his voice a little thick and unintentionally husky. "Got it. We don't have to land on our belly. You're off pilot duty now."

But she was looking at him with those dreamy eyes, and with a soft sound of sympathy, she touched his lip.

He'd nearly forgotten. "It's nothing."

"I'm sorry," she whispered in a voice that for some reason

nearly undid him. Then she shifted, meaning she once again pressed that honey of an ass into his crotch, and then she finally, *finally*, went still. Stared up at him.

Yeah, babe, that's exactly what you think it is.

"I, um—" She scrambled to get off his lap. "You—"

Uh huh. He was.

While she turned away, he busied himself with the controls, a little unsettled that he could possibly be turned on by her, here, now.

Another air pocket pitched them a few hundred feet, and with a gasp, she fell back into the copilot's seat.

He wanted not to care. Instead, that caring barreled through him with shocking strength. "Stay down," he said. "Buckle in."

"You aren't going to turn me in when we get down, right?"

"Let's just land."

"Noah. *Please.*" Her voice was low, sweet. *Desperate.* "I don't have anyone else."

Under entirely different circumstances, he'd have enjoyed her begging him in exactly that voice, the circumstances being her naked beneath him, but then she covered her face with her hands and sagged back in utter destitution.

And he felt like a jerk. He, the hijacked one. "Prepare for landing."

She lifted her face. "And then what?"

"I'll let you know."

Chapter 5

Ignoring Bailey and her palatable desperation, Noah went into landing mode, maneuvering the plane in the fading daylight, talking to ground control as they came into view of the small, private Mammoth airstrip where he always landed.

As the sun sank below the mountain line, he touched down and taxied them in, while Bailey sat still, white-knuckled, white-faced.

Finally he shut down the engine.

She didn't move.

He stood, then crouched at her side. "We've landed."

She nodded, but didn't look at him until he slid his hand along her jaw and tilted her head down toward him.

"I'm sorry," she whispered, her hair falling over his hand, her skin creamy soft beneath his fingers.

Sorry for coming along, he wondered, or for running out on him, which she'd most likely do while he arranged for the plane's tie-down and complete recheck of the landing gear.

"I didn't mean to ruin your night," she said. "I didn't know it was your plane I was getting on."

"Whose plane did you mean to get on?"

"It was going to Mammoth. That's all that mattered."

Their faces were level. He was close enough to see that her

baby blues were outlined in a ring of midnight blue, and that she had a light smattering of freckles high across her perfect nose. Close enough to see the pulse beating faster than a hummingbird's at her throat. Without conscious thought, he stroked a thumb over that beat.

Her gaze caught his, and held.

Their mouths were nothing but a whisper apart. He knew it was crazy, but he wanted to close the gap, wanted to put his mouth on hers as he'd so pathetically fantasized about on more than one dark, sweaty, sleepless night. The only thing that stopped him now was the knowledge that she didn't want anything but her freedom.

But her gaze lowered to his mouth, too, and her tongue darted out to moisten her lower lip.

He nearly moaned. Instead, his hand slid from her jaw to the back of her neck, his fingers slipping into her silky hair, which was now teasing his forearm.

She said his name again, just a whisper of a sound this time, and her eyes fluttered closed, which sent a ridiculous surge of lust coursing through him.

She wanted him, too.

This was crazy, *crazy*, and yet he leaned in.

So did she.

He'd never be sure which of them closed that last inch between them, but it didn't matter because suddenly her mouth was soft and warm on his. He had one last blinding thought before he went under—one kiss would never be enough, not with her, his walking/talking/breathing wet dream.

Then she let out this breathless little sound, and her tongue was so hot and sweet he could have sustained himself on that alone. She slid her fingers up over the back of his head to keep him where he was.

As if he'd move.

Fat chance. He was kissing Bailey Sinclair; he wasn't going anywhere. He glided his hand up her side, over the curve of her waist, just barely skimming the bottom curve of one soft breast.

She seemed to hold her breath for more. Instead, he slid his hand over her shoulder, closing his fingers in her soft, wildly tousled hair at the back of her neck, gently drawing her head farther back, which rocked her body into his.

In sweet, undeniable, erotic response, she arched into him, pressing her breasts into his chest, then tilted her head in a way that more fully sealed their mouths together and caused him to pretty much lose all ability to think about anything other than heat and hunger and sex and Bailey—

Then his cell phone rang, shattering the silence, and she jerked as if she'd been shot, scooting back from him, all the way back.

Feeling inexplicably like a perv, he pulled out his cell. "Fisher."

"Something interesting," Brody said. "My Aspen-bound passenger vanished."

Noah cut his eyes to Bailey. "Is that right?"

"Yep. She just up and left, though it would have been nice to be notified."

Noah didn't take his eyes off Bailey. Jesus, had they really just kissed, or was he losing his mind? "Maybe she had other plans."

Bailey met his gaze straight on, her cheeks pinkening. *Please*, she mouthed, bringing her fingers up to her lips.

Her still-wet lips.

Yeah, they'd kissed. And he knew what she really meant; it wasn't *please kiss me again* but *please don't tell.*

"How was your flight?" Brody asked him.

"Besides the landing gear sticking?"

"Holy shit."

"Yeah, it was interesting."

"Anything else interesting?"

"Plenty."

Brody, one of the smartest guys Noah had ever met, went silent a moment. "Interesting, as in get-struck-by-lightning-and-crash-into-the-side-of-a-mountain interesting, or . . . interesting, as in an unexpected-passenger interesting?"

Noah slid his sunglasses over his eyes. "You're quick."

"*Holy shit,*" he said again. "Really?"

Noah didn't say anything.

Bailey just kept looking at him with her heart in her eyes.

Damn, she had a lot of heart.

"What's up with that?" Brody asked.

"Got me."

"You okay?"

Noah hadn't taken his eyes off Bailey. Nor she him. She was taut as a drum and looking more than a little frazzled around the edges. He suspected if he so much as said, "boo," she'd fall apart. "Always."

Brody let out a low laugh. "Right. Well, I'll just put the million-dollar plane away and bill her for the services. For *both* planes. You know, sometimes, the erratic behavior of the rich and famous really works for me."

"Yeah." Noah shut his phone.

Bailey didn't move.

He gave it a long beat, then straightened to his feet. "I have to tie-down." He paused, brow arched. "You going to try to stop me with your pen?"

She had the good grace to blush as she rose, too. "No."

He watched as she pulled a small backpack from beneath the seat in the back. "Are you going to be here when I get back?"

Suddenly, she was very busy playing with the zipper on her backpack.

Jaw tight, he pulled her around to face him. Beneath his fingers, she felt thin. Fragile. *What is she going off to face all on her own?* "Let me rephrase. *Be here* when I get back." He took his hands off her while he still could, gave her one last long look, then exited the plane.

Cold air smacked him in the face. He was in the center of the sharp, craggy Sierras, and at just over six thousand feet altitude, it showed. Piles of fluffy snow lay along the outer edges of the runway, lining the tarmac. The mountains surrounded him in a three-hundred-and-sixty-degree view of jaw-dropping gorgeousness, every one of them white.

Just what he'd come for. Snow, skiing, snow bunnies, beer, sleep. *Not* a crazy heiress with haunted eyes and a tendency to hold people up with pens.

He handled the tie-down and spoke to a lineman about getting the landing gear fixed, all while keeping an eye on the plane. She was going to bolt, he just knew it.

And sure enough, not sixty seconds later, she came out of the plane as if she owned it. Not as the bag lady she'd been hiding as, but as the gorgeous, swank Bailey Sinclair. The loose sweats were gone. Her head was back, chin high, eyes flashing as though she was queen bee as she carried her bag. She wore designer jeans that fit her like an old friend, fancy boots up to her knees, and a snug, shimmery siren red sweater, all of which screamed class and sophistication. Her hair had been tamed in a sleek ponytail, and she'd put on some gloss that made her mouth look . . .

He had to tear his gaze off the mouth. It didn't matter what her lips looked like, or even what they said. He wasn't buying any story she was selling.

But she wasn't leaving. Not without some answers.

Maddie had called ahead and ordered fuel and overnight hangar storage for the Piper. She'd also gotten him a Jeep. She had the unique ability to locate anything, obtain it, and have it delivered in a blink, and in the year since they'd started Sky High Air, she'd made herself invaluable to both him and the guys, and also their customers. Now all he needed to do was get into the Jeep and drive off. It was what Bailey wanted him to do.

Too bad he'd never been so good at doing what other people wanted. He strode back toward the Piper and met her just as her expensive boots hit the tarmac.

"Thanks for the ride," she said, staring at his throat, carefully not meeting his eyes.

How, he wondered, had he ever *not* known that soft, sweet yet somehow outrageously sexy voice? Her long side bangs blew into her face, and she shoved them free with fingers that had gone white with cold. "I'll never forget it."

They had a past, a professional one, and in that past he'd never called her anything but Mrs. Sinclair.

But now they had a decidedly unprofessional past as well, and he couldn't bring himself to call her Mrs. Sinclair ever again. "Bailey, wait."

"No, I've got to—"

He put his hand on her arm, and she looked at him then, from eyes so filled with worry and fear and terror that he put his other hand on her as well.

He couldn't say why, but he was not letting her go.

"You turned me in, right?" she whispered. "The police—"

He slowly shook his head.

She just stared at him from wide eyes. "Why?"

"Why what?"

A shudder wracked her frame, and he didn't blame her. It was butt-ass cold. "Why didn't you turn me in?" she asked.

Hell if he knew. Maybe he was just thrown by the circumstances, the coincidences . . . maybe it was that in spite of himself, he really was just curious. *What threw a poor little rich girl over the edge?*

Okay, no. That wasn't it. He was curious, yes, but he was also . . .

Concerned.

Sincerely, extremely concerned about her. For some inexplicable reason, he wanted to get to the bottom of this freaked-out, sexy as hell, hurting woman and her problems.

"You could have overpowered me on that plane," she said as a particularly icy wind blew between them. "I know you could have. If not when you were flying, then when I was." She hugged herself. "Or on the radio. Or on the cell phone. Or a million other times. You could have easily given me away, but you didn't."

He had to shove his hands in his pockets rather than stroke her bangs out of her face—*what the hell was that?*

She wrapped her arms around her waist. "So why didn't you?"

"I have no idea." But he did.

She was freezing, and so was he, which was stupid. He grabbed his duffle bag, then hers, and led them both off the tarmac, toward the rented and waiting Jeep, where she dug her heels into the crunchy snow and balked.

"I don't need a ride," she said.

"No? So your plan was to get here, to the airport, then freeze to death? *That's* why you hijacked me?"

She looked away.

"Truth, Bailey. You owe me that."

"Okay, truth. The truth is you have to get far, far away from me. I mean it. I'm like a bad luck charm. Trust me. Being with me, here, is going to get you hurt." She swallowed. "Or worse."

He stared at her as that soaked in. She was trying to protect him? "I'm a big boy," he assured her. "Just tell me. What are you doing here?"

"I already said. I'm here to pick something up."

"Fine." Any second her teeth were going to rattle out of her pretty head. "Get in the Jeep, I'll drive you to get this 'something.'"

She pulled out her cell and read a text message.

"What is it?"

She didn't answer, but thumbed some sort of quick response.

"Bailey—" Knowing she wouldn't tell him a damn thing, he snatched the phone.

She'd typed: YES, I'M IN ASPEN. HAVE 2 TRY 2 FIND IT.

"Hey!" She grabbed the phone back, hit send, then glared at him.

"Who are you texting with?"

"Kenny."

Her brother. Okay, but if the guy cared so much, where the hell was he?

Bailey glanced back at the terminal.

"What, you going to go hijack a taxi now?" he asked.

"This isn't funny."

"You're right there. Nothing about this is even remotely funny. You could have gotten into anyone's plane. Hell, I always assumed you were richer than God himself, so—"

She interrupted him with a harsh laugh as he unlocked the Jeep. He held open the door, the interior light casting her face in bold relief. "You could have gone to any airport," he said again. "Into any plane, but you got into mine. So now get into my Jeep."

She stared at him for a long beat, then surprised him by slipping inside. She started to look up at him, but her gaze snagged on a neighboring parked car, a nondescript SUV, and she frowned.

"What?"

"There's someone in that car watching us," she whispered.

The SUV started up, but the lights didn't go on.

Very interesting, he thought. "Why would anyone be watching us?"

"Just get in," she said urgently, sinking low, reaching back for the hood of her soft, angora hoodie sweater, putting it on over her hair, and slipping on a pair of wide sunglasses despite the fact that the dusk made them unnecessary. "Please, Noah! Just get in and get us out of here as fast as you can."

Something had changed in her body language, and since he'd had his gaze pretty much glued to her body nonstop, he couldn't miss it. Everything had gone rigid, her shoulders, her face, and her hands were white-knuckled on the dash. Most telling, the utter, sheer terror was back. So much so that he took a good long second look at the SUV.

With the sun sinking below the horizon, long shadows cast across the parking lot. He couldn't see through the windshield to the driver, or if there was a passenger.

But his gut told him there was at least one passenger, and his gut was rarely wrong.

And she was still trying to protect him. Hell if that didn't sting. He walked around to the driver's seat, casually but quickly, then started the engine. "Where to?" he asked when he got them on the move.

"Uh . . ." She was looking in the rearview mirror as he pulled out of the parking lot.

The SUV followed.

Oh, yeah, things just kept getting better and better. "Friends of yours?"

"No."

"So you have no idea who they are?"

She didn't look at him. "No."

Shit. Another omission, he was certain. He turned down a side street.

So did the SUV.

Could be a coincidence. A strange one, but still. . . . He made another unscheduled turn.

So did the SUV.

"If you don't know them, why are they following us?" he asked, dividing his attention between the road, the rearview mirror, and Bailey's very tense face.

She still had white knuckles on his dashboard, neck craned as she watched behind them with a growing expression of dread and renewed fear. "Don't know."

Gritting his teeth, he made a quick turn.

And still the SUV kept up with them.

"I don't suppose calling the police is an option."

She didn't say a word to that.

He glanced at her as he pulled out his cell. "Speak up or forever hold your peace."

"No," she whispered.

"Even if I leave out the hijacking part?"

"*No.*"

"Why not?"

"Because then you might as well just kill me yourself."

He shot her a look, but she wasn't kidding.

"Noah, did Sky High Air figure out I wasn't on that flight to Aspen?"

Noah divided his attention between the rearview mirror and the road, while trying to think with his mind racing at eighty-five miles an hour.

"Noah?"

He glanced at her, knowing the truth was in his eyes, and not sure that he cared.

She just stared at him, horror dawning. "Oh, boy. Well, that's it then. Now I've done it."

"Done what?"

"Gotten you good as dead, too."

Chapter 6

Maddie Stone closed down her computer and walked through Sky High Air's building, turning off lights and making sure everything was shut down for the night to her specs. She had high specs—for herself and everyone else—higher than was asked of her as a concierge and personal assistant to three adventurous, gorgeous rebels.

But she loved it here, loved it more than any job she'd ever held, and she'd held a lot of them, carrying far more experience than any twenty-six-year-old should.

Everyone deserved a second chance, she reminded herself, and that Sky High had given her hers . . . well, she'd never forget it.

At first she'd found it odd that out of everything she'd done, both legal and not, both good for her and most absolutely not, stuff she was proud of and stuff she'd rather forget, she'd ended up on a private airstrip watching over three of the wildest, most outrageously sexy men on the planet.

But then again, that actually fit.

The four of them fit, a surprising wonder she marveled at every day.

Noah, Shayne, and Brody, three childhood buds in crime, had quite the history together. According to legend—or so

Shayne had told her after a few beers one night—they'd met on one fateful day in middle school detention; Shayne having been nailed stealing a chemistry test cheat sheet, Brody for getting caught naked with a girl four years his senior in the supply closet, and Noah, fresh from England, having gotten himself in a fight. The three of them, unlikely friends from entirely different walks of life, had bonded that day over a shared love.

Airplanes.

Maddie had never actually given airplanes much thought, seeing as all her life she'd never been able to afford hopes and dreams. But that had changed.

Thank God that had changed.

Still, she held no illusions. She knew she was different, knew, too, that with her funky, out-there clothes and tendency to change her hair to colors not quite on the chart of acceptability, she didn't look the part of the concierge. But since the day she'd walked in here and proven herself competent, not a single one of them had ever judged her.

She could love them for that alone.

And she did. She loved the carefree playboy Shayne, the intellectual adventurer Noah Fisher.

Which left Brody.

Did she love the edgy, dangerous, bad boy Brody?

Hard to say, as every time she was anywhere near him she lost control of her thought processes and her body went all tingly and weird.

Pathetic, secretly lusting after one of her bosses. Pathetic, and not going to happen.

Ever.

A thought that Brody seemed to share as well, since he did his best to avoid her. Assuring herself that didn't hurt, that it didn't matter, Maddie lifted her chin and reminded herself that for the most part, men sucked anyway.

Well, except for Shayne and Noah. The two of them had

never been anything but kind and wonderful to her, which was why her heart ached for Noah these days. When she'd first begun working here, he'd been quick to smile, fast-witted, and always the center of the fun. A wanderlust at heart, he'd traveled the globe many times over, and was perpetually adventure ready. His zest was intoxicating, and he'd given her a renewed lust for life by just being himself.

She wanted to see him smile again, wanted him to find joy in life and flying and Sky High Air again. Somehow, she had to help him, *would* help him.

In any case, she was done here for tonight. The doors were all locked, Shayne had taken a last minute client to Santa Barbara, and Brody . . . well, Brody was holed up in his office as usual, working himself into an early grave.

She walked by his office door, shut of course, then nearly jumped out of her skin when he whipped the door open.

Just over six feet of sexy-as-hell male stood there with a frown on his face, his dark hair in wild waves from frustrated fingers, his even darker eyes filled with secrets she'd never managed to plumb. Around his neck were his earphones, from which Lincoln Park blasted out at decibel levels uncharted.

How the man hadn't gone deaf was beyond her, but that wasn't what she wondered when her gaze ran up his body, which was built like the tough, leanly muscled athlete he was. Nope, what she wondered was why, if she was so damn attracted to him that her brain cells melted into a little pool of longing every time she looked at him, did they drive each other so crazy?

Brody clearly wasn't wondering any such thing. He had only one question, spoken tersely. "Has he called?"

She knew he was worried about Noah, and she knew why. They'd all spent a considerable amount of time in the past six months worrying about Noah, the third Musketeer, the sexy Indiana Jones who had always been the grounded of the three, the one most likely to hold them all together.

But then had come the crash, and the death of a dear friend and client, and he hadn't been the same ever since. She knew Noah blamed himself, just as she and everyone else knew how ridiculous that was. No one could have avoided that crash, and no one could have kept Sheila alive. "No, he hasn't called. You said you talked to him after the landing and that he was fine."

"No, I said I talked to him and he was *alive,*" Brody corrected. "*Fine?* I don't think so."

She didn't question him. No one knew Noah as well as he and Shayne did. If he thought Noah had been more off today than usual, she believed him.

And truthfully? She was worried, too. "I can get him on the phone for you if you'd like."

Hunching his broad-as-a-mountain shoulders, he shoved his hands into his pockets. At some point he'd changed from his pilot's uniform back into a pair of beloved old Levi's, washed to the point of buttery softness, and faded white in the stress points, of which there were tantalizingly many. "He said I was acting like a woman."

Maddie laughed.

Brody's frown deepened.

"Sorry," she said, anything but.

"If you're sorry, then why are you grinning from ear to ear?"

Uh, because you, a walking, talking attitude, are the farthest thing from a woman I've ever seen. "You should see your face."

Standing there with his attitude blaring as loud as Lincoln Park, with that scowl on his face, looking every bit the wild, rebel pilot that he was, he positively gave her shivers.

Damn, but she had a thing for all boys bad, the badder the better. *Yes, but you gave all that up, remember?*

And then she saw it, in Brody's stormy gray eyes. He knew something and was holding back. "What is it?" she asked.

"He's got Bailey Sinclair with him."

"*What?*"

"She didn't just vanish on me. She vanished into Noah's

Piper. I think she hid out, or Noah would have said something before takeoff."

"You're saying he took off without knowing she was on board?"

"Yeah. And when I called, he evaded."

Maddie stared at him. They all knew about Noah's not-so-secret crush. "Why would she stow away?"

"I can think of several reasons, none good."

Oh, boy.

"Call him," he said, and turned to go back into his office. "Work your magic."

He thought she had magic? Well now, that was interesting. She thought *he* was magnificent. "What should I say?" she called out. "That his momma is worried?"

She thought she heard him growl as he shut his office door, which made her smile. If she couldn't have him drooling over her the way she secretly drooled all over him, she did enjoy irritating him. She pulled out her cell and called Noah, thinking he'd take one look at the ID and not pick up, but he surprised her.

"Yo," he said softly. "Everything okay?"

"That's my question to you," she said.

He didn't respond to that.

"Noah? Whatever's going on, you're not up for it. Get your ass back here."

He let out a quiet laugh. "What happened to talking to me with kid gloves?"

"I'm not Shayne or Brody," she said. "Put simply, I don't have a penis and therefore can actually say what I mean. You are not fit to be doing this."

"And what am I doing?"

"I wish to God I knew."

More silence.

"Noah."

"Gotta go, Maddie. See you Monday."

"*Noah.*"

Nothing.

"Don't you hang up on me—"

But it was too late. She looked up and found Brody standing in his open doorway. "You're right," she agreed. "Something's off."

He didn't move so much as a muscle, but she could see the tension increase in his big, tough body. They just stared at each other, and for that one moment at least, they were united in their concern for Noah.

They hadn't lost their tail; the SUV's lights were always back there.

After them.

Bailey gripped the Jeep's dash as Noah drove the mountain passes like a man who knew what he was doing.

But he didn't. He couldn't.

Because she hadn't told him what they were up against. Oh, God, if something happened to him, she'd never forgive herself.

But then again, if something happened to him, she was going to be dead, too.

How did they find her so soon?

How was she going to lose them?

The road narrowed, a sheer cliff on their left, a heart-stopping drop-off on their right. She closed her eyes. "Noah. I can't let you do this."

"A little late now, Princess." His long legs worked the clutch and accelerator as he handled the Jeep with easy precision. "You picked my plane, remember?"

"Yes. And God. I'm sorry. I'm sorrier than I can tell you, but it's not too late to get as far away from me as you can."

He slid her an assessing glance. "I can take care of myself."

Bailey didn't doubt that, but he had no idea what she—they

were up against. She eyed the dark evening sky, the mountains that were nothing more than inky shadows looming tall and large. "Can you go faster?"

He had one hand on the wheel, the other on the stick shift, his long legs working the clutch and acceleration with a confidence she'd never mastered. "Sure," he said. "If I want to careen off the road and down that cliff, plunging us to our certain deaths."

Good point. They'd been swallowed up by the darkness now, complete except for the two headlights spilling from the Jeep, highlighting the curvy two-lane road and the sharp fall off to their right. Couldn't forget the drop-off. She tried to keep breathing.

Noah downshifted and took a turn just hard enough to have her bumping up against the door. An oncoming vehicle briefly lit up the inside of the Jeep, slashing across Noah's face, probably lighting up her face as well.

His eyes met hers for one beat, his brow furrowed, mouth tight and grim. "What do they want?" he asked.

"It's complicated."

He swore beneath his breath. Shook his head. "Okay, let's set aside this pointless argument for another. Who are they?"

"I'm not exactly sure."

He used sheer strength to handle the car around a tight hairpin turn that nearly had them on two wheels. "How did they find us?"

"I'm not—"

"Exactly sure?" He shot her a scathing look across the console that might have withered her, except that she was still shaking and so beyond exhausted and terrified, she had nothing left.

"Where are we going?" he asked tightly. "And don't say you're not sure, because—"

"In two more miles, you're going to turn left."

"There's nothing left except an unfinished resort."

"That's the one. It's one of Sinclair's Fun and Sun resorts. Alan's."

"And that's where you have to get your 'something'?"

It's where she *hoped* to get her "something." Something green. As in US dollars that she could then hand over to the men presumably following her.

And then, hopefully, as in please God, she could live the rest of her life in peace, maybe even find some semblance of normality.

Damn it, Alan, I can't believe you did this to me. . . . She closed her eyes and pressed her forehead to the cool glass window at her side. She should have believed it. Hell, she should have expected it. Her entire life she'd been manipulated by the men in her life, first her father, then Alan. Charming, elegant men, the both of them, but beneath their veneer had been an edgy danger she'd never guessed at.

How had she not?

But oblivious, she'd gone in search of the easy love she hadn't found with her father, and had mistakenly believed Alan would offer it. In reality, she'd just exchanged one charming, wealthy, smooth-tongued man for another, like a meek little puppy searching for that elusive acceptance.

Alan had treated her well enough, if not a little distantly, until the day he'd gotten himself killed.

Now she was left to face the music. But even bankruptcy and social humiliation didn't touch the fact that the very people that had once kissed Alan's ass now expected her to lead them to the money she'd never even seen. It was beyond a nightmare at this point because she couldn't wake up.

The road opened up, and instead of a cliff on their left now, they were passing a vast, unending forest. Dark. Scary. On the next sharp turn, the Jeep slid on a patch of ice. She gasped, but Noah had the wheel in a firm grip and muscled the vehicle, keeping them on the road.

She let out a low breath. "Close."

"What's closer are the guys on our ass."

Whipping around, she saw the headlights behind them and chewed on her lower lip.

"Who knows you're here?"

"Only apparently everyone at Sky High Air."

"No one there told a soul. Who else, Bailey?"

"No one!"

"Kenny."

"Kenny is my brother. He's on my side."

He said nothing to that.

"Turn left," she reminded him when she saw the large hanging sign up ahead: *Sinclair's Fun and Sun.*

"With them right behind us? No way." He went straight past the turnoff, speeding up until her blood pounded in all her pulse points.

"Oh, my God," she whispered, forcing her eyes open so she could see it when they plunged off the road.

"Yeah, we're not going to be so lucky as to get divine intervention tonight," he said tersely, watching the rearview mirror instead of the road, which was giving her more than a few bad moments.

"Noah—"

"The cops would be pretty welcome about now—"

"What are we going to tell them, that someone's tailgating us?"

"I don't think that's all they have in mind—*Shit.* Hold on." In one sudden movement, he flicked off the headlights, whipped a U-turn at speeds that rolled the eyes in the back of her head, and yanked the Jeep to the side of the road and into the woods.

Bailey thought maybe she screamed, but couldn't be sure that wasn't just her brain imploding. She had no idea how Noah could even see—she sure as hell couldn't—but she could hear branches of trees slapping and scraping the sides of the Jeep as they drove into the woods.

Then he hit the brakes and jerked up on the emergency brake at the same time, sending them into a careening, spinning stop. Bailey's seat belt tightened painfully over her ribs, but before her momentum could take her forward enough to kiss the windshield, Noah thrust out an arm to hold her back.

Her breasts pressed into his biceps, his hand flattened on her belly, and it seemed in slow motion that she settled back into her seat and turned her head to look at him.

Unbelievably, her belly quivered. Her nipples hardened. She didn't understand the reaction—or hell, maybe she did. She'd gone a long time without sex, maybe too long, and now her body was going to take whatever it could for pleasure.

In the dark, he slid his big palms up her torso, pulling the seat belt loose. She thought for a second maybe he'd been taken over by aliens.

Or maybe that was her, because suddenly she was leaning into him, her gaze glued to his lips, the lips she wanted back on hers.

Crazy.

They were in the Sierras, on the run from some big badasses who wanted her dead.

And she wanted another kiss.

His head was bent. He was trying to see her, and meanwhile his fingers—

She actually closed her eyes to better absorb the sensation, which if she could think, would mortify her. It'd been too long, much too long, since she'd been touched in any pleasant way.

And the truth was, she *wanted* his arms around her, wanted his mouth back on hers, and wanted him to never let go while he was at it.

Insane.

He lifted his head and in the dark met her gaze. "You okay?"

"Yes."

He was quiet a moment. "How do I believe anything you say?"

Not knowing how to respond to that, to the absolute truth, she just swallowed and looked at him.

He shifted closer, a small movement that upped her pulse rate. "A beautiful liar," he murmured, a mere breath away and getting closer with each passing heartbeat, which, granted, came fast enough to warrant a heart attack warning.

He was looking at her mouth, his eyes sleepy and sexy enough to have her closing the gap herself, just shifting a little bit closer—

"But still a liar," he whispered, and then in direct opposition to those words, he kissed her.

Chapter 7

Noah's mouth was warm, deliciously warm, against Bailey's frozen one. All of her was frozen, and as she pressed close to him, she wished that they could stay like this forever.

And for one glorious moment, he did stay, kissing her long and wet and deep, oh God, so deep. She could feel his arms around her, and nothing, nothing had ever felt so right. She slid her hand across his nape, through his silky hair, holding his head because she didn't want this to end.

Obviously her brain wasn't firing on all cylinders. But then Noah changed the angle of the kiss, and a sound of pure pleasure escaped her, and then again when one of his hands slid down her side and up, beneath her sweater, his fingers fanning gently across her ribs to barely, just barely, brush against the underside of her breast.

The sensations were so lovely, she prayed they would never stop.

But then he pulled back, and she saw why.

A car went whipping down the highway. A nondescript SUV, moving way too fast.

Looking for her and Noah . . .

That had her brain firing at top speed, and she let out a breath, trying to control her racing heart. She carefully drew air into her lungs, uncomfortably aware of her body, quivering and tense and still straining toward his. "Smart move, hiding."

Noah didn't say anything, didn't move.

How did he do that? she wondered. Was he totally and completely unaffected by this odd and inexplicable attraction? Or maybe it was all adrenaline for him, a release of that energy, nothing more. She slid a glance his way and found him looking at her with such a great intensity it blew her hair back, and . . . and when she took a peek at his button fly, she found something else.

Okay, he *wasn't* unaffected.

That shouldn't have made her feel better, but selfishly, it did. "Can we go now? And get to the resort?" She needed to get there. She had no idea how she'd gotten so lucky as to have him get rid of the bad guys for her, but he had, and she had things to do. "Noah?"

"Not yet."

Not yet? Maybe he somehow missed her urgency—

A second car whipped by on the highway. Also a nondescript SUV.

She stared after it in shock. "Two? There were *two* of them?"

Noah waited until the taillights faded from view, then started the engine of the Jeep.

"How did you know there was a second car?" she asked, dazed.

"Wrong question." He maneuvered them back onto the highway, going back the way they'd come.

"What do they want?"

"Yeah, there's the right question." He looked over at her, because they both knew the truth. She knew what they wanted. She'd taken too long getting the money, and Stephen and his thugs had gotten antsy. They didn't trust her.

And now they wanted her blood to go with the cash.

Noah turned into the resort. The road in was a mile long, lined by a vista of rugged mountain peaks that couldn't be seen on a dark night like this. Thick with snow, the road forced Noah to take it slow, utilizing the four-wheel drive. Finally the tight, narrow curves opened into a large parking lot at the base of the resort. Though the buildings were unfinished on the inside, in true Alan style, the outside of the place looked ready and welcoming. Always the cart before the horse with Alan. The main lodge was a four-story cabin-style building with snow three feet thick on the roof and icicles hanging down along the eaves, making it look like a gingerbread masterpiece. A deserted one—there were no lights, no other cars, nothing.

Noah pulled into the front row. "It looks finished."

"Not on the inside." Turning in her seat, she glanced uneasily behind them. "We lost them?"

"No. They're still back there, lying low."

Her stomach dropped at his easy acceptance of the trouble they were in. "I don't see them."

"That's because they don't want to be seen." He had one arm along the back of her seat, the other on the console in front of her. He looked big, bad, slightly attitude ridden, and . . . worried.

About her.

She didn't want to see that, didn't want to know he cared.

"Truth time," he said quietly.

He was surrounding her. It would be so easy to sink into his strength. Instead, she fumbled behind her for the door handle, pressing away from him. "Thanks for the ride, I'll just—"

He slid his warm hand to hers, halting her movements. "What? What exactly are you going to do, Bailey?"

Find the money.

Turn it over.

And then hopefully live to a ripe old age somewhere warm, somewhere quiet.

To that effect, she shrugged off Noah's hand and opened the door of the Jeep. Icy night air instantly hit her in the face, sapping the very breath from her lungs. Her feet sank into the snow. Already she couldn't feel her fingers, but she managed to grab her bag. "Take good care of yourself."

"Bailey, wait—"

"I can't. But thanks. Thanks for . . ." She offered a feeble smile. "Everything."

"Damn it, hang on—"

She shut the door. She imagined him swearing colorfully, but it was now or never because she was losing her nerve. The strain of keeping the truth to herself, and therefore keeping herself alive, was seriously beginning to wear on her.

She turned toward the gigantic resort in front of her. With Alan's death, construction had come to a grinding halt.

Actually, that had happened when it had been discovered that he'd siphoned all of his money out of the business accounts. He owed millions of dollars, and yet the money had vanished into thin air.

Or so she'd thought.

Now Stephen was out there, sure she knew where Alan had hidden it, and he was on her tail.

Literally.

If she hadn't already felt like a frozen popsicle, the thought of what he'd promised to do to her would have made her blood go cold.

But she couldn't get any colder.

Behind her, the driver's door to the Jeep opened. Refusing to acknowledge the small, tiny beat of hope, not to mention relief, she began walking, fast, toward the buildings, her every step sinking into the snow so that it crept up her boots, and then inside them.

"Goddamnit," Noah muttered, grabbing her arm, bringing her around, his free hand coming up to her hip to hold her still. "I said wait."

She wondered if he really did that on purpose, took such care in order not to hurt her, but even as she wondered, she knew it was true. He *did* take care not to hurt her. Just the thought brought a lump to her throat. She was so glad to have him here, with her, but she needed to get rid of him before they arrived, before they hurt him, too. "Go back, Noah."

"No."

"I mean it," she said, her voice quivering. "You don't know. You—"

"*Shh.*"

"Need to go back—"

"No, I mean really, *shut up.*"

Oh, God, now she heard it. An engine. Accompanying this was a beam of headlights, a car making its way up the road.

Toward them.

"*Hurry.*" He pulled her stumbling through the snow, slipping an arm around her to rush her along. Her bag banged painfully at her side, and she was so cold each movement was agony, but she didn't slow down, couldn't with the grip he had on her.

"How do we get in?" he asked as they reached the closest structure.

"This way," she said, and they ran past the large double front doors, along the side of the building.

The headlights bounced off the snow in front of them, and she whipped around to look. It was one of the SUVs. The driver made his way across the parking lot, using his high beams to scan the buildings.

Noah pressed her back against the corner of the building, where they were hidden from view. He held her there with his body, the same body she'd lusted after more than once. She was so cold she felt as if she could shatter, yet being against him was heaven. A half-pained, half-aroused sound escaped her, one she was helpless to control, and he immediately pressed his mouth to her ear. "Don't move."

His body heat began to sink into her, so delicious she nearly opened her frozen lips and said, "I won't move ever again if you don't." Every inch of him was pressed snugly up against her: chest to chest, thighs to thighs, and everything in between. . . .

The sound left her again, horrifying in its neediness.

"Shh," he said again, and slid a finger over her lips in warning.

Or so she assumed, because she doubted he'd meant the touch to feel like a caress, like a prelude to another kiss. God. One would think she'd been starved for sex.

Alan's touch had been pleasant enough, even lovely, but never . . . *necessary*.

Noah's touch felt *necessary*, and another involuntary sound left her—

The headlights scoped the side of the building, uncomfortably close to where they were hidden. Noah tightened his arms on her, either in warning or comfort, she didn't know, but she took both, pressing her frozen face into his throat, reveling at the welcome heat she found there. There she stood, in the dark, wishing she could tuck her fingers and toes inside his clothes, wishing . . .

It was crazy, but she wanted to press her lips to his skin.

So she did.

He went utterly and completely still.

Time stopped.

Never in her life had she felt so aware of anyone, of his hands on her, of his heat, his strength, and when he lifted his head to stare at her, the air so cold their breath crystallized in front of their faces, she couldn't tear her gaze away. They were both breathing a little more quickly than could be attributed to just adrenaline now, and he slowly reached out, stroking a stray strand of hair off her cheek. "Did you just kiss my neck—"

"No." She shook her head, and that stray strand of loose hair flew around her face again, catching on him, sticking stubbornly to the stubble on his jaw. "I didn't."

Cocking his head, he just looked at her.

Oh, God, okay, she'd kissed him. She'd kissed him, and

even now, with the embarrassment creeping up her face, she wasn't sorry.

In fact, she wanted to do it again.

Clearly she'd sustained a head injury at some point along the way. . . .

The headlights vanished.

Noah pulled back, and she bit her lip rather than let out a sound of regret at the loss of his body's heat. "Let's go," he said. Once again grabbing her hand in his, he pulled her along as they ran through the snow toward the back of the building.

Here, the snow on the sidewalks was thicker, and they sank into it well past their calves. Still, they ran. Bailey's sides burned, and she could barely catch her breath. The boots she wore were high-heeled and utterly impractical, and if Noah hadn't had a grip on her, she'd have fallen on her ass.

"Where to?" he asked.

"Around to the back," she said, gulping for air.

"You have keys?"

He wasn't even breathing hard, the bastard. "I know the code." Or so she hoped. It could have been changed myriad times by now.

Behind the lodge they came to a large open courtyard. In better times, this place would have been hopping, filled with tables and outdoor heaters, a stage for a band, the sidewalks lined with shops and cafes and galleries all lit up like Christmas, all year long.

Above were two tall buildings designed to look like a Swiss ski resort, filled with condos, but now they resembled two towering dark, looming ghosts.

Both were empty, she knew, except the penthouse, which Alan had designed and furnished for himself because he liked to visit during construction, and he expected to be kept in style when he did. The penthouse was huge, ridiculously luxurious, and overwhelmingly opulent.

He'd brought her here once, a few months before his death,

to show her off at an investor tour. She'd worn a sexy cocktail dress and smiled as directed, and had felt like a piece of meat.

If the money was hidden here, then it had to be there, in the only finished area—Alan's penthouse.

At the door, she hit the keypad with frozen fingers and clicked in Alan's favorite number: 6-9-6-9.

"You're kidding me," Noah said, watching over her shoulder.

She felt her face heat, wishing some of that would make its way to her fingers, but then the doors clicked and she shoved them open.

Noah pulled her inside and shut the doors behind them. It was pitch dark, and they took a moment for their eyes to adjust. There wasn't much to adjust to. She knew they stood in a reception area that had been planned to be filled with upscale sophistication and elegance, but for now it was nothing more than expensive tiles and wood and unpaid bills.

"Elevator," she said. "To the penthouse."

"The elevator works?"

"Everything works, this place was nearly complete, all except the designers and furnishings, when . . ."

When Alan had bitten the dust.

He held her back from turning to the elevator. "We have to stop them from getting in here." His voice was disembodied in the dark. "Or we're sitting ducks."

A grim reminder that they were being followed. She resisted grabbing him and never letting go. "They won't know the code."

"That won't stop them."

His grim certainty, in a cool, calm voice, gave her a shiver. No, that wouldn't stop them. "What are you going to do?"

"Whatever I have to."

Horror filled her. "Kill them?"

"Hell, no." She felt him shudder, and his reaction might have been funny if anything about this situation could have possibly been funny. She'd been surrounded by bad guys for so long now, she just assumed everyone was one. "Sorry."

"Forget it. Let's just get what you need."

She'd have sworn she'd become immune to emotions after all she'd been through, but like before with him, her throat tightened. "Thank you."

"Don't thank me. If anything more strange happens, I'm calling the cops."

Panic filled her. "The police can't help me."

"Of course they can."

"No." She wouldn't give Stephen a reason to go after Kenny. Or now Noah. "No police. Trust me. They can't help."

His gaze slid over her. A muscle in his jaw bunched. From inside his shirt, he pulled out what looked like a pen, but when he flicked a switch, it lit up like a flashlight.

"Stay back," he said as he turned to some sort of electrical panel next to the doors. Opening it, he began punching numbers on the keypad. "Away from the window."

"What are you doing?"

He shut the panel. "Gaining us some time."

He'd messed up the code somehow, and she just looked at him, stunned. She'd have sworn she'd had him pegged, with that gorgeous smile, his careless, easy way of wearing clothes, the light stride, as if he'd never had a care in the world.

But he kept surprising her, leaving her off center, and completely unable to peg him. And damn, if she didn't find herself with the tragically ridiculous realization that she was nursing a serious crush. Hell of a place to be, considering she'd practically kidnapped him. "Who are you, MacGyver?"

With the glow of the penlight, she saw a ghost of a smile curve his lips. "Come on."

"They'll just break the glass to get in."

"Maybe, but they'll have to dismantle the alarm I just reset first, and that's going to buy us a few."

She moved to the elevator, which he studied for a brief moment. "No," he said.

"No?"

"The stairs."

She looked down at her worthless high-heeled boots. Of course, the stairs. "It's nine flights."

"Then we'd better hurry."

"But—"

"Look, getting stuck in the elevator because they've cut the electricity doesn't appeal much."

No. No, it didn't.

"Nor does the idea of the doors opening to surprise goons, if they somehow beat us up there. Come on." He opened the stairwell door and looked back at her.

She sighed, then entered. The first flight wasn't so bad, and she began to think maybe she could do this without even breaking a sweat.

Then halfway up the second flight, she began to huff and puff. Oddly enough, she remained cold, so cold she still shivered hard enough to rattle her teeth together.

"Shh," he murmured.

Shh? *Shh?* She'd like to shh *him!* But then he went still, and she plowed into his back.

He reached back to steady her, his arm wrapping around her hips. This action glued her to his side, which in turn left her feeling extremely clumsy, and yet . . .

Utterly female.

She couldn't help it, pressed against him as hard as she was, inhaling his warm scent. Absorbing his body heat, she felt distinctly protected. Worried about.

And for the first time all night, just a little bit heated. But even all the body heat in the world couldn't fuel her engine. They kept moving.

On the third-floor landing, she was breathing so hard, she

thought she might die. On the fifth floor, she came to a gasping halt, knowing it. "Can't."

"Only four more flights."

She would have laughed if she'd had the breath. Four more flights? She'd have better luck at Mt. Everest. "I definitely need . . . to get back to . . . those yoga classes."

He let out a soft laugh, and she felt his gaze run up her body. "I thought you were a model."

"Yes, but my metabolism is hereditary. I'm in terrible aerobic shape."

"You look like you do all right."

As before, her body tingled with an awareness that felt a little bit shocking given she was in the middle of the most terror-filled night of her life.

"Come on," he said. "Let's do this." And taking her hand, he tugged her up another flight.

She did her best, but she was definitely lagging. He simply pulled her along, practically carrying her. "What's up here?" he asked.

"A penthouse suite."

"No, what's up here that we can't leave until we get it?"

We.

For so long she'd been an *I*, all alone in this. But he'd said we. He wasn't going to abandon her, no matter what she deserved, and she put a hand to her pounding heart. She'd swear she could feel it trying to leap out of her chest. She couldn't even answer. She could barely keep air in her lungs. Instead, she went to follow him as closely as she could, which since he still had a grip on her, was pretty damn close.

"Bailey?"

She had no idea what to say, so she said nothing.

Finally, at the ninth floor just outside the penthouse door, he stopped.

Pressed her back to the wall.

Then held her there.

Waiting.

The only light came from the windows at either end of the hallway, where the snow's glow lit up the black night with a blueish tint. Adding to the odd lighting, the hallway was lined in mirrors, and shadows cast from them, reflecting the fancy brass trim all around, and the look of concentration on Noah's face.

"Talk to me," he demanded very quietly. "In ten seconds or less."

"I'm not exactly sure what I'm getting," she admitted.

He just looked at her.

"Okay, it's . . . complicated."

"No shit, Princess. Eight seconds."

She had to tell him something. "It's not only complicated; it's a long story. Much longer than eight seconds."

He didn't look happy at that answer, but honestly, she didn't know how to explain the situation quickly. Hell, she didn't know how to explain the situation with all the time in the world. She had no idea exactly where to look, or even if the money was here. "I'm sorry, I—"

Noah slid a hand to her mouth.

And that was when she heard it.

The ping of the elevators.

Someone was in one of them, maybe several someones, coming up.

Chapter 8

Bailey felt as if she'd swallowed her tongue. Or maybe that was just her heart, which had landed in her throat.

They were coming.

The day had just been one long Mr. Toad's Wild ride.

Still holding her immobile and silent, Noah flicked his light over the penthouse door and found the keypad. Reaching out, he hit 6-9-6-9.

The door clicked open.

"At least he was consistent," he murmured, and pulled her inside. "Listen to me," he instructed over his shoulder as he kept guard at the door. "Hide. Don't come out until I come for you."

Through the dark she looked at him making a stand at the front door, shoulders broad, body braced.

He was going to try to protect her.

But he had no idea what he was up against. Hell, she barely knew. She was too exhausted to think. She was cold and tired, and truthfully, just about ready to give up. "No," she whispered, shaking her head. This wasn't going to happen. "No way. You can't do this for me; you have to—"

"*Hide*, Bailey."

She grabbed his hand to try to turn him to face her, desperate to make him understand. He had to hide, too. "Noah—"

"And *stay* hidden." He shoved something into her hand. His cell phone. "If I don't come for you in ten minutes, call for help."

"Where are you—"

The door shut in her face.

"Going. Ohmigod." If he got hurt, or worse . . . With a half sob, she whipped around and used the penlight to view the penthouse condo.

She couldn't see much with the narrow beam of light, but it appeared the place was still overly done in wealth: cool tiles, warm woods, expensive art on the walls, and a ridiculous amount of silk pillows on the overstuffed furniture.

Stay hidden.

Noah wanted her to stay hidden while he, an innocent in all this—never mind that there didn't seem to be an innocent bone in his very fine body—dealt with her mess.

Hopefully while staying alive, very alive.

Please, Noah. Please stay alive.

She moved down the hallway toward the master suite, which she'd never actually slept in. Alan had never invited her, other than the time she'd toured the place at the inspection phase.

Now she wondered why. Had he stashed his hidden fortune here? If so, she'd know soon enough because Alan enjoyed keeping his safes behind his pieces of art.

It'd amused him to keep his private things in plain view.

The master bedroom was so big she couldn't span it all within the small beam of light. She took in the artwork on the walls, then began pulling out the pictures to peek behind each.

At least two minutes had gone by. She knew Noah had said to hide, but she had to finish looking.

She moved back down the hallway into the living room and

checked beneath the art there as well. Nothing. She went to the front door, put her eye to the peep hole, and saw . . .

Nothing, just an inky blackness.

A third minute had gone by, possibly a fourth.

Oh, God.

Where was he? The thought of something happening to him because of her made her feel sick.

And where were the people on the elevator? Was it possible they didn't know what floor she and Noah had gone to?

Or maybe they'd sent up an empty elevator to trick them, and they were taking the stairs, too, in which case Noah had walked right into a trap.

She put her hand to the handle and nearly wrenched open the door, but managed to get a rein on her panic. Running out into the dark hallway wasn't going to help anyone.

Think.

Alan had spent some time here. He'd probably had meals . . .

Using the light to find her way into the gaping huge kitchen, she eyed the walls. No pictures. No safe—

Wait. Had she just heard something?

Heart in her throat, she eased open a drawer. And then another, and another, until she found what she'd been looking for—a steak knife. Fisting it, she whirled around, ears straining.

The sound came again, so slight she couldn't be sure she'd really heard anything. She gripped that knife like a lifeline. *There.* There it was again, but she couldn't pinpoint the location. Hide. Trying not to hyperventilate, she hunkered down, her back to a cabinet, trying to make herself as small as possible. Plus she wasn't sure her legs could support her weight. She clicked off the penlight. Reaching behind her, she opened the cabinet doors. *Please don't let there be spiders in here*, she thought, turning to crawl in. It smelled musty, and—

And she nearly jumped right out of her skin when from behind her, fingers wrapped around her ankle, then tugged her back against a hard chest. In one motion, she was unceremoniously relieved of her knife. She braced for a stabbing pain as she opened her mouth to scream, but a hand clamped over it. An arm came around her hips, holding her immobile.

She'd seen all the horror movies, she knew what came next, so she bit his hand.

"Ow, goddamnit!"

Noah.

He hauled her back up against him. "Goddamnit, I told you to hide."

Adrenaline whipped through her. He'd scared her half to death—a real feat tonight. "I *was* hiding! Are you okay? Are you hurt? Did they get you? Oh, my God, you're in one piece, right? Where are they—"

Again his fingers covered her mouth. "Momentarily stuck in the elevator. The keyword here being momentarily. Now, can you please stop moving?"

Got it. Don't move. Not a problem, he had her back to his chest, her butt to his—

Um.

Oh, boy. And now that she knew it was him, she became aware of his hands, one across her front, just above her breasts, the other low on her belly, which she sucked in as she tried not to wonder what he could feel through her sweater.

"What part of don't move didn't you get?" he asked, tightening his arm, making her realize she was wriggling all over the place.

And that her wriggling had . . . affected him.

Now neither of them moved. In fact, she barely breathed.

He was hard.

He was hard, and if she turned her head, she could kiss him—

"We're going to get what you came here for," he said in her

ear, his voice a mere whisper. "Then we're going to go back down the stairs. Silently."

How could he concentrate on their situation with an erection pressing into her bottom? She couldn't. She couldn't think of anything but what it would be like to go for it, right here in the dark, just two strangers in the night. She had a feeling he could show her all that had been missing from her life, that he could relieve this odd and building pressure within her, or at least try.

"No noise," he reminded her. Taking the penlight back, he gave the kitchen one quick glance-over. Outside the kitchen window, the night was utterly black. No moon, just a foggy layer that blanketed most of the stars from view. Inside, things felt uncomfortably close and intimate.

Having circled the room, he came close again. She could feel the heat of his body, and given how chilled she felt, she almost wished he'd come in even closer.

"Your move," he said.

She wet her suddenly dry lips and watched his gaze dip down to take in the movement. "I . . . don't have a move."

He stared at her, his tension making him look pretty damn scary. If he hadn't taken such good care of her, she'd be shaking in her boots because he now appeared incredibly intimidating. But he *had* taken care of her. He'd done everything he could to keep her safe, and also . . . he'd kissed her. "I can't find . . . what I'm looking for."

"Bailey—"

But just then, from the other room, the front door opened with a shockingly loud click.

Hell, Noah thought. More trouble. Why was he not surprised?

Bailey was shaking, and not just a few little tremors, but full body shudders that were knocking her pretty teeth together. He ran a hand down her arm, which felt way too cold through her sweater and made him frown. Yeah, she was soft in his grip, her hips nicely curved, her breasts mashing into his side, the sweet scent of her skin teasing his nostrils, but it also appeared she might be in shock. Not good. "Don't move," he said in her ear. "I'll be right back."

She clutched at him. "No—" But then she purposely clamped her lips shut and shook her head, her hair flying into his face, the silky strands clinging to his jaw. "Nothing."

Nothing, his ass. She was holding on by a string, and desperately trying to be strong while doing it. Good. They were going to need her strength and all of their wits put together to get out of this, and he still had no idea what "this" even was. Noah squeezed her arm gently, trying to signify that he really would be right back. She nodded, but didn't let go. He stroked a finger over hers, which were currently embedded in his shirt.

"Right," she whispered, but it was another second before she let go.

He told himself this was her own doing and shifted silently to the double kitchen doors. What they needed was time, but that wasn't going to happen.

The handles were western style brass pulls. Pretentious, not to mention ugly as hell, but perfect for slipping the knife through and barricading the door closed. It wouldn't hold against brute force, but it would gain them the few seconds they needed.

Hopefully.

Because for whatever reason, gorgeous Mrs. Sinclair had four extremely goon-sized knee-cap breakers on her tail, and while they weren't exactly fast on their feet, they were as persistent as bulldogs.

Two of them were downstairs watching the exits. The other two had made their way out of the elevator and were now inside the penthouse. Armed to the teeth.

Apparently Bailey's "something" was something extremely valuable, and he'd bank on the fact that it involved money. Bags of it.

That Bailey wanted it so badly bothered him.

Distance, he reminded himself. *You need distance.* Like miles and miles of it . . .

Okay, things were far too tight in here for him to risk leaving her. Backing to the cabinets, he pulled her to his side and once again put his mouth to her ear. "Another exit?"

"Patio deck," she breathed. "But—"

They didn't have time for buts, and he dragged her out of the kitchen, wincing at the sound of her heels click, click, clicking across the fancy tiles. He was all for a woman's high-heeled fuck-me boots, especially hers because they made him hot. Probably, she could wear steel-toed work boots and he'd get hot, because the truth was, it was Bailey herself that did him in. She could just stand there and breathe and he'd react, but his point was that he wished she'd been wearing running shoes.

Hell, he wished she wasn't here at all, but instead safe on the Learjet heading to Aspen. That was what he wanted—her far away from all this shit.

They got through the kitchen just as someone tried to get in the double doors. From the other side, a radio squawked. Then a voice softly said, "Get your ass up here, we've got 'em."

Not yet, you don't, Noah thought grimly, relieved about one thing. If the two men from downstairs were being called up, that meant there was no one watching the perimeters of the building.

That would work in their favor.

"Den," Bailey whispered, sounding as if she was hyperventilating.

In the den he spotted the reflection from double French

doors that probably cost more than he'd made last year. He headed for them, hoping like hell there was some sort of fire escape plan.

From behind them, the kitchen doors splintered open, and Bailey gasped.

Don't fall apart on me now, he thought, and pulled her along. She pushed ahead of him and shoved open the French doors. There were a few inches of snow on the covered deck, only what had been able to blow in sideways, but the sharp slap of icy air sucked the air from his lungs.

"Hurry," she said.

That was his line, but he moved out after her and carefully shut the doors behind them, pushing her out of the line of sight from inside.

There wasn't much to see in the pitch-black night. No moon, no stars . . . just a storm moving in.

Yeah, that was just icing on his big fat cake tonight. But there was, hallelujah, a fire escape, which consisted of a narrow ladder from each deck to the one below. "Down we go," he told her.

She stared at him blankly.

"Down the fire escape."

"Down the fire escape." She looked over and gulped. "As in *down the fire escape?*"

He pulled her toward it. "There's no way around this one, Princess." He manhandled her to the edge and physically lifted her leg over.

As she caught a glimpse of the ground far, far below, she froze. "Ohmigod."

"Don't look down."

"My boots—they're high-heeled. Noah, I'm going to slip and fall."

Holy hell. The fuck-me boots. Were they going to catch absolutely no breaks tonight? "Yeah, okay. Move over."

"I can't—"

Not waiting for her, he swung his own leg over, which left him pretty much straddling the princess ninety feet above the ground. *Still* not enough to make him forget that she had a soft, sweet body that fit perfectly to his. Ignoring that, he slid down that soft, sweet body, his cheek rubbing up against all sorts of interesting parts that flipped his senses into overdrive, until his feet were several rungs below hers on the ladder.

This left his face right about tight, amazing ass level. Okay, he hadn't thought this through. His jaw brushed one denim-clad cheek, and for just a second, he closed his eyes.

He wanted to nibble. They were ninety feet above the fucking ground and he wanted to eat her right up. Yeah, Shayne and Brody had definitely been correct—going six months without having sex with anyone other than his own fist had been a colossally bad idea.

He needed to get laid in the worst possible way.

"I'm scared," she gasped, and executed a careful turn so that she faced him.

Perfect. Now her crotch was right in his face. Not exactly a problem, except he was having a little trouble concentrating.

"You can't fall now," he said, feeling like a perv, telling himself to keep breathing, not to go nuts now. "I'm just below you. I'll catch you." He helped her turn back around, which of course involved lots of touching. Now his face was once again two inches from her ass, and his mouth was watering. "Start going down with me."

Or *on* me . . .

Still breathing as if maybe she'd already climbed this building, she nodded. "Just go down with you," she repeated.

Christ, the words sure did conjure up an image. He shifted down a few rungs so that, thankfully, his mouth came level with the backs of her knees. Nothing sexy about the backs of anyone's knees.

Nope, not a damn thing.

But then she did as he'd asked, she followed, so that she

shifted right back into the circle of his arms, and once again he was staring at her most perfectly delectable ass. Closing his eyes would be a bad thing, he reminded himself, and stoically, he kept his gaze on her as they crawled down.

The things he had to do.

"Are we almost there?" she asked breathlessly.

He looked. Not even halfway. "Nearly," he lied. "Keep moving."

"I wish he wasn't dead so I could kill him."

"Who? Alan?"

"And my father."

This was a new one, but now wasn't exactly the time to point out she'd been less than forthcoming with certain vital information.

From in his back pocket, his cell phone vibrated. He had no doubt it was someone at Sky High Air with more demands that he come home now. And it made perfect sense, except for one thing. For the first time in far too long, he felt . . . alive.

That was when the bullet pinged right past his ear.

Chapter 9

Shit, someone was really shooting at them. Noah hated that; he hated that it was starting to snow like a mother. He hated that he couldn't enjoy his view of Mrs. Sinclair's world-class ass, and he hated today.

He really, really hated today.

"Was that—"

"Yeah," he said, his heart racing, his breath coming hard and fast. That had been close, waaaay too close for comfort.

Another shot ricocheted past his nose, and Bailey screamed loud enough to blister his ears. Hell. Wrapping an arm around her hips, he yanked, sliding her down into the protection of his body. Ignoring the fact that she fit against him as if she'd been made for the spot, he took a look over his shoulder. Eight feet to the balcony of the fifth floor. Or was it the fourth?

Wincing, because this was going to hurt like hell, he held onto his bundle of woman and leapt toward the balcony.

Bailey screamed again, but Noah was too busy hitting the deck, then having the air sucker punched out of his lungs when she landed square on top of him, to tell her to shut up again.

Honest to God, she was the noisiest woman he'd ever been shot at with.

Oh, wait. She was the *only* woman he'd ever been shot at with. One more whizzing bullet and his heart nearly lurched to a complete stop, starting up again on a staccato beat when Bailey covered her own mouth with her hand to keep in the next scream.

"Good girl," he wanted to say. But with a groan, he rolled over in the snow, finding one hand full of soft breast. Christ. Yanking his hand back, he went up to his knees, keeping her tucked in front of him as he quickly crawled toward the balcony door, not an easy feat with the few inches of slippery snow. Pulling her up, he sandwiched her against the wall. "Wait here," he said in her ear. "Don't move, don't breathe, and for God's sake, don't scream."

"But—"

He put a hand over her mouth. "Princess, goddamnit, for once, just do it, no discussion."

Only when she gave him a jerky nod did he run back to the fire escape ladder, where he slid down one more floor. Once there, he braced himself and kicked in the sliding glass door.

Glass shattered, and he toed out the rest, making sure to walk through and traipse as much snow inside as possible. With his penlight, he rushed through the opulent, ridiculously large, empty condo and opened the front door into the dark hallway. *There. Follow that lead, assholes.* Then he whipped back through the condo, back through the broken glass door, where he shimmied up the fire escape to the deck where he'd left Bailey, thinking, *Please still be there, please don't have done something stupid.*

She was a mere shadow squishing herself back against the wall as close as she could get in the falling snow, practically hugging the plaster, hair wild around her face, which was as pale as the wall behind her.

When he loomed close, her eyes went wide, her hands flat on the wall on either side of her as she gasped, looking as though she expected him to rape and pillage.

It brought home the very sobering realization that he really had no idea what she'd been through, but whatever it'd been, it had been bad.

And he'd been flinging her around, pushing, shoving, pushing some more. . . . Feeling like the biggest jerk on the planet, he lifted his hands. "Just me," he said very softly.

Some of the terror left her eyes but not all, and she straightened. "I know that."

He moved in close, stealing a precious few seconds to look her over, assuring himself she really was all right.

"Are you okay?" she asked, shaking like a leaf as she got a good hold of his shirt.

That she could even ask told him a lot about her. "That was my question to you," he said, still holding onto her, needing to hold on to her.

"I'm fine."

"I set up a detour." Hopefully. "It'll give us a few extra minutes. Come on."

She tripped on her heels, then caught herself, doing her best to keep up, and he slipped an arm around her, trying to help.

The door to this level was locked, too, no surprise. But there'd be no glass breaking, not this time. The last thing he wanted to do was attract more gunshots. He fiddled with the lock on the slider. Yeah, he could pick this one. He'd seen several bobby pins in Bailey's hair, and turning to her, he slipped his fingers through the silky strands. Silky, *frozen* strands.

"What are you—"

Jackpot. He yanked out a pin and dropped to his knees. "Remember the no-talking part?"

She held her silence for all of three seconds. "I don't think those locks are going to be pickable—" She broke off when he shot her a dry look, and she tightened her mouth as if to say, *Done talking.*

Yeah, right.

Turning his attention back to the lock, he put his tongue between his teeth and concentrated.

"Noah," she whispered.

Ignoring her, he set his ear against the wood to listen for the lock tumbling into place—

"Noah."

Jesus. Tipping his head back, he went to give her a long, frustrated, shut-the-hell-up look, but she seemed so small and wet and miserable, not to mention off-the-charts freaked out, he just sighed. "Almost got it."

"Yes, but those are state-of-the-art locks—"

It clicked open.

"Oh," she murmured in surprise, a sound that turned into a gasp as he yanked her inside with him, carefully shutting and relocking the door behind them.

"Hurry," he said.

"But I thought you sidetracked them."

"They won't stay that way if we don't get out of sight and out of hearing range." The condo was pitch-black, but he didn't turn on his penlight, not yet. Not when the bad guys had guns and were on a scavenger hunt.

Not when he didn't know what the fuck was going on. From the scent, he could tell the place had been dry walled, probably textured, but not painted.

Just like the condo above.

It meant no furniture. He knew they had to be in a living room, so he strode forward, one hand out in front of him, the other gripping Bailey, which proved unnecessary because she hadn't let go of him since he'd found her against the wall.

She hadn't spoken again, which he appreciated, but she was breathing like a misused race horse, and he knew it was only a matter of time before she hyperventilated herself right into a faint. "It's okay," he said. "It'll take them a few minutes to figure out which floor we're on."

"A few minutes," she repeated like a parrot.

He found a wall, an open doorway, and thought they probably stood in the hallway, near the front door. At least he no longer felt uncomfortably exposed, or braced for a bullet in his back.

But something about that whole situation bothered him. The goons had missed. Several times.

What kind of paid goons missed?

Answer—they didn't.

Which meant one thing. The shots hadn't been meant to kill, but to terrify.

Given the way his pretty little hijacker was gasping for air, he had to concede they'd done their duty. He was more than unnerved himself.

And for more than one reason.

She was holding on to plenty of secrets, which in no way explained why, instead of wanting to ring her pretty little neck, he had the urge to wrap his hands around her hot little bod and not just squeeze.

But stroke.

Lick.

Nibble.

Yeah, he'd lost it completely.

He figured they were far enough away from the windows now and pulled out his penlight. They stood in a foyer bigger than his entire house, complete with vaulted ceilings and a hoity-toityness that was provided thanks to too much money. Not the kind of place where he wanted to come ski, thank you very much.

Next to him, his hyperventilating hijacker shivered violently, reminding him that while she might be a pain in his ass, a gorgeous pain, she was also wet, frozen, and in danger from shock. He wanted to get her back to the Jeep, pronto, and then the hell out of here, but there was one little problem.

She hadn't gotten what she'd come for.

"Okay, Princess, truth time."

She didn't respond. Either she didn't want to, or she couldn't because her teeth were threatening to rattle right out of her head. Not good. He moved in, putting his hands on her arms. Christ, she was drenched, her sweater almost frozen into ice. He rubbed up and down trying to keep her warm.

"They—they're g—going to f-f-find us—"

"Not if I can help it." Cupping her icy face, he tipped it up so he could see into her eyes. "They could have killed us, but they didn't," he said. "Why not?"

She looked away.

"Want me to guess?"

More nothing.

"They're not going to kill us until you give them what they want."

Something on the floor simply fascinated her.

Perfect.

He stared at her, waiting, but she'd gone mute. Frustrated, he grabbed her hand and opened the front door.

"W-where are we g-going?"

Somewhere warm. Somewhere safe. Or at least relatively so. He had no idea where until they got out onto the floor and saw a set of double glass doors lined in enough fancy, expensive brass to fund a third world country for a year. "What's that?"

"A d-day spa. Each r-r-resort has one."

"With its own separate entry for employees?"

"P—probably."

It took only a second to get them inside the nearly completed spa, and another to find what he'd been looking for. The employee entrance, which thank you God, led directly to its own set of stairs. With his penlight, he lit the way and pulled her along with him. He made her run the entire four flights without stopping, and when they'd exited out into the night, they were on the far side of the parking lot, squinting into the snowflakes falling big as dinner plates. "Get ready."

"For what?"

"To run." Flattening them both back against the building, he searched the area and saw no one. Not that he could see far with the white, fluffy snow. He looked up. There were lights flickering in the . . . he counted . . . fifth and ninth floors.

That was the good news. They hadn't figured out that they'd been on the fourth floor yet, much less that they'd left the building entirely. One thing in their favor tonight.

The bad news? They still had to get out of the lot without being detected. "*Now.*"

He pulled her with him as he ran toward the Jeep through the snow, holding her against his side with one arm, the other digging into his pocket for the key. He took her to the driver's side, unlocked the door, shoved her in, and then followed, nearly sitting on her when she didn't scoot in fast enough.

As it was, her scent got caught up in his nose again, and her hair, her wild, glorious hair tangled in his watch, where he spent a few precious seconds bent over the thing trying to get her free, their faces close enough to share air.

She was panting to draw it into her lungs and shaking hard enough to break bones. Her lip gloss had long been chewed off, and the rest of her make-up was gone. She had a smudge of it beneath her eyes, making her look even more fragile, more vulnerable.

Christ, she was a mess. A heart-stopping, beautiful mess. And he wanted her, wanted so badly *he* was shaking. Starting the engine, he shoved the Jeep into gear and took them the hell out of the parking lot.

"I n-need to get to—"

"We're not going anywhere tonight. I'm way too tired to fly."

"But I—"

"Later." He drove them down the windy, icy roads at speeds not exactly legal, especially in the snow, but he wanted to get as far ahead of the goons as possible. His eyes were gritty, grainy from exhaustion and adrenaline. Yeah, flying out of here tonight would be suicidal.

So he took them to their only other option—the house Maddie had reserved for him. It was secluded, and better yet, empty.

And no one would think to look for Bailey Sinclair there.

He hoped.

"W-where are we going?"

"Where I meant to go all along."

"Wh-what if they find us—"

"Not tonight, they won't." It took only ten minutes to get there, during which time he aimed all the heater vents on Bailey and hoped she didn't freeze before he could get her warm. When he pulled up—bless Maddie—the driveway had been cleared, and the house porch lights blazed through the falling snow in welcome. The house was a two-story cabin-style, with snow a foot thick on the roof.

He pulled into the attached garage. "Now," he said, turning in the driver's seat to face his soggy, wet, cold passenger. "We need to talk. And when I say we, I really mean you."

Bailey's pulse was thundering, her body shuddering from cold and who knew what else.

And Noah wanted to talk.

"I think I deserve to know what's going on," he said into her silence.

He did, she knew it. "It . . . it begins with Alan."

In reality, it began far before that, with her father, but she didn't want to sound so pathetic as to have been screwed over by the only two men in her life.

"Alan's dead," Noah said bluntly. "He died months ago. An accidental shooting during hunting season."

"Actually, that's not quite true." She knew she had to tell him something. He did deserve to know. "He died months ago, yes," she agreed. "During a hunting trip. But not from an *accidental* gunshot." With a shaky hand, she pushed her wet hair from her face.

Noah caught her hand in his. "What did he die of?"

"He was shot, but it had nothing to do with an accident."

Noah was quiet a moment. Considering. She couldn't tell if he believed her or not, and was surprised by how much she wanted him to. "Interesting how that missed the news."

"I know." She chewed on her lower lip, pulling it between her teeth, wetting it with a nervous tongue. "But it's true."

Noah's gaze was locked on her mouth. "More," he said, and when she shivered, he ran a warm hand up her arm. Never mind that she knew he was doing it to give her some badly needed body heat, it felt like more. "Alan had a little gambling problem," she admitted.

His gaze held hers for an interminably long moment, and once again time seemed to do a little song and dance and then stop completely.

Her own gaze didn't hold steady through that beat. It couldn't, not with his hand on her, the heat from it seeping into her like a soothing balm.

"Is that how he went through his trust fund?"

"Yes. But he went through it a long time before I ever knew it."

"How long?"

"Before he married me. My father . . ." She shook her head. Here was the hard part of the confession. "My father screwed him out of a bunch of money. He never recovered from that."

"So what, your father gave him you?"

At that humiliating truth laid out bare, she closed her eyes. But there was no more hiding what her life had been. He'd seen the proof in her eyes. "You could say so, yes," she said, remembering the feeling of betrayal when she'd found out the truth.

But now she felt as if the cold night had gotten inside her

bones and was going to rip her apart. She heard Noah swear, the rough sound from deep in his throat only making her shiver yet again. She turned her head to the window and stared into the black, stormy night.

She felt stripped bare, and more vulnerable than she'd ever been in her life.

"Bailey," he said very quietly, reaching out for her hand, rubbing his fingers over hers, clearly trying to infuse her with his heat.

Helpless against the pull of his voice, she looked at him.

"There's more."

Yeah, there was more, lots more, including the answers he wanted. It was just that she didn't have as many as he might have liked, and she didn't intend to give them to him in any case. "Alan owed people big. And when he couldn't pay, they killed him."

"And now they're after you. Which makes sense if they'd killed you, but they didn't."

She just looked at him, warring with her own serious trust issues. Luckily for her, he seemed to take this all in with a grim composure that was somehow, shockingly, like a calming balm on her panic.

"They want something from you," he said, watching her very carefully. "Whatever it is, they want it badly."

"Yes."

"And they're not going to give up until you deliver."

True enough.

He looked resigned. "So where are you headed next?"

"To either of the two remaining resorts in Alan's name."

She watched him absorb that, then slowly shake his head. "You're still hiding."

"Yes, because if they catch me—"

"No, from me. You're still hiding from me."

What could she say to that? To the utter truth? "It's nothing personal," she said quietly.

"Yeah, it's personal. It's very personal." And he got out of the Jeep.

Frustrated, uncharacteristically uptight, and the capper . . . inexplicably aroused, Noah came around the Jeep for Bailey, leading her through the garage to the inside of the house.

He had no idea what it was about her, either that fierce pride in her eyes that said she'd rather not have needed his help, or the way he felt when she laid those eyes on him, or maybe it was more base than that; maybe it was simply her mouth-watering body.

He had no idea, but he tried to put it, and her, out of his head.

He'd stayed here before, many times, and was already familiar with the house. He cranked up the heat, all while holding on to the soggy, still shivering woman.

The people who owned the house were incredibly wealthy but not showy. As usual, the place was clean, warm, and cozy. Just as he liked it. The living room opened into the kitchen, and on the counter was a basket filled with his favorite junk snacks: cookies, donuts, and chips. Maddie had had it stocked for him. "Hungry?"

Bailey looked at the offering and shook her head.

"Don't tell me. Health food nut."

"Good food never hurt anyone."

He, not nearly so picky, grabbed a large chocolate chip cookie, and munching, found her an apple in the refrigerator, which she took with a wild shiver.

"Come on." He led her through the house and up to the master bedroom, where he would have pulled her into the bathroom, thinking a hot shower was what she needed, but she dug her heels into the carpet and shook her head more violently than the rest of her was shaking, which was really saying something.

"You need to get warm," he said.

"I'm fine."

Bullshit, she was fine. The car ride might have begun to warm her up, but it hadn't fully done the job, and he needed to do something. Clearly she was pulling the shy card, but it was too late for that.

"N—no need for a shower," she said through chattering teeth.

"You have to get warm." He lifted his hands to his own shirt, which he unbuttoned.

Her eyes widened. "Um—what—"

"I don't know about you, but I'm just about done with being cold and wet."

"Yes, but—"

"Hurry."

Her gaze locked on his chest. "H—hurry to what?"

"*Strip.*"

Chapter 10

Bailey could not have possibly heard him right. Strip? *Strip?* Was he insane? Suddenly being too scared to think and too frozen solid to imagine ever being warm again took a backseat to this new and entirely disconcerting situation.

She was alone in a house with a man she hardly knew, a big, strong, tough man who knew his way around trouble, who looked like sin on a stick, oh, and he'd *unbuttoned his shirt.*

Strip . . .

How was it even possible she wanted to do just that? She'd seen men naked before, so she had no idea why the sight of Noah undoing his shirt, revealing a wedge of bare torso, made her mouth suddenly dry, but she wasn't sticking around to find out. "Noah—"

He took a step forward, and she took one back, which had the high mattress hitting her in the butt.

As if that had been his plan all along, his hands went to either side of her hips, resting on the thick bedding, his body close enough to share some of that heat he had radiating off of him, not to mention the sheer, hard strength of him pressing against her.

Strip . . .

She wanted to, she really did, and it had nothing to do with impending hypothermia and everything to do with how he made her feel when he looked at her, touched her.

Kissed her.

God. She was really losing it here, as surely as the room was beginning to warm from the hot air coming out of the heater vents, enclosing them in an intimacy she wasn't sure she could face. He couldn't really want her, could he? Not after what she'd done, dragging him here.

Putting his life in danger.

That last thought made her breath catch, made her hug herself and close her eyes until he lifted her chin. He was close enough that his broad shoulders blocked out the light. "Just want to warm you up, Bailey."

She *was* cold, *beyond* cold, and shaking so hard she could feel her brain cells rattling together.

And still, she could think.

And what she thought was that things were worse than ever. She hadn't found the money. One resort down, two more to check. And now that Noah had helped her lose the men on her tail, she should go immediately. That meant going back out there. . . .

Closing her eyes again, she weaved in exhaustion, then felt his hands on her arms again. "Hey," he said, bending a little to peer into her face. "Hey, it's going to be okay."

"Really? How?" She didn't pull away. She no longer had the energy; the cold had sapped it right out of her. "I'm sorry," she whispered. "I have to go. I need to call a cab, or—"

"No. Hell, no." With that he dropped his shirt to the floor and pulled her into the heat of his body. "No one's going anywhere, not tonight."

She resisted—barely—the urge to bury her nose against him and inhale him up like a forbidden treat. But she couldn't resist the heat of him. "I have to—"

"Stay," he commanded quietly. "You have to stay. Tomorrow is soon enough to figure it all out."

At the thought of turning it off for the night, she nearly melted. She was helpless against the pull of him, and couldn't help but lift her arms and wrap them around his waist.

When she did, he sucked in a harsh breath. "Your hands are frozen."

Yes. Yes they were, and to prove it, she ran them up and down his back, gliding them against sleek, smooth skin and sinew, thinking, *Yum*.

"*Christ*, woman."

At his tortured tone, she laughed. *Laughed*. She couldn't believe she'd managed to find anything funny about this night, hell, about her *life*, but he'd made her laugh.

But then he wrapped his fist in her hair and gently tugged her head back to meet his gaze. His eyes weren't laughing, but oh, so serious, and her smile slowly faded.

He just looked at her, a look that brought a whole new meaning to anticipation, and she shivered, a bone-deep quiver that had him letting out a low sound filled with regret, concern.

And arousal.

It brought her own to the surface, and then suddenly he was even closer, running his nose along her jaw, pressing his cheek to hers, and then finally, *finally*, kissing her.

There was nothing, nothing in the entire world, like kissing Noah Fisher. His mouth touched hers at the corner, and then his tongue, and she opened for him, opened and dove in, and lost herself. The night had been so monumentally bad, a nightmare. The only thing holding her together was him: his heat, his strength, his unbelievable wit and ease in any situation.

Only when air was necessary did they break to breathe, and again he lifted her face to his, gaze serious. "Back to that whole stripping thing." He stroked a finger ever so lightly over her jaw, then down her throat, her shoulder . . . nudging her sweater off as he went.

Oh, God. She'd never toggled back and forth between fear and arousal before, but she'd been doing just that since she'd stepped onto his plane, watching him pilot without knowing he had an audience.

He was looking into her eyes, and whatever went through his mind, his jaw went tight, and he moved into the bathroom and cranked on the hot water in the shower.

"Kick off your boots," he said, coming back to her.

"Um—"

His eyes held . . . things, lots of things, and that was when she realized. She wasn't so much in danger from the bad guys at the moment, but from within her own self.

Serious danger.

"Bailey—"

Just then, from inside her pocket, her cell phone vibrated and chirped, signaling she had an incoming text message.

Noah watched Bailey debate with herself on whether to look at the message in front of him or not, but she finally reached into her pocket and opened the phone.

WHERE R U?

"Where is *he?*" Noah countered, reading over her shoulder.

"Hidden." She looked away, and chewed on her lower lip in a gesture of nerves. "Hopefully."

"What does that mean?"

She said nothing, and he sighed. "Bailey."

"After—" Her mouth tightened. "I told him to stay away. But now I'm afraid he'll get so worried about me he'll come back."

"Why didn't you go with him?"

"He's fine moving around doing carpentry, which suits him. But my life is in California, Noah. I teach here. . . ." She shook her head. "I really thought I could handle this."

She had courage and guts, and he didn't like the way that

softened him even further toward her. "Don't," he said when she hit reply. "Don't text him back."

"What? I have to."

"Fine. But don't tell him where you are."

"Why?"

He just looked at her.

Still shivering, she looked shell-shocked, frozen to the spot. "Are you kidding me? You actually think he—"

"I don't know what I think. Keep your location quiet." Hating the fear on her face, he had to temper down on his bottle of emotions, of which frustration and impatience were leading the way. "If he's really gone, then it doesn't matter. Right?"

She hadn't moved other than to keep shivering. Her eyes were dilated, and she looked near shock. Steam drifted in from the opened bathroom. She nearly dropped her phone, she was shaking so hard. He had to get her into the hot water.

To that end, he took the cell phone out of her hands and set it aside. *Clothes next*, he thought.

"C—cold," she said.

"I know." He shouldn't care. She'd hijacked him, had really thrown a wrench in his whole ski-and-screw-his-brains-out weekend, but she'd been desperate and terrified, and he'd been helpless against those things. Still having no idea exactly what she'd been through, but more determined than ever to find out, he dipped down a little to look directly into her eyes.

She tried to look away, but he simply cupped her jaw. "I'm going to help you," he said, and ran his hands down her arms. "Starting with a hot shower."

"I don't need help."

"Could have fooled me."

A sound of extreme exasperation left her lips, which he figured was a good sign. If he could piss her off, she wasn't dying of hypothermia.

"Okay, up until this point I needed your help," she conceded. "But I'm fine now."

"Okay." Leaning back, he crossed his arms. "Go ahead, get yourself warm, then."

She glanced through the open door at the shower, at the steaming air rising from it, and walked into the bathroom. She lifted her fingers to her sweater as she looked pointedly at the door, which he ignored. "I'll be fine," she said, her fingers trembling so that she could hardly grip the buttons on her sweater. "Just fine."

"Uh huh." He followed her. Brushing her fingers aside, he went for the buttons, but there were a million of them, and they were tiny and slippery. He got two undone, just enough for his fingers to brush creamy, soft skin beneath. A muscle in his jaw began ticking. "Do these buttons even function?"

"They did this morning."

He sighed. "Your lips are blue." So was her skin, blue and mottled.

"We're not . . . doing anything."

Other than getting naked. That would probably be enough for him, after six months. "I know."

"Good. Because it's been so long, I've forgotten how."

He stared at her, his brain whirling from the quick subject change, not to mention the subject itself. "How long?"

"Really long."

"Really long," he repeated, a little dumbfounded, still holding on to her sweater. He could feel her smooth skin beneath his fingers. Just from that, he got hard.

"He lost interest," she whispered.

Jesus, how was that even possible? "Don't take this the wrong way, Bailey, but Alan was a complete idiot."

She lifted a shoulder, and he vowed right then and there to somehow make sure she knew that there was nothing wrong with her, to prove exactly how desirable she was, but right now, he had another mission.

Get her warm. Make her feel safe. Without letting her think on it too long, he tightened his fingers over the hem of the fuzzy soft material that had been clinging to her breasts for the past hour—not that he'd noticed.

Shit, he was such a liar. He'd so noticed.

He'd noticed and had found himself nearly poleaxed by the way her nipples, two tight peaks, pressed against the thin, wet, soft material.

Alan had lost interest? Noah would have to lose his head. Both of them. The hot, brain-cell-melting kisses they'd shared hadn't helped. No, those hadn't done anything but make him want more.

Then her eyes met his, wide and half wild, and he tempered down on himself and his ridiculous thoughts. This was about getting her warm.

Not about the fact that he was hard from just looking at her.

Nope, his needs had no place here, no place at all. Repeating that like a mantra inside his head, he lifted up on her sweater, forcing her arms up over her head.

"Are you hurt?" he asked.

She said nothing to that, which sent a foreboding down his spine. If someone had laid his hands on her . . . well, he didn't want to think about it. He'd spent his entire life hating violence, and yet it was pouring through his veins now.

"I just don't want to be dead," she whispered. "I want to stay alive."

He stared into her eyes, seeing all sorts of things there, things that somehow soothed the beast roaring within him, things that made him incredibly aware of his fingers resting on her sides, spread wide so as to touch as much of her as he possibly could. "Alive is excellent." His thumbs were just beneath her breasts. If he moved them, he'd be able to feel those curves, take the weight of them in his palms and—

And she was breathing erratically again, so he swallowed his own emotions, his arousal, and kept going.

He pulled the sweater off over her head.

Her bra . . . it was a barely there number, a pale, pale pink thing that just skimmed her nipples with satin and lace, like in his fantasies. Her breasts were two perfect pale curves plumping out of the bra, tipped with small, tight nipples poking at the satin, and her quickened breathing didn't help any.

Truth was, he was breathing as wildly and as loudly as she was. He could hear them both over the water hitting the tiles in the shower.

Bailey stared at his throat while he took in the button and zipper on her jeans. Since she didn't reach for either, he sucked in a breath and did it himself, trying to ignore the way her belly fluttered when he touched her skin.

Pop went the button, and with a hard swallow he reached for the tab of her zipper.

The rasp of the metal sounded incredibly loud in the room.

Then he dropped his gaze to look down at what he'd exposed, and what he'd exposed was a wedge of soft, creamy, pale skin that he wanted to put his mouth to so badly he was shaking for it.

For her.

Yeah, way to keep your distance.

Tightening his mouth, he hunkered down before her and pushed her jeans to her thighs, trying not to notice that he was at eye level with the most beautiful, erotic sight he'd ever seen—a pair of absolutely heart destroying pale blue string bikini panties with a satin ribbon over each hip and a little triangle that barely covered her mound. Trying not to stare, he shoved the denim farther, to her knees.

Looking at her perfect body, it was a moment before he was able to speak. He wanted to hold her. God, he wanted that so much he ached. Surging to his feet, he looked into her eyes and felt his heart engage.

Hard.

Which was some pretty damn bad timing.

With the slow, exaggerated movements of someone either sick, drugged, or exhausted beyond all sense, she kicked free of her boots.

And then stepped out of her jeans.

His heart stopped, then kicked back into action, going from zero to sixty in two-point-one seconds. Maybe less.

Oblivious to his reaction, she turned her back and afforded him a front-row-seat view of a world-class ass.

Weaving, she grabbed the shower door. He lurched to help, but she held up a hand to hold him off, and he forced himself to stand very still rather than put his hands all over her.

"I'll be quick," she promised, glancing at him over her shoulder as she gripped the shower door. "So you can warm up, too."

Before he could do anything stupid, like suggest they conserve water and shower together, or better yet just get down on his knees and beg to worship at the temple of her body, she stepped into the water and shut the glass door.

"Okay, then," he said, and backed to the bathroom doorway, running into it like an idiot. "I'll just be out here if you need anything." *Please need something.*

Me.

She didn't answer, so he stepped outside the bathroom. Paused. Waited. She still said nothing, so with no choice left, he shut the door. Leaning back on it, he surveyed the master suite and let out a slow, deliberate breath.

Because he wasn't seeing the huge bed, piled high with luxurious bedding. He wasn't seeing the gorgeous oak furniture, or the huge picture window revealing the dark, dark night.

He could see only Bailey, and how she'd just looked beneath the streaming, steaming hot water running in rivulets down her body—

He thunked his head back against the door, but the image

didn't dispel. It seemed like days ago since he'd gotten onto the Piper to come here. Days since he'd first looked into Bailey's eyes and been drawn in . . .

Since that thought brought him back to her naked and wet and gleaming, he tightened his jaw and stalked out of the bedroom, making his way through the house, checking each door and window lock.

The shower was still running.

In the kitchen, he put water on to boil, got out a mug and found some tea. When he had it steeping, he picked it up and headed back to the bedroom. He looked at the bathroom door. She'd been in there long enough to broil herself. "Bailey?" He knocked twice.

Nothing. Just the water hitting the tiles.

And suddenly, he got worried. Or *more* worried. "Bailey? You okay?"

Again with the no-answer thing.

The hell with preserving her privacy, he thought, and helped himself to the door.

Chapter 11

The shower looked empty. Heart in his throat, Noah set the mug down on the counter and yanked open the glass door.

And felt his heart crack.

Bailey was huddled on the floor in a ball, her head bent over her knees.

Yeah, all distance had definitely gone out the window. He'd done as she'd wanted; he'd gotten her to Mammoth. Now he should turn around and get her the hell out of here, or walk away.

But he couldn't.

He couldn't walk away from her and didn't know who could.

She hadn't moved. Concerned, he stepped right into the shower and squatted down at her side. "Bailey."

She jerked as if she'd been shot, and then stared at him from hollow, haunted eyes.

She'd fallen asleep, he realized, just sitting right there, too exhausted to even move.

He knew how she felt. Even now, with the water beating down on his back, soaking into his jeans, he felt the same.

The water was beating down on her as well, and with her

hair in her face, and the little bit of mascara she'd had left smudged beneath her eyes, she looked like a drowned rat.

Ah, hell, who was he kidding? She looked hot. Way too hot to touch, but he couldn't just leave her there. He stood and turned off the water. "Come on, Princess," he murmured, and scooped her up into his arms. *Not* noticing how her bare wet skin felt in his hands, he told himself. *Not* noticing that her pale blue satin panties and pink bra had gone sheer, and snug as a second skin, revealing far more than they hid.

Christ, she was mouth-watering.

Nope, *not* noticing. He tossed a towel around her, did his best to dry her off some, and carried her into the bedroom. He went to set her down on the floor next to the bed so that he could pull back the comforter, but she tightened her grip around his neck and burrowed in, making a soft little sound that tugged right at his gut.

"I've got to set you down," he said. "And get your wet things off."

She loosened her hold, and he let her slide to the carpet, maybe coincidentally keeping her snug against him as he leaned over the mattress and yanked down the covers.

Or not coincidentally.

Dropping the towel, she moved to crawl into the bed, but he stopped her. "Your things . . ." He gestured to her bra and panties, which were outlining every curve and nuance. Her breasts were pushed up, her nipples two tight points. Her belly rose and fell quickly with her stressed breathing. And those panties, the way they clung to her every single jaw-dropping, sexy, erotic inch.

But he might as well try to stop breathing.

Or to not get impossibly hard at the sight of her.

Yeah, like that was in his control.

"Sorry," she actually said, and reached behind her to unhook her bra, while he stood there afraid his tongue would fall out and embarrass him.

A man should not go six months without sex, he told himself. Should. Not. Because now, suddenly, the only thing that was going to make him feel better was exactly that, complete with a mind-blowing orgasm, the hotter, the sweatier, the wilder, the better.

It was crazy, beyond crazy, but after the unexpectedly rough flight with the landing gear troubles, then the goons with guns, the wild goose chase . . . they were finally going to end up naked.

Just to prevent hypothermia.

A big, fat lie, by the way. He hated liars, and he'd become one, but with the feeling of Bailey wrapped around him like warm honey as she'd been, he didn't give a shit.

She was struggling with the clasp on her bra, her motions lethargic, as if she was so out of energy she could barely move. In the meantime, with her arms behind her, her breasts were thrust out like two ripe offerings. Water from her hair dripped down her belly and into her panties, which concealed exactly nothing, not the fact that she was neatly trimmed or that she was a natural strawberry blonde.

Jesus.

"I can't—" Her voice was slurred with sheer exhaustion.

"Here." Putting his hands to her shoulders, he turned her around and brushed her hands aside. Her shoulders and neck were bared because her hair had fallen to her front, showing off her smooth, beautiful back, the way her sexy-as-hell panties had given her a world-class wedgie—

"Noah?"

Right. The bra. "Yeah," he said, tearing his eyes off her ass and the wet satin invading it, his voice sounding rough even to his own ears as he unhooked her bra.

Head bent, she let the material fall to the floor. Unable to help himself, his gaze slid back down. "Uh—"

Her fingers hooked into the little wisp of material still at her hips.

Again, he stopped breathing.

With a tug and a little shimmy, she began to slide the panties off.

And for just a moment, he actually died.

Oblivious, she bent over, and he realized he hadn't died, not yet anyway, because there was blood rushing through his veins, beating with a loud BOOM, BOOM, BOOM at the sight of her as she bent, naked, totally exposed—

"Tired," she murmured, and straightening, crawled up onto the mattress, nearly making his eyes pop right out of their sockets at the sight of her briefly on all fours as she moved to the center of the bed.

She was the most gorgeous, sexiest thing he'd ever seen.

Then she slipped beneath the covers, turned on her side away from him, and didn't budge.

"Yeah, uh . . . I'll just crank the electric blanket." He did that, then stood there like the fool he was, dripping all over the carpet, shivering, hard as a rock.

And there was nothing, nothing in the world, worse than being in wet Levi's when hard as a rock.

She didn't move.

"I'm going to get out of my wet things," he heard himself say.

She didn't care. Or at least she didn't say a word.

He unbuttoned his Levi's and grimaced as he attempted to shuck himself out of the wet denim. He'd already kicked off his shoes, so hc tried to get his drenched sock off, but that turned out not to be a good idea with his jeans stuck wet and clinging to his thighs, and he fell over.

Lying on the floor, his ass hanging out, his legs caught in the damned wet jeans, he sighed. "I'm okay," he said.

To no one.

When he managed to kick free of the jeans, he stood up. All he could see of Bailey was the top of her still damp hair, but he could have sworn he could hear her teeth chattering together.

Damn.

Well, that left him no choice, right? He had to warm her up, ward off the impending hypothermia. It was his civic duty. So he quickly dried off, lifted the edge of the comforter, and slid in. Oh, yeah, the sheets were warm, thanks to the electric blanket and the down comforter.

So he had no idea why he breached the halfway point of the huge bed and bumped up against a nude, curvy, deliciously warm Bailey. Oops. He was on her side. Unfortunately, his arms slid around her before he could stop himself, and he pulled her back against his chest and thighs, snuggling in.

"Mmm," left her lips, but other than that, she said nothing.

Nor did she move away. In fact, she didn't move at all.

Encouraged by that, he braced his head on one hand, the other skimming up her side as he looked down at the only thing visible outside the covers—her face.

And had to laugh.

She was asleep. As in dead-to-the-world, one-hundred-percent asleep, while he was hotter than he'd ever been, harder than he'd ever been. . . .

For a woman so terrorized, she didn't even realize he was in bed with her. He didn't care. He had no idea how sick that made him, but was fairly certain it made him pretty sick.

In her sleep, she snuffled and made some sort of soft whimper. "Shh," he murmured, hand on her belly, stroking lightly up and down. "I've got you."

Absorbing his words, she sighed, and wriggled just a little bit closer, which involved her sweet bare ass pressing into his hard-enough-to-hammer-steel self.

She slept on.

Yeah, *that* was good for the ego.

She sighed again, wriggled again for more. Her hair tickled his nose, and instead of brushing it away, he buried his face in the rioted mess, then found himself pressing his mouth to her neck.

God, she was sweet. Sweet and pale with exhaustion, and he just breathed her in. He needed to let her sleep. But unable to resist, he smoothed her damp hair off her face and let his mouth take itself on a little trail down her throat and back up to her ear, breathing her in as if she could be his air.

Her hand squeezed his, and another little sigh escaped her, though she didn't awaken. He thought of the night she'd had, of the days leading up to it that he still didn't know enough about to suit him, and understood whatever happened had been brutal, and she'd been through hell. Empathy swamped him, and he rubbed his jaw down the side of her neck.

"Mmmm," she sighed again, with another enticing wriggle, and this time something else rose within him, something far more physically based.

He danced his hand up and down her belly again. Up, up . . .

To the very undersides of her breasts . . .

Oh, God, she felt like heaven . . . and down, down low enough to run into the very tippy top of her strawberry blond mound . . .

Again she rocked her bottom against him, making him twitch.

A little whimpery sound that in fact could have been a half sob escaped her and tore at his gut. He pressed his lips to her jaw, her cheek, helpless to resist her smooth skin. Her breathing evened out at just the feel of him, and that, too, brought a deep surge of satisfaction. "I've got you," he murmured.

"Noah," she murmured, not moving, not even to open her eyes.

"Yeah. Me." Feeling the weight of her exhaustion, he was glad she didn't move. He kissed her jaw again, and then her throat, groaning when she took his wandering hand in both of hers and brought it up to her breasts.

His fingers stroked her hard, pebbled nipples as his mouth worked its way to her shoulder, nudging the covers down as he went so he could lean over her and get a good look at what he exposed. He completely melted at the sight of her pale breasts and his own tanned fingers playing with her nipples. He let the blanket fall to her waist.

And the truth hit him like a one-two punch—the more he saw of her, the more he wanted, and the stronger the need for her became.

What was that?

He had no idea, but neither did he have any resistance to fight it. It was a wrenching realization of how bad he had it for her. "God, you're beautiful."

In answer, she burrowed back beneath the covers so that he could see nothing now but a cloud of strawberry blond waves, but . . . but she didn't let go of his hand. Instead, she pushed it down, while he tried to keep from drooling all over her, tried to keep from begging her to continue letting him touch her because her nipples were the most gorgeous nipples he'd ever seen. . . .

But where she pushed his hand—past her quivering belly into the slippery satin and between her thighs—worked, too, and he spread his fingers to touch as much of her as he could.

She let out a needy murmur, one that had his name on it, and nearly had him coming right then and there.

"Noah," she gasped, her body arching up when he moved his fingers, increasing the rhythm. God, he still couldn't get enough of her.

Still fully covered by the down comforter, she rolled to her back, giving him better access.

Which he gladly took.

Keeping his hand on her, he slid his face just beneath the blanket, pressing his mouth to her shoulder while working her into a feverish pitch with his fingers. Another soft sound came from her throat, and she blindly turned her face toward his. An invitation if ever he'd seen one, and he snatched it, lowering his mouth to hers.

She made the sound again and opened her legs for him, and

he didn't hold back, running his tongue over her lower lip, drawing it into his mouth to suck, then caressing it again as he glided his fingers over her. Into her.

She gasped his name, and he leaned over her, inhaling her scent, the soft feel of her beneath him, the way she panted in his ear, how her mouth clung to his as if maybe, just maybe, he was a lifeline for her, the way she'd become one for him.

Her breathing had turned into a mantra of his name, and he increased the pressure of his fingers, making her cry out, a needy sound that went straight to his groin. The covers slipped to her shoulders. Her eyes were open, glossed over and disoriented with sleep and desire, and he didn't care. He kissed her again.

And again.

Her face was flushed, her mouth wet from his, and that wasn't the only place she was wet. She was drenched, for him, and the knowledge brought a surge of pleasure so sharp he couldn't contain his groan, or keep his fingers from playing in her slippery heat.

"Please," she whimpered into his mouth, rocking her hips in tune with his fingers, urging him into her rhythm, but he already knew it. Somehow he already knew her, knew what made her hum with pleasure, knew how to turn her moans into gasping, hungry cries, how to drive her up higher and higher until her body went tight and then even tighter, until her hands came down over his as if to hold him there, as if afraid he'd pull away and stop.

Not going to happen. He kept with her, increasing the pressure and pace as she wanted, tugging the blanket down so he could watch, which nearly had him losing it.

Her eyes were closed, her mouth open as she gasped for air, her breasts full, her nipples peaked tight, her belly quivering as he moved his fingers on her, in her. Bending, he took one of her nipples in his mouth and sucked hard as he stroked her, and she went taut as a bow, and then burst.

He couldn't tear his eyes off her as she exploded for him, on him, all over him. It was the hottest, most erotic experience of his life, and he hadn't even been touched.

Her hips slowed, and she released his hand, probably as reality hit. She made a sound, one that held more than a touch of embarrassment, and without looking at him, rolled to her side, away from him.

He didn't react as fast as she, and was slow to take his hand off her, letting it glide up over her hip, over her ribs, barely skimming the very bottom curve of a breast before he withdrew. Though it was the last thing he wanted to do, he covered her back up, covered them both back up, and by the time he snuggled in behind her, she was dead asleep again, lost in dreamland, hopefully where there were no bad guys with guns, and most likely where there was no him either.

Nothing showed of her now except the very top of her head, but he could feel her every single silky inch, and his body hadn't yet gotten the message that he wasn't on the same path to release that she'd gotten.

It didn't matter.

He wanted to turn her over to talk, to make her trust him with all her secrets. He also wanted to make her come all over him again, as many times as possible, and then he wanted to bury himself inside her so only the two of them existed, so that she could lose herself in him.

And him in her.

Her breathing slowed even more, evening out in the cadence of someone deeply asleep. Which she needed, he reminded himself. He took several deep breaths of his own and forced some grim thoughts to help ease his desire, such as the events that had transpired since leaving Burbank, leading up to him being here in this bed.

It was sobering. But not sobering enough, not with her hair in his face, the taste of her still on his lips, the scent of her consuming him. Not with the hard-on he had raging even right this moment, nudging her in the ass on its own. With a sigh, he pressed his face into her hair, letting it drift down over him, and tried to follow her into dreamland.

Bailey couldn't catch her breath. She was running, running at top speed, or at least as top speed as her ridiculous high-heeled boots would let her in the snow, which had seeped into her clothes, down her boots, into her hair and face so that she was so frozen solid she couldn't feel anything.

She couldn't see either; a fog had settled all around, and panic gripped her in its icy fist.

"Bailey!" Kenny called from somewhere in the fog, somewhere close.

He was in danger, terrible danger. She hadn't gotten him far away enough, safe enough, and on top of that, she hadn't been able to find the money.

Now he was going to die, because of her, and no matter how fast she ran, she couldn't catch up with him. "I'm here!" she cried. "I'm right here! Where are you?"

"Bailey?"

He sounded farther away this time, and her heart sped up as she ran harder, faster. She had to find him before they hurt him. She had to.

Then she plowed into something—*somebody*.

Reaching out, she dug her fingers into Kenny, sobbing in relief, only . . . only this person was bigger, taller than Kenny.

Alan.

"But you're dead," she said inanely, staring up into his face.

He grabbed her arms, gave her a little shake, and smiled, and the teeth fell out of his mouth. Before she could so much as draw a breath to scream, the skin slid off his face, and his hair slid away, revealing a skeleton, a horrible, terrifying skeleton smiling at her. "And you're next," it said evilly.

She found the breath to scream, but it came out as a sort of pathetic little whimper because he was going to kill her. At the knowledge, she began to fight, kicking, biting, scratching, and when he dropped her, she whirled and ran for her life.

Any minute now she'd feel a bullet tearing into her flesh, which spurred her on while striking terror into her heart. Each breath was a sob for help, for mercy, for this nightmare to be over—

"Bailey."

"Get away from me!"

"Princess, it's just me. I've got you."

Bullshit, he was going to get her. Confused, disoriented, she fought with every ounce of her being—

"*Bailey.*"

The voice was different, and penetrated through her panic. Not Kenny's . . .

"You're okay," Noah said. "It's just me."

With a gasp, she opened her eyes, but it didn't help. It was still pitch-black, and panicked, she sat straight up and bashed her forehead into his. Seeing stars, she fell backward to the pillow.

"Jesus. Fuck. Christ." He sounded as if maybe he was in considerable pain.

Pain she'd caused.

But at least he was alive, and then he proved it by pinning her down with his big, tough, gorgeous body.

"Talk to me," he said.

Chapter 12

Talk to him . . . the one thing she didn't want to do, not when still gasping from the dream and seeing stars from bashing her head on his, hard. She couldn't see a hand in front of her face either, which didn't help.

She could feel, though. Feel Noah sprawled over the top of her. All of him was hard, and sharp, far too sharp for her to get anything past, though she wished she could, because she didn't want to discuss this.

Or anything.

It was too much, it was all too much, and she shoved at him, needing to roll over and lick her wounds in private.

"Bailey," he murmured, holding on to her, stroking his hands down her body. "You're okay."

Her naked body.

Oh, God. She'd let him—at the memory, she squeaked in humiliation, which he must have taken as fear because he whispered, "It was just a dream." He kept his hands on her, not letting her go, even though she wanted to roll into a tight ball. "Just a dream."

"But it wasn't." She hated that her eyes burned, that her throat was so tight her every breath hitched. "Kenny was there, he was hurt, and then Alan—"

"A dream," he said again firmly. "I promise."

"But it all really happened. Alan did leave me in this mess, and it's going to keep happening, don't you see? It's going to keep happening until I—"

Find the money.

She closed her mouth, wishing she could find an escape, something to take her out of this existence of terror.

His hand stroked her hair, and she closed her eyes, thinking if he kept doing that, maybe for the rest of the night she could pretend none of it had ever happened, that they were here together because they wanted to be.

That she was safe.

"It's going to keep happening until . . . what, Bailey?"

And even though he couldn't see her, she shook her head from side to side. She couldn't tell him. The less he knew, the better. She was still breathing kind of crazily, as if she'd really been running in the woods from Alan. It had seemed so real, but truthfully? Lying in bed with Noah like this, tucked beneath his long, tough, sinewy body, it wasn't Alan she was in danger from now, but her own heart.

Noah stroked the hair from her face. She still couldn't see him, but she didn't have to; she could feel him. He'd kept his word; he'd kept her safe. It was like her own little miracle.

He brushed his nose along her jaw toward her ear, where he slowly exhaled and brought an entirely different kind of shiver to her body, one that had nothing, nothing at all, to do with fear.

Not a little miracle, she corrected when she felt something pressing into her thigh. A *big* miracle with a long, tough-built body more than capable of doing whatever was needed.

Including, apparently, her, and in spite of herself, she felt her body heat up in memory.

"You're safe here," Noah said, his voice coming disembodied in the dark. "Believe that much, at least."

"I do." Her voice was raspy, telling her she'd slept long and hard. A shock. She hadn't slept long and hard since Alan's death.

His fingers sank into her hair as his thumbs stroked her forehead. "That's got to hurt," he said, and she heard the wry smile in his voice. "You hit my chin hard."

"Seeing stars," she admitted.

"You really are safe here, you know," he said, sounding sure and confident.

What she'd give for half of that confidence. "Still, I should go. I have to—"

"It's only five. Sleep some more first, then I'll take you where you need to go."

"Five . . . *in the morning?*"

"Yeah."

With a squeak, she pushed him aside and sat straight up again. "We slept all night?"

"What was left of it."

She felt the mattress give as he stretched for something, and then she heard a click, and a soft light flooded the room.

Then an entirely different nightmare came to her. Because she'd kicked away the covers while running in her dreams, and she wore only a set of goose bumps, and nothing else.

She grabbed for the down comforter to pull it over herself, but Noah beat her to it, holding the blanket away, his gaze running over her breasts, her ribs, her belly, his eyes dark, so very, very dark.

But that wasn't what made her breath catch in her throat, what had her nipples hardening in spite of herself.

No, that came from the fact that he was also completely, gloriously, one-hundred-percent naked.

And aroused.

Oh, good Lord, was the man aroused, and built, not to mention completely at ease with his body in a way she would have admired if she wasn't suddenly so aware of how exposed she was, and vulnerable.

And needy.

With the light on, she felt extremely . . . vulnerable. She covered her breasts with her hands and closed her eyes, concentrating on breathing and not on the image she presented him with.

But then she felt his hands on her, turning her to him. "Bailey."

"We shouldn't have slept together—"

"We were chilled, and you were near shock. You needed body heat."

Again she felt the mattress shift beneath his weight, and then she was tucked back beneath that admittedly warm, deliciously warm, hard body.

The man was her virtual opposite, not a soft, giving, cushy inch on him. "You're not wearing anything," she said breathlessly.

"I was soaked all the way through. I couldn't sleep like that."

No excuses, no apology.

He'd stripped down, slipped into bed to keep her warm, and she'd let him. She squeezed her eyes tighter, knowing he was looking at her, that she was just about as bared and exposed as she could get.

He said nothing, and when the moment stretched on past bearing, she cracked open an eye.

And met two orbs of heated jade. Oh, God. Yeah, he was looking at her, but not her body. Nope, he was looking right into her one eye, and suddenly she couldn't look away to save her life. "The covers," she said.

"You want to cover up to hide."

"I'm cold."

"Then I'll keep you warm." And that said, keeping his gaze locked on hers, he slowly but inexorably pulled her closer, ignoring the fact that she resisted slightly—only slightly because being against him was hardly a hardship—ignoring everything until he'd sat back against the headboard, with her in his lap.

Only then did he pull the comforter up over the both of them, but by then she didn't need the warmth of the down; she had the blazing heat from his body, and it generated a heat of her own, one that started deep within and burned outward.

"Okay?" he asked.

Her breasts were mashed up against his hard chest, reminding her that while she was soft and feminine, he was sinewy and tough and hard as nails. One of her hands was trapped at her side, the other between them, pressing into his corrugated abs. Beneath her hip she could feel—"Either you're still carrying that flashlight," she said, still breathless. "Or—"

"Or I'm happy to see you?" he asked dryly. "Take a guess."

Her entire body went on red-alert status, complete with happy nipples and some sort of fireworks between her thighs. She didn't mean to, she really didn't, but she wriggled, just enough to wrench a low, rough sound from his throat.

And the "penlight" swelled to full-blown searchlight size. "Oh, boy," she whispered.

"That's what you do to me, Bailey," he said, keeping her close when she might have scooted free. "I can't help the reaction, but I'm not going to hurt you, or make you do anything you don't want to do."

At the unexpected gentleness of his voice, her gaze whipped to his. Slowly he reached up and swiped at a tear she hadn't even known she'd shed.

"Can't you talk to me?" he asked quietly.

Throat nearly closed, she could only stare up at him, never so aware of a man in her entire life. Aware and alive, two beautiful things.

But this was not meant to be. She'd committed crimes to get here. She'd lied, and though he knew of both, *he'd* been the victim, *her* victim, and when this was over—assuming she managed to survive—nothing could come of this rather startlingly explosive attraction.

"You can trust me," he said.

It made her heart hurt, physically hurt. All her life she'd been controlled, first by her father, and then by Alan, almost without her even realizing it. She'd been on her own for months now, and though it had been terrifying, it had also been exhilarating. Making her own decisions, accounting to no one . . .

Trusting went against the grain. Even for a man who'd gone over and beyond the duty, who'd been forced here against his will and yet continued to do everything in his power to help her, to keep her safe.

Even when he didn't know the whole story.

He just wanted to help her. That was all.

In light of that, some of her unwavering determination stalled, and as she watched him, she softened some more.

And melted.

As if sensing it, he dipped his head and stroked his thumb over her ribs, his eyes so dark and deep she could have drowned. His shoulders were certainly broad and strong enough to take the weight of her problems.

Was he going to kiss her?

She shouldn't have been able to even think such a thing, but looking into those mesmerizing, melting eyes, it was all she could think about.

He slid his hand into her hair, cupping her nape, urging her closer, his thumb stroking her skin. Her heart sped up as anticipation swam through her.

She wanted him. She wanted his hands back on her.

"Trust me," he whispered again. "Talk to me."

She'd never been so torn in her life, wanting to do exactly that . . . and also wanting to jump him.

Devour him. "I've . . . sort of sworn off all men."

"Including Kenny?"

"No. He's all I've got."

His voice was grim and solemn. "That's what I was afraid you were going to say."

"Kenny wouldn't hurt me."

"Well, Princess, I hope to hell you're right." He shifted even closer if that was possible, the blanket completely sliding off them. Oblivious, he looked at her, his hair falling into his eyes, making her want to touch.

But she didn't.

She didn't dare because she didn't know if she'd be able to stop.

"What about your mother?" he asked.

"Oh, you know, it's just the same old classic poor little rich girl story," she said with a laugh that didn't ring true even to herself. "She died when I was young. My father traveled a lot. I shifted from nanny to nanny until I got too old for such company, and then I went off to college." Without really mastering the whole letting-people-in thing.

Which hadn't mattered once Alan had come into her life. He'd come with a full social calendar and in the beginning had readily included her in everything. And had included Kenny, too, when he'd expressed interest. "All in all, a rather lonely childhood," she admitted.

"I know how that feels." He smiled a little grimly at her surprise. "See, we're not so different. Except that I wasn't a poor little rich girl."

She was smiling, she was naked, and they were talking. "What were you? Seems a little late now, but I really do want to know."

"I was born in London on the wrong side of the tracks. My mother was just a kid herself and not into the whole maternal thing. So I begged, borrowed, and stole my way here, where I landed pretty quickly in a series of decent foster homes until I struck out on my own." He smiled. "I did okay."

"I'd say you did. Though you're not alone, you have Shayne and Brody to watch your back."

"Why isn't Kenny watching yours?"

"Because I don't want him to."

He just looked at her.

"Don't say it," she said fiercely. "He's not behind any of this."

He looked as if he might want to argue with that, but changed his mind. "Just promise me not to use your cell phone anymore. Don't give anyone a way to track you."

"I . . . I didn't think they could do that."

"We don't know what they can do," he said, and a shiver raced down her spine.

But she did know what they could do to her. What they *would* do if she didn't somehow fix this. "Kenny is *not* the one trying to hurt me, Noah."

"I didn't say he was. But it's possible, if they got a hold of him, that they're using him to get to you. You have to know that much."

Horror filled her. "He would never give me up."

"Just keep the phone turned off." He tugged her down to lie alongside him. She managed to keep the covers over her, but he slowly slid his hand up the blanket, closing his fist in the soft material.

"You told me they want something," he said. "I'm assuming you were told to help or else, right?"

He held her gaze until she nodded, and then in reward, bent and gently, so gently it brought the sting of tears to her eyes, pressed his lips to her heart over the blanket, and then slowly pulled it free.

She could have stopped him, but she didn't, not as the down scraped over her nude body, or when the air brushed her skin.

He kissed a bared rib now, then murmured, "Who are they?"

All she could see of him was his broad shoulders and back as he bent over her, his muscles flexed taut, and she stirred, from the inside out. "I . . ." Couldn't think. "I really didn't get a good look at them." She *hadn't.*

But she hadn't needed to either, she knew exactly who was in charge.

Stephen.

Another soft kiss, lower now, on her belly, while his hand danced down her thigh. "You sure?"

She knew she had to give him something, had to let him in, even if only a little. "Y—yes," she whispered, stuttering because his mouth skimmed over her hip on his way down, his wavy hair tingling her skin, making her belly jump and quiver.

She knew his eyes were open, that he could see her up close and personal. With a touch so light she couldn't believe her body followed his direction, he nudged her thighs open. "Where did they come to you before?"

"Uh—" Hard to talk when he dipped farther down, his shoulders holding her legs open. Shocked that she'd allowed this, she stared down at the top of his head, watching him press his lips to her flesh. His mouth was soft, so achingly soft, as were his hands. Never in her life had she been so aware of her own body.

"Bailey?"

"The house." She closed her eyes. "I'd fallen asleep on the couch, and when I woke up—" She'd been petrified to find herself facing three men, two of them huge and menacing and armed, one standing at either end of the couch. The third man had been Stephen. He'd sat on her coffee table at her shoulder as if he'd been invited in. And he had, many many times, by Alan. He was polished, elegant, and utterly, terrifyingly, smoothly dangerous. He'd said hello politely, while turning a very wicked looking knife in his fingers.

"They were just there," she said now to Noah. "They wanted—" Money, of course. "They wanted to warn me. If I didn't do what they said, they'd come back."

"And kill you."

If that was all it'd been, it wouldn't be so difficult. But when she'd shaken her head, saying she didn't have the money, didn't know where to find it, he'd nodded, then stood and said that he hoped she'd said good-bye to Kenny.

And her second graders.

Because, he'd said, she wouldn't be seeing them ever again, since his men would be killing them.

One by one.

Then he'd leaned over her and said that he'd be in touch, and she'd better hope he didn't find out she was holding out on him. He'd nodded to the two other men, one of whom held her down while the other had crawled up on top of her, between her legs, wrapping his fingers around her throat, squeezing until she'd blacked out.

When she'd come to, she'd been alone.

She'd been on the run ever since. She'd gotten a hotel room, hadn't gone back to the house or to work, and now she'd gotten Noah involved. "They'd kill anyone I cared about."

"So you have to do what they want. You have to find something." Turning his head, he kissed her other inner thigh.

With his mouth on her, she could hardly breathe, much less talk. "Hence the whole hijack-the-pilot thing."

"Yeah." He stroked his thumb lightly over her skin, his voice a sleepy, sexy whisper. "So why me?"

She wished he'd turned off the light, or that he'd stop talking and start kissing her again. "Your plane was there, ready to go."

"So was Brody's," he reminded her.

"Yes, but . . ."

He kissed her again, lightly, softly, sweetly, and yet nothing in her reaction felt sweet. A new tension had gripped her body, one that had nothing to do with fear, and she found herself arching up into him, her fingers digging into the comforter at her sides.

Noah lifted his head, waiting for an answer.

"I wanted it to be you," she admitted.

"Because I'm an easy mark?"

"No. God, no." She closed her eyes. A hiding habit, she knew, an especially silly one since she was as exposed as she could get, but she needed a minute for this one. Because if she couldn't give him the truth about what she had to do, she was going to give him the truth about this.

Needed to give him the truth about this.

But then he stroked her again, his touch still light and easy, and once again she lost her grasp on her thought process. "You are not an easy mark," she managed.

She had no trouble reading his expression when he lifted his head, no trouble seeing that his features had softened, heated. His fingers were still on her thighs, his thumb gently stroking, and her body, with a mind of its own, twitched, letting her legs fall farther open.

Crazy, she thought. She was crazy wild to expose herself this way, letting him see . . .

Everything.

His gaze dipped, looking directly at what she'd revealed, and then an almost unbearably sexy sound left his throat as he slowly . . . dipped . . . his head . . . and touched his lips to the groove at the very top of her thigh.

"I—I wanted it to be you," she managed. "Because I felt like I knew you, like we had a connection."

He shifted his lips along her hip, her belly, to her other hip. While she didn't so much as breathe.

"We've never talked about anything other than the weather and the route you wanted me to fly," he said directly against her skin. "Which begs the question . . . why me?"

"I . . ." His mouth was working for her, it really was. "I felt it." God, had she felt it. She wanted to pull him up so that she could think, so that she could make some sense. Instead, she continued to fist her hands in the down comforter at her sides and let him drive her to the very edge. "I kn—knew you'd help me."

"Yeah." He let out a short breath and touched his forehead to her belly, his lips tantalizingly close to ground zero. "Do you know why?" he asked.

"Um—"

He slid his fingers beneath her bottom, cupping her, then lifted his head and leveled her with those melting eyes. "Do you know why?" he repeated.

"No."

"Because I had a crush on you."

"You—" *He had a crush on me.* "Noah—"

"A big, fat crush."

Whenever she'd seen him at Sky High, he'd been courteous, professional, distant.

And sexy as hell.

"You never gave me the time of day," she said.

"No, Princess, that was you. You were always dressed to the hilt, looking hot enough to melt butter right off your skin, and yet you never seemed to know it. You'd smile, but rarely speak to me."

"I liked you."

His laugh was soft, and self-deprecatory. "Yeah, well, I fantasized about it being more than like. I wanted to kiss you. I wanted . . ." He tugged, and his face was right there, between her legs.

"This," he said. "I wanted this." With characteristic bluntness, he looked at her. Looked for a long, breathless beat with his hair brushing her belly, his breath warming her skin.

She knew what he saw. A woman's body, up close and personal, complete with flaws.

He didn't say a word.

And she couldn't take it, she just couldn't, so she wriggled up to reach the light and turned it off.

With a low laugh against her skin, he surged up and flicked it on again.

Oh, God. She tried to relax, but she just couldn't, and knowing it, she reached up and flicked it back off.

Silence reigned.

And then it grew, and grew some more, until it was like another person in the room. Realizing she was holding her breath, she let it out.

And Noah sighed. "Hiding again."

"No, I . . ." Okay, yes. Yes, she was.

But he left the light off, and she breathed some more, her entire body quivering with anticipation.

"After all we've been through, you don't have to hide, not from me." Dipping his head, he stroked his thumb unerringly over her, just where she needed it, and then—oh, God, and then—his tongue.

He did it again, and then again, just a little harder, a little faster, and she gasped and arched up, right into his mouth.

"Ah, yeah. That's perfect. You're perfect." And holding her open, he proceeded to drive her out of her own mind and straight into another mind-blowing orgasm.

While she was still shuddering, he crawled up her body, nudging at her center with a most impressive erection.

"Tell me the rest, Bailey."

Was he kidding? She couldn't even put a thought together, much less a sentence.

"What else are you hiding?" he wondered with another nudge that made her want to wrap her legs around his waist and draw him inside. "Bailey?"

"Nothing."

Liar.

He didn't say it, but the word danced around them in the dark as if he had.

"I need to know," he said. "To keep us safe and happy."

And then reaching out, he once again flicked on the light. Settling between her legs, he looked deep into her eyes. "And I want to keep us very, very safe and happy."

Chapter 13

Bailey arched up, helplessly opening for him, but he held back, damn him.

"I guess the next question," he said in a thick voice, pressing his lips to her throat, "is are you going to help me keep us safe and happy?"

"Noah—"

But he pushed inside of her and all thought capacity shrank to the pinnacle of sensations running through her.

Their twin sighs of pleasure comingled in the air.

"What else, Bailey?" he managed. "What else are you hiding?"

"Nothing," she gasped. Everything.

Then he rocked deeper and she could scarcely breathe because he felt so good filling her, so right. *Right.* She'd never felt anything like it. He was inside her, thick and full and heavy. *Perfect.* She had to abandon all thought, abort all reason, because there wasn't room for anything with what he was making her feel, which was alive, gloriously alive.

"It's just you and me," he ground out as he moved within her. "Just us. You can tell me."

She clutched at him, needing him to move again. Then he did just that, his thrust scooting her up on the bed. She might have hit her head on the headboard if he hadn't slapped his hands against it, bracing them as he slid in and out of her. Even as she lost her mind, she shook her head. Surely it couldn't really be like this, this good, this amazing. They were two virtual strangers, and yet . . . and yet she'd never felt so in tune with anyone in her life.

Somehow he knew her, knew her body, knew what she needed, when she needed it, and how to give it to her. He filled her senses, had her writhing, arching, begging. *Begging* in some wordless, gasping voice she hardly recognized as hers, all while he brought her to the very edge and then, damn him, held her there, a panting, dewy, sweaty mass of nerve endings, reduced to total dependency . . .

"Come," he demanded in a rough, low voice, and stroked a thumb over where they were joined.

She saw stars, and when he did it again, with slightly more pressure, she went off like a bottle rocket, coming, going . . . coming again. Or still . . .

Vaguely she realized he had stopped moving, except for the trembling of his arms where he held himself rigid above her, and she opened her eyes.

His expression was one of fierce concentration, his brow damp, his jaw bunched. "I can't believe I nearly forgot—"

She looked at him blankly, on sensory overload with the feeling of him stretching her so deliciously.

"Condom."

She closed her eyes. This. See, *this* is what happened when one went too long without sex. Severe brain cell loss. "I'm on the pill," she whispered.

"Pregnancy isn't the only reason for a condom."

She wished the light was off again. "I'm . . . safe."

When he didn't say anything, she admitted to yet another truth. "I told you it'd been a long time. Almost two years long," she admitted softly. "And I've been checked since then."

He lowered his weight to his forearms, his fingers gliding into her hair, his face close to hers. He kissed her jaw, her ear, her mouth. "It's been over six months for me," he said softly. "And I'm safe, too."

A long time for a man who probably had women throwing themselves at him, but she set that thought aside because her brain simply didn't have room for it, not with him filling her so completely that she had to feel him move again.

Had to.

She glanced toward the lamp, but he shook his head. "On."

"But off would be so much better."

He didn't say anything to that, instead began a set of hot, wet, open-mouthed kisses along her neck to just beneath her ear. She'd never thought of herself as a particularly sensual creature. Sex was very nice when done right, but it wasn't always done right, and truthfully? In most cases, she'd found better release from a battery operated toy than a man.

But not tonight.

Tonight she had Noah, who knew his way around her body better than she did. How else to explain why just a kiss made her ache for more, or why her body felt fluid in his arms, or how mind-blowing it was to have him move within her, in a perfect rhythm that she never wanted to end?

He would never hurt her. He would never disappoint her. How she knew these things about him, she had no idea, but she did.

She knew them as certainly as she knew he'd give her his last breath.

He slid his hands down to the backs of her bare thighs, spreading them wider, allowing for a deeper penetration, which wrenched a groan from him and a matching one from her. No one had ever been so deep inside her before; no one had ever made her thoughts dissolve into mindless sensation and need, such desperate, clawing need.

He whispered her name and the sound alone had her body going taut again, her breath coming in pants as she heated, slickened.

Still on his forearms, his hands in her hair, his eyes locked on hers, he let her see everything he felt as he slid in and out of her, in and out in that mindless rhythm that brought her right back to the very edge.

And then he dipped his head and took her breast into his mouth, and she fell right off that edge back into the abyss, and this time, he followed her over, rocking into her, pumping hard and deep, her name on his lips, his body rigid as his release poured out of him, and somehow she knew . . . that dependence she'd been reduced to . . . he'd felt the same.

It united them, and if her heart hadn't caught before, it was snagged hard now as she drifted back to earth locked tight in his arms.

"Jesus," he breathed when he finally relaxed and rolled to his side, taking her with him.

She had her face pressed against his chest. She could feel the erratic beat of his heart, and a little dazed, she shook her head. "That was . . ."

"Defies words, doesn't it?"

Defied logic, too. Or maybe in her mixed-up world, this at least, out of everything, made sense.

"Know what I think?"

She didn't know, but hoped it was that they should do this again.

He pulled her over the top of him, his hands running up the backs of her legs, urging them to straddle him as his mouth cruised down her collarbone.

"That's what I was thinking," she gasped.

He let out a soft laugh. "I should be thanking my lucky stars I happened to be on the tarmac yesterday."

"I was waiting for you," she murmured, eyes closed, body already humming, or still humming—

He'd gone still, so utterly still. Why? When she opened her eyes, she found his locked on her.

"What did you say?"

Oh, God, what had she said? The sensual haze began to dissipate. "Um—"

"You said you were waiting for me."

"Yes."

"But before, you said you didn't know it would be me."

"Right, but—"

He rolled her off of him, then slid off the bed. "But you did know, didn't you?"

And here was a prime example of why sex shouldn't be mixed in with deep conversation. She didn't have enough blood in her body to work her brain and her other parts at the same time.

"You waited for me," he said slowly. "*That's* why you kept canceling those other flights. I didn't show up. And you picked me because . . . because Brody or Shayne would have turned you in."

"Yes. No. *Damn it*," she said when those green eyes froze to ice. "Noah, I picked you because—"

"No. Don't say it. Don't come up with yet another lie, or omission, or whatever the hell you do." Unself-consciously naked, and looking like a Greek god while he was at it, he grabbed his jeans. "Time to roll, Princess. If you want a shower, now's your chance."

"Noah—"

"Hurry up. It's dawn."

Stomach jangling, she looked out the window and saw the purple and pink streaks across the sky. She couldn't believe it, but she'd survived the night.

All thanks to the six feet of sexy masculinity standing next to the bed, staring down at her, still and tense and gorgeous.

"Where to next?" he asked.

"Noah—"

He shook his head. "Forget it. No doubt it'll just be some Bailey mixture of the truth anyway." He tossed her clothes at her. "Let's get a move on."

She hugged her clothes close, aware of the irony that she'd been so terrified of their close intimacy, and yet now she feared its loss. "I won't go back. I can't—"

He whipped back, eyes furious. "You think I'd take you back and turn you in now? Knowing you'd face—*flattering*, Bailey." He scrubbed a hand over his face and sighed. "Look, I'm not taking you back. I'm taking you on your mysterious scavenger hunt."

Relief rushed through her so fast she felt faint as he went to the bedroom door and yanked it open.

Relief, and a regret so big and strong and overwhelming it nearly choked her. She stared at his back, her vision blurred by the tears she refused to shed. "I can't believe you're still going to help me."

He shoved his fingers through his hair, holding it off his face, making quite the picture as he did, arms raised, body hard and practically shimmering with tension. "Yeah, I'm going to help you. And I know exactly how big of an idiot that makes me, so you'd better hurry the hell up before I change my mind."

She wanted him to look at her all soft and sweet again. She wanted him to hold her, stroke away her fears.

Touch her. Kiss her . . .

But to get those things again, she had to trust him, really trust him, and tell him everything.

She knew this. Do it, she told herself. Try him. "Noah—"

"Don't." He shook his head. "Don't look at me like that, with your heart in your eyes. Too late. Just get ready so I can help you, and then get you the hell out of my life."

And with that, he walked out of the room.

Chapter 14

Noah entered the spare bathroom and cranked on the shower. Dawn had sneaked up on him, and with it came a whole host of things he'd rather not think about with his heart still beating like a drum and sweat cooling his body, which even now was half ready to go again.

In fact, with just one encouraging word from Bailey, he'd—

Hell. He'd have done whatever she wanted, and more.

Sap. Sucker.

Idiot.

But she hadn't given him any encouraging words at all. She'd sat up, and he'd known without even looking at her that she was thinking so hard her head hurt, because the tension radiating off her had filled the room.

He'd never met a woman who could think so damn hard.

He stepped into the shower and scalded himself, and when he was done, he went downstairs to the kitchen and straight for the chocolate glazed donuts.

On his first bite, his cell phone began vibrating. He heard the master bedroom shower go on, and he thought of Bailey, naked beneath the streaming water, and his entire body tensed because apparently, his dick hadn't gotten the memo that Bailey was bad for him.

Extremely bad.

He opened his cell. “What?”

“Why aren’t you sleeping?”

Shayne.

Noah rubbed his temples. “How do you know I’m not?”

“Because you wouldn’t have answered. You having wild monkey sex with a snow bunny yet?”

He glanced upward at the ceiling and once again pictured Bailey. Wild monkey sex? How about the best sex of his life? “Uh . . .”

“You did not catch a bunny that fast.”

Noah had to let out a short laugh. “You would have.”

“Yes, but I haven’t gone six months without so much as looking at a woman either.”

Noah didn’t know what to say to that.

“Listen, Noah.” Shayne paused. “I know.”

“Yeah? You know what?”

“That you have Bailey Sinclair with you.”

“Jesus, Brody is such a woman. Tell him that for me, would you?”

Shayne didn’t bite. “You still have her, right?”

The shower turned off. She was probably reaching for a towel to rub all over her body, a body that he could be rubbing all over himself right this minute if he hadn’t been such an idiot.

“She’s trouble, Noah. As in she’s in it up to her eyeballs. And if she’s hanging with the same crowd her husband was, she’s no good for you.”

“Yeah, listen, I’ve got to go.”

“She stowed away on you for crissakes.”

“She had . . . reasons.” What the hell was he doing, defending her? But he couldn’t seem to get around the fact that she hadn’t been in cahoots with those men; she’d been on the run from them. He believed in her. He just didn’t know why.

"I don't know what kind of sob story she gave you," Shayne said. "But we should be calling the authorities. We should—"

"I can handle this."

Shayne was quiet a moment. "I fueled up the Moody. I'm coming up there."

"I can handle this."

Bailey walked into the kitchen then, looking like a million bucks, though how she'd done it in so short of a time was a marvel. She'd obviously gone through her duffle bag and created another heart-stopping look for today: a pair of black jeans and a soft, white fuzzy sweater, this one with a zipper running down her torso, everything hugging her curves well enough to make his mouth go a little dry. Her hair was relatively tamed, which meant it flew around her face in alluring waves. She'd put some glossy stuff on her lips that made them difficult to tear his eyes from, but he managed, and then found his gaze snagged on hers, which was filled with all the little mysteries that made up Bailey Sinclair.

And suddenly he didn't care about any of that. He wanted her. He'd just had her, and he wanted her again.

"Gotta go," he said to Shayne.

"Noah—*Goddamnit.*"

Noah shut the phone, watching Bailey as she managed to not meet his eyes. "Your next move."

"Excuse me?"

"What is it?"

She looked away, and that was the topper on the Not Trusting Cake, so he bent down into her face and showed her his. "Look, Alan was an asshole. Your father? *Asshole.* I wish they were both still alive so I could pay each a visit and tell them personally. But—" But she wasn't listening, so he put his hands on her arms. Not a good idea because then he automatically pulled her in, tucking her up against him. "But not all men are assholes."

Wide-eyed, on her tiptoes because he was holding her there, she blinked once, slow as an owl. "I know that."

"Do you? Do you really? Because it sure as hell feels like you've lumped me into that whole men-are-all-untrustworthy-dickwads, and while I've definitely got my faults, I'm not going to play with your head, leave you stranded, or put your life on the line for my own stupid mistakes."

Given that he was saying he wasn't an asshole with his mouth and yet manhandling her all thc same with his body, she did the last thing he expected. She put her hands on his shoulders. Slid them up to cup his face. "I know," she said softly.

Undone, he let her feet hit the floor but didn't take his hands off her. Setting his forehead to hers, he found himself taking in a gulp of air, of her. "Then let me help you."

She stared at him for a long, long moment, during which time he held his breath.

"I'm going to charter another flight," she said.

"On your own."

Surprising him again, she didn't break eye contact. "It's for the best."

Hell no, it wasn't. On her own, she'd run into those guys again, and he doubted a warning would be all she suffered this time. "You can't walk back to the airport."

"I'll call a cab," she said quietly, looking unsure of her welcome.

His fault. "Sure, you could do that. And risk being found through that trail."

She looked dejected, and scared again, and damn if his heart didn't squeeze. "Just tell me where you're headed, damn it."

Her eyes went stubborn. "I can take it from the airport."

"Like you took it the other night at your place when they came to warn you?"

She paled, and he felt like the biggest jerk on the planet.

"Fine," he said. "Let's do this one step at a time. You need a ride to the airport. Let me take you that far at least."

They got into the car in the garage, with Bailey picking at the bagel Noah had insisted she eat. He knew when he pulled into Sky High, she'd probably run out of the Jeep before they could even say good-bye, and it was making him very uptight. Hating that, he leaned in and looked into her eyes. "When we get there," he said. "I'll-"

"No."

"No?"

"I am going to make this easy," she said, shaking her head. "You need to let me."

Her hair was in his face, again, and he tried not to notice that he loved the way it felt clinging to his day-old beard. "Easy went out the window yesterday. Tell me where you're running off to, Bailey."

She looked out the Jeep window, even though her view consisted of bare garage walls.

Turning her to him, he gave her a little shake. "After all we went through yesterday, and then last night, you still can't tell me? Are you kidding me?"

She squeezed her eyes shut, and her voice wobbled when she spoke. "I'm trying to protect you, Noah."

No one had ever said such a ridiculous or touching thing to him before, and right then and there he fell a little bit in love.

But just a little bit.

Certainly it was reversible, or at least survivable.

Or so he told himself.

"That's stupid," he said. Granted, it was an unfortunate word choice, but he couldn't help it; he was getting mad.

Her eyes flashed, too, and she shoved free of him. "If something happens to you, I couldn't bear it, okay?" she cried. "And if that's stupid, then I'm sorry, but—"

"It won't. Nothing will happen to me."

"You can't make that promise."

He realized she'd been through too much for her to trust that far. She simply couldn't do it, he hadn't earned it yet. "You'll see," he said very quietly.

"Noah . . ." She looked baffled. "Why would you do this for me?"

Why? Because he couldn't not. Because she was something to him. Everything. To show her, he pulled her over the console and into his lap. She opened her mouth, probably to come up with more reasons not to trust him, so he put his mouth over hers.

She went still with shock, but he didn't care. He just wrapped her in his arms and nibbled at her, first one corner of her mouth, then the other, until with a soft whimper, she let him in. With another soft sound, her hands glided up his chest and snaked around his neck.

Pulled him close.

"Bailey," he murmured, groaning when she bought into the kiss, lining up their lips, hers parted, warm and welcoming. He'd have staggered if he hadn't been sitting down. "This," he told her roughly, kissing her jaw, her neck. "Because of this."

She sank her fingers in his hair—he loved it when she did that—and pulled back a fraction, to see his face. "Because of . . . sex? With me?"

It'd been more than sex, far more, and he looked at her until she closed her eyes. "Okay, yes," she whispered. "Because of this."

"And more, damn it."

To prove it, he kissed her again, slid his tongue against hers and tasted her, filled himself up with her, which he, realized, was all he wanted. Needed.

It shouldn't bother him that after all this time, all his life really, he'd kept his heart intact, and that she'd not only cracked it open, but had also taken it in the palm of her hand.

But it did bother him, big-time.

"Noah," she whispered in a voice designed to make him instantly hard, except that he already was.

He had his tongue in her mouth, a hand tangled in her hair, his other gliding down her back, then lower, until he cupped the sweetest ass he'd ever had the pleasure of squeezing. "Tell me where you're going."

Panting a little, she wriggled around to fully straddle him, which good Christ, had the hottest part of her gliding over the neediest part of him.

"Catalina," she whispered, and pressed her face into his neck. "There's another nearly finished resort on the island, and I . . ."

"Need to find 'something.'" Yeah. He knew that part. "I'm flying you."

"You don't have to—"

He shut her up with his mouth, until they had to break apart for air.

"Promise me you won't do anything stupid," she said.

Do something stupid? The only stupid thing he was in danger of doing was drowning in her eyes.

Oh, and falling for her.

Details.

"See," she whispered, cupping his face. "If something happens to you, I won't be able to live with it."

Because things happened to the people in her life.

He knew that now and understood her fear. "Nothing stupid," he promised, mentally crossing his fingers. Because he'd already done something stupid. And was in the middle of something else even more colossally stupid. That being sliding his hands beneath her sweater and up her back, then down, and into the back of her jeans as far as he could get, which admittedly wasn't far enough.

She wriggled a little bit more, giving him better access so that his fingers encountered something silky, something that, oh God, felt like an itty, bitty, tiny thong.

God bless the thong.

"Nothing's going to happen to me," he whispered roughly. "To either of us. Except . . ."

"Except?" She sounded as if she'd been running uphill for miles.

"Except this—" And he slipped a finger over the silk barely covering her.

"Ohmigod." Her hands fisted in his hair, her arms tightened around his head, placing his mouth at, ah yes, right at her breast. With his nose, he nudged the neckline of her sweater aside and gently closed his teeth over her silk-clad nipple at the same time.

Because of the grip she had on his head, he couldn't see anything but her beautiful nipple, and he flicked at it with his tongue as he fumbled with his left hand for the seat lever. When he hit it, his seatback flew backward, and so did he, flat to his back.

She fell over him.

Perfect.

Nudging her up his body, he unzipped her sweater, opening it so that he was able to glide his mouth past her breasts, her ribs, to her belly, and then he pulled on her jeans, working them down to her thighs so he could kiss even lower . . . kiss every inch of skin that passed him . . . and then lower, oh yeah, *lower*. Scraping her panties aside, he stroked her with his tongue.

"*Noah—*"

Reluctantly he lifted his head, but he could still taste her, which worked for him. His gaze ran up her glorious body to her face. Her eyes were still the bluest on the entire planet, glazed with desire.

For him.

That shot a surge of pure lust straight through him. Her hair was adorably rioted as usual, all around her face, and she licked her lips in a nervous gesture. "Are you okay?"

"Yes. But I don't think . . ."

"Perfect," he said, holding her above him with his hands on her hips. "Go with that." When he used his tongue again, she gasped. When he sucked, she cried out and arched right into his mouth.

Nice. He was going to make her forget, for just a few minutes if nothing else, the horror she'd been through, what she was still going to have to go through.

"We've got to go," she managed, her hips rocking restlessly.

"Not go. Come." He unbuttoned his Levi's, and with her help managed to liberate the essentials. She bashed her knee on the console, and he hit his elbow on the window, but finally, oh, God, finally, he pushed up into her and proceeded to make them both forget everything but this.

Chapter 15

Bailey had never been a particularly good flyer. Being in the air always made her nervous, but when she'd been with Alan in the back of a private jet, she'd been able to draw the shades and somehow pretend she wasn't really thirty thousand feet above sea level.

There were no shades in the copilot's seat.

Noah glanced at her. His eyes were covered in his aviator sunglasses, but the amusement was clear in the quirk of his mouth. "A lot more relaxing when you're not hijacking someone, huh?"

Regret slashed through her. "Noah, I—"

"Hey." Reaching over, he put a hand on her thigh. "That was a joke. Not funny, huh?"

"It's just that I'll never be able to tell you how sorry I am."

"I don't want you to be sorry. Let's just get this done."

She'd let him talk her into flying with him, and was torn between terror and relief that he'd be at her side in Catalina.

He got on the radio and called ahead to the airport there, asking if any other private aircraft had flown onto the island that morning.

They hadn't.

He also checked in with the two local island charter services. They'd had two flights since dawn, one filled with a group of businessmen for a conference, the other with tourists. There were no cars on the island for visitors, only rental golf carts, and no one could say if anyone had gone exploring near Alan's resort in one. But no one remembered four goons in black.

He called air traffic control next, because even though he was flying them directly to the private strip at the resort, he wanted to check on cloud coverage, or any other inclement weather.

Everything was clear.

Noah looked at her. "After this is over, you'll be able to go on with your life."

She'd been scared so long that being safe seemed completely out of the realm of believability, so much that she couldn't wrap her mind around it. Going on with her life . . . What would that entail? Teaching? Yes.

Noah?

Terrifying how much she'd like that. But would he? How could he after what she'd put him through? And yet the way he looked at her said otherwise. Or maybe that was just wishful thinking on her part.

But surely he couldn't look at her like he did and intend to walk away. . . .

Reaching for her hand, he pressed his lips against her palm, giving her stomach a little flutter.

And south of her stomach? More interesting reactions.

It still shocked her how with just a touch from him, she let go of all inhibitions. Last night had been so far out of her league that little tremors of sexual zings still coursed through her.

And then this morning in the Jeep . . . well. Just thinking about that had her squirming some more. No doubt, he could just look at her, and her body reacted. Proving it, he glanced over at her, and as if he could read her thoughts, cocked a brow, his eyes heating just a little.

Her nipples went hard.

Damn, she was easy. Ridiculous. She tried to distract herself with concentrating on what would happen to her if she didn't lay her hands on the money, and that was indeed sobering enough to work. "I'm not sure this will ever end."

"It will," he said with such confidence, she wanted to believe. Oh, how she wanted to believe. "Shayne's brother is a cop," he said. "He could—"

"No." She'd been warned what would happen if she did that, and she believed them. Shuddering, she hugged herself. "That won't help me."

"You're not alone in this anymore, Bailey." He tugged her hand until she looked at him. "I won't leave you alone."

Oh, God, he was something. Strong, sure. Amazing. What she'd ever done to deserve his belief in her, she'd never know. "Let's just do this and see what happens."

"And if it's not there?"

"I have one other shot." The Baja resort.

"What will you do with yourself?"

She realized he meant afterward, when this whole thing was over. It hadn't been a dream she'd allowed to form. "I . . . I don't know."

His eyes narrowed as he turned his head from his controls. A frown tightened his mouth. "Damn it. You still don't actually believe this is going to be over."

She looked away, but he tugged her hand again until she craned her neck, looked him in the eyes—those amazing eyes—and sighed. "No," she admitted.

Mouth grim, he checked his instruments, the horizon. "Don't you give up on me now."

Beneath them, the Pacific Ocean shimmered a brilliant blue. "I'm trying not to."

"Trust me, we can do this.'

"You know I'm not so good with the trust thing. I . . . I need time."

"How much time?"

"More than a day."

"You've known me for more than a day. You knew me enough to make sure it was me on that plane yesterday, and no one else." He looked at her, his eyes steady and sure. "Why was that, Bailey, if you didn't trust me?"

The question caught her breath. Or maybe the man did that. But in any case, it became difficult to draw air into her lungs.

Because it was true. She *was* beginning to trust him. "It was almost easier before," she said, watching the island in front of them get bigger and bigger as they got closer, lifting out of the water, its mountains reaching high up into the sky. "When it was just me in danger."

"Bailey—"

"No. I hate knowing I'm putting your life on the line as well."

"I'm a big boy, and can take care of myself."

Yes, he'd proven that, hadn't he? But it didn't ease the worry, not one little bit. She watched him go through the landing procedure. Ahead, the island was lush, gorgeous, and she wished they were coming here for any other reason. "This resort is bigger than the Mammoth one."

"Which means . . . ?"

"It won't be as easy as last night."

A harsh laugh left him at that. "And last night was easy?"

Right. The truth was, it was only a matter of time before the goons caught up with her, and she wanted to have their money when they did. Looking into the warmest eyes she'd ever seen, she realized how very badly she wanted to live.

"Get ready," he said. "We're going in."

* * *

Catalina Island was 42,000 acres of mostly craggy cliffs. Landing was always a bitch, made tougher by the winds and unsettled air currents.

But he'd experienced worse. A lot worse. Noah shut down the engine and looked at Bailey.

She was a little green, so he helped her out of the plane, where they stood on a large plateau and took in the view.

To their right, about three hundred feet straight down, lay the Pacific Ocean. On their left rose a set of jagged peaks, reaching for the sky in a huge half circle, protecting a valley, and a jaw-droppingly gorgeous if not slightly ostentatious resort.

He eyed the buildings from where they stood, noting that the place looked completely deserted, but then again, so had the Mammoth resort yesterday.

Next to him, the wind ruffled Bailey's hair, plastering her sweater to her curves as she studied the resort, which was two buildings connected by a skyway between them, all overlooking the cliff and the jaw-dropping view with a steep road up to it. The road itself was gated, and appeared to be paved, or at least graveled, but there wasn't a vehicle in sight.

Going to be quite a climb, he thought, and wondered if that part had occurred to Bailey yet. He eyed her high-heeled boots. "Ready?"

"There used to be a cart to take us up . . ."

Noah took in the small, one-story hangar at the side of the tarmac. No lights or movement there either. No bad guys with guns, though honestly, given the way things had been going, that meant jack shit.

They could be anywhere, waiting.

He liked the locked gate, though, a lot. Anyone following them would have to break through it. Good odds, but he kept watchful just the same because he knew it wouldn't take much for anyone to discover where Alan's resorts were, nor would it take much more to put someone in place at each, where they could sit back and wait for Bailey to come get what they wanted. "The hangar first."

"Why?"

The door was locked, but as he led her around the perimeter, he found a gold mine. "Because of this."

Bailey stared at the golf cart, which looked as though it had seen better days in the previous century. "This is the one."

He helped her into it and proceeded to hotwire the thing to life, while Bailey just looked at him. "Who are you anyway, Superman?"

He'd been on his own a long time, and had learned a whole host of useful skills with which to survive. Once upon a time, some of those skills might have occasionally been illegal, but hey, he'd been young, scared, and starving.

He'd evolved since then, mostly, but this called for old drastic measures. "Superman would fly us up to the hotel."

He stomped on the gas and they hit the gate which broke open.

"Hey, that works," he said with a grin, and pushed the accelerator to the floor, which didn't accomplish all that much as he drove them up the hill.

And actually, *drove* was a bit adventurous for what they really did, which was putt-putt up the mountain on the single lane rocky road at the same pace they could have jogged it. Noah would have liked more horsepower and speed.

Hell, he'd have liked to still be in bed. *In Bailey*, for that matter. "You okay?" he asked her over the sound of the rackety engine and the wind in their faces.

She nodded, but didn't speak. He supposed that was as much nerves for what lay ahead as the fact that her teeth were rattling in her head as he bounced them along.

She was holding her hair back from her face with one hand and straightening her sunglasses with the other because they kept sliding down her face. She looked like the sexiest, cutest thing he'd ever seen, and right then and there his heart squeezed hard enough to hurt like hell. "So we'll just go in, get out," he told her. "We'll be back on the plane in—*holy shit*!" He ducked as a bird, a *huge* bird, dive-bombed them.

She laughed. *Laughed*. The sound was so musical, so damned beautiful, he turned his head and just stared at her, and in doing so nearly crashed them into a rock.

"What?" she asked, self-consciously running a hand over her wild hair.

"I've never seen you do that."

"Do what?"

"Laugh." Smiling, he reached for her hand, and squeezed. "I love it. Do it again."

With indeed another laugh, this one startled, she shook her head. "You're crazy."

"Of that, there's never been any doubt." He found himself grinning like a fool for no reason other than he was with her, on Catalina Island, with the glorious afternoon sun beating down on him.

But the road was tricky, and required both hands, so he had to let go of her, something he really didn't want to do. Halfway up the mountain, he felt her looking at him, and he glanced over.

"Why six months?" she asked.

"Huh?"

"Why six months since you've been intimate with a woman?"

"You're kidding me."

"I'm just wondering."

She'd found some gloss in her purse and put it on her lips so that they looked shiny and wet.

Good enough to eat.

She was good enough to eat, and he knew exactly how she tasted.

The thought would have been enough to stir his body, but she was more stubborn than a mule and wasn't going to be side-tracked.

"Noah?"

His smile faded because he didn't want to talk about the crash. He never talked about it; there was no need. It'd happened, it'd been a tragedy, one he couldn't avoid, and it was over.

Over.

But she was still looking at him, head cocked in that endearing way she had, with her long bangs falling over one eye.

Sighing, he turned his concentration back to the road in front of him, taking the last hairpin turn into the resort a little sharper than he should have, causing dust to rise up and choke him as effectively as his regrets of the past did. "I haven't had time to date."

"Now who's the liar?" she asked softly.

Damn if that didn't cut deep. He hated liars, and yeah, he'd just become one. But she was looking at him, waiting, and she wasn't going to let him get away until he said something. Anything.

So he shocked himself by putting it out there between them, in real words. "My last date went . . . bad."

"And you haven't dated since?"

"Really, really bad, Bailey."

Not giving her a chance to ask anything more, he took the last turn and parked beneath the shadow of the first building. Getting out of the golf cart, he peeked through the double glass doors to see inside.

The place definitely wasn't as far along as the Mammoth resort. It was dry-walled, and probably had electricity, but that was about it. "There was lots left to do here," he said when he heard Bailey come up next to him. The doors were locked, not surprisingly. And sturdy.

"Yeah. So exactly how bad was that date?" she asked single-mindedly.

"What? Jesus, Bailey." He let out an annoyed sound but she

didn't budge, just stood there looking at him. "Now's not a good time," he pointed out.

She lifted a shoulder. "Seems like a great time to me."

He stared at her, and she smiled sweetly.

Waiting.

Fine. "I killed her."

"I . . . I don't believe you."

"Well, you should," he said grimly, but before they could continue this ever so lovely conversation, he heard a very unwelcome sound.

The *putt-putt-putt* of another cart somewhere close by.

Chapter 16

Noah couldn't tell if the cart was coming or going, but he didn't take the time to find out. He just grabbed Bailey's hand and began running. "Where's Alan's suite?"

"Near the spa," she answered breathlessly. She was huffing and puffing. "It's behind these buildings, in a separate building beyond the pool."

They moved that way. Here, the buildings were butted up to the mountain, with only a path between them. There was heavy growth all the way down to the path, mostly manzanita bushes, so it was likely they could vanish effectively if it came to that.

He pulled Bailey along the trail, which as it rose became narrow and rocky. The view would have been breathtaking, maybe on a day where they weren't on the run from the unknown, a scavenger hunt for God knew what. They ended up behind the first building, which opened up into a huge courtyard pool, and yes . . . spa.

The pool was built but not filled, surrounded by rocks and alcoves. Beyond the pool, directly against the mountainside, was a smaller building.

The spa.

"It'll be locked," Bailey said as they headed toward it.

But it wasn't, because the doors had been shattered open. Noah couldn't see what had been used to do so, but he was thinking a bullet.

And he'd bet it'd been shot from the same gun that had shot at them last night, possibly the same gun even now after them.

Not. Good.

"Oh my God," Bailey said, coming to the same conclusion, pressing closer to his side. "That's who we just heard."

Probably, he thought. He pulled her away from the open doors. They moved back around the pool. "Hurry," he urged, practically dragging her, not taking a breath until he had her behind the two large buildings of the resort, and behind some relative shelter.

"Maybe it's not what we think," she said. "It could be anyone."

Yes, except there was no sign of anyone, or on-going work, no plane other than his.

They heard the cart again.

Bailey covered her mouth with her hand to hold in her panicked gasp. He put his hands on her shoulders and looked into her eyes. "Could they have already gotten what you came for?"

Distress crossed her features. "I don't know."

"If they did, it's over, right?"

She bit her lower lip. "If it's over, why haven't they left?"

Yeah. Exactly what he wanted to know. "I need the full story, Bailey. You know I do."

"It's money," she said.

"I figured that, Princess. And it must be a hell of a lot."

"Alan screwed them out of it."

"So they're pissed to boot. Terrific." Holding her hand, he stepped through the broken glass door, which tinkered at their feet. They stood in what looked to be an elegant, sophisticated reception room. Like the Mammoth resort, it was painted, half-tiled, the reception desk only half-installed. Clearly, construction had abruptly come to a halt.

Behind the reception area was a wide, long hallway, which they followed past a group of rooms for spa treatments, then several others, which opened to a hallway that had a single door at the end.

Pushing Bailey behind him, Noah flattened them both against the wall and listened.

He could hear nothing now.

"Noah?"

With their cart way out front of the two main buildings, it was possible that no one realized they were back here. He wanted to get Bailey back in the Piper, but they couldn't leave, not until she searched the damn suite.

"*Noah.*"

"Yeah?"

"What do you mean, you killed her?"

He stared at her. "Are you kidding me? Look, do your thing, search the place for the money and let's go." The suite door was locked with a keypad. He punched in six-nine-six-nine, and it clicked open.

He entered, and shook his head. Like at Mammoth, this suite had been finished down to a fine fault, glimmering and shimmering with all the best money could buy.

He glanced at Bailey, who was still looking at him, still waiting for him to—unfuckingbelievable—discuss his "bad date." "Seriously. We are not doing this now."

Miraculously, she let it go, and walked farther into the spacious living room, going right up to the prints on the wall, peeking behind each and every piece. "It's not here," she said after a minute.

"You sure?"

"Alan loved to hide his safes out in plain sight. It always amused him to sit in his living room surrounded by company and be able to lay his eyes on his fortune and feel superior."

"Nice."

"Yeah, I tend to hang around real winners. Rat-fink bastards. Murderers." At this, she looked at him, baiting him, but hell no, she wasn't getting information out of him that easily, not with the goons still on their tail and closing in, and his own pride prickling because it had taken this, yet another close encounter with gun-toting idiots, to force her to trust him.

Money.

Shit. People got good and dead over disputes with money, and he didn't want to be one of them.

"You did not kill anyone," she said.

He sighed again and went to move around her. But she stepped in front of him, and despite the fact that she came up to only his chin, she blocked his path and held her ground. "I just don't believe for one second you committed murder. I do not."

His gaze slid to hers and locked on tight. She was serious, standing there with her hands on his chest to hold him there—as if she could really hold him—her attention one-hundred-percent focused on him and not on the fact that they could be shot and killed any second themselves.

You did not kill anyone.

The words she'd spoken had far more meaning than they should, because whether she realized it or not, it meant she believed in him.

Trusted him.

"It was a plane crash," he heard himself say.

"Oh," she breathed, her hands softening on him, a gentle caress now instead of fists. "Oh, Noah."

Why her horror and compassion nearly undid him, after six months of nothing reaching him, was beyond Noah. But he wanted to bury his face in her hair and hold on tight, and never let go. "Look, later, okay?" he ground out instead. "Say, after we get the bad guys off our tail?"

She nodded, but it was a moment before she let go of him, and when she did, he had to fight the urge to grab her back.

Clearly, he'd not gotten enough sleep.

She checked the other rooms in the suite, then shook her head. "It's not here."

That was all he needed to know. "Okay, let's get the hell out of here." He grabbed her arm when she would have gone back the way they'd come. "They know we're here somewhere. We have to go out a different way . . ."

"The kitchen," she said, and took them there. It led into a private courtyard. From behind the privacy fence, Noah surveyed the area. He could see the pool, the entrance to the other building . . . and no bad guys.

Bailey came up behind him. "Were you the pilot when you crashed?"

He shot her a look of disbelief. "What part of *later* didn't you understand?"

"Were you?"

"Yes."

She put her hands on his back. "I'm sure you did the best you could."

He had. He goddamn had, but his best hadn't been enough. And he sure as hell didn't want to think about this now.

"I don't see them," Bailey whispered, looking over his shoulder. "I don't see anyone."

Which didn't mean a damn thing, unfortunately. All he had to do was get them around the pool and back around to the front of the resort to their cart. Then drive it down the hill to the plane.

Without getting shot.

Flattening himself against the corner of the left main building, he peeked out front. Ah, shit. Next to their cart was another.

Empty.

And now the front doors here were broken, too, completely shattered. Someone had gone in there, probably looking for them. "Wait for my signal," he said, gaze glued on the empty cart. "Then run like hell for our cart." He wished the cart had a souped-up engine because their getaway was low on horsepower.

"How did it happen?" she whispered. "The crash?"

Craning his neck, he looked into her eyes. "Jesus, you have a one-track mind."

"Maybe I just care." She smiled, but it seemed a little uneasy. "More than I wanted to."

Something to think about. As was the way his heart kicked hard. "Wait here."

He dodged toward their old putt-putt cart. Reaching beneath it, he disconnected the battery cable, then for good measure, pulled out his penknife and cut through the coil wire.

That should hold them.

He hopped into the goons' cart, started the engine, and hit the gas, heading toward Bailey. "Get in!"

She leapt over the side, and before her butt even hit the seat, he'd whipped them around and toward the road.

"Get down," he said, dividing his gaze between the rocky road and their back. Any second now the men would appear—oh, shit, there they were, racing out of the building and toward the old cart. "Get onto the floor, head down!"

"Oh, my God."

"Do it." Lifting a hand off the wheel, he fisted it in the back of her sweater and dragged her off her seat and onto the floor. That done, he concentrated on driving them back down the crazy one-lane road toward his plane, which sure as hell better be in the same shape they'd left it because take-off was going to have to happen in a hurry.

From her perch on the floor, Bailey stared up at him, eyes huge. "Are they back there?"

"Yes." They were attempting to start the cart that Noah had just "adjusted." "But I disabled our cart so they'll have to run." He grinned down at her.

She blinked, then shook her head, then surprised him by grinning back. "You really are Superman."

No. Hell, no. But if she wanted to think it . . .

He got them as close to the Piper as he could, coming to a skidding halt and grabbing for Bailey. "Go, go, go."

Together they ran to the plane. He shoved her inside, then began his precheck at Superman speed, keeping one eye on the road as he did, finally leaping into the pilot's seat just as he heard voices. The men had given up on their cart and were running down the road toward them, guns out.

Shit.

He'd never flown without a preflight check, never, but he did now, doing his best to rush the take-off without doing anything stupid. He got them in the air and then looked back to find the goons standing in the middle of the runway, clearly furious.

Noah let out a long breath, relaxing marginally. "Safe again."

Bailey was white-knuckling the armrests, face pale, breathing a bit unevenly, but she nodded. "Yes." She pressed her face to the window and looked back at the island. "For now," she said quietly.

He wanted to hug her. Kiss her. Never let her go. He reached for her hand and squeezed. "You okay?"

She looked at him. "Could be better." She dragged her teeth over her lower lip and gave him an openly coy, sexy look.

He laughed in disbelief. "I can't—I'm flying, Bailey."

"No." She blushed. "Not that! I was thinking it's a good time for the later thing."

"Good God, woman, you are seriously tenacious." But he sighed. "Fine. The crash." It felt odd to say the word he thought so much about but never said. "I was flying a friend to her condo. There was a storm. I wanted to turn around—" He shook his head. Damn.

Her eyes remained solemn. "You realize this is not a normal bad date story. This is a life-affirming story."

"Life affirming? She died, Bailey. How is that life affirming?"

"You didn't," she said simply.

And wasn't that just the crux of everything that had been torturing him for six months.

Sheila had died.

And he hadn't. He, the son-of-a-bitch who'd spent his life cheating death one way or another, hadn't died.

And a small part of him had thought he deserved to.

Now she reached for him, touching his shoulder, his jaw. "You're here. Alive. Do you have any idea how glad I am?"

Because that reached out and grabbed him by the throat, he didn't speak.

Couldn't.

He slid his sunglasses over his eyes and told himself it was because the ocean sprawled beneath them, a brilliant blue far too bright, and not because he needed to hide a moment. "Where to next?"

"Baja."

His stomach sank. "What?" She was kidding; she had to be kidding.

"The last resort. It's in Cabo."

Shit. Of course. Why would it be anywhere else than the place of his nightmares? He carefully schooled his reaction, which was a hell of a lot harder than he thought. "They're going to be waiting."

She looked at him a long moment, and he knew he must have given something of his nightmare away. "I know."

He fought the useless battle against those soft, drown-in-me baby blues. "It's just money, right?"

"*A lot* of money."

"Whatever. Let it go, let them find it."

"I don't think they can find it without me."

A muscle in his jaw ticked as he realized he still, goddamnit, *still* didn't know the whole story. If that didn't just make his day complete. "Fine. Then it's off to Cabo."

"Noah, I can't ask you to—"

"Then don't ask." Turning his attention forward, he concentrated on flying and not, absolutely not, begging her to once and for all *trust him*.

Chapter 17

They landed at Sky High Air at dusk. Noah tied down the plane himself and looked up at the steel-and-glass building that was his real home.

He wasn't at all surprised to find Shayne waiting for him. "Don't start," he said when Bailey had vanished inside the terminal, heading toward the ladies room.

Shayne shoved all ten fingers through his hair, holding it off his face while he stared at Noah. "Don't start? You're supposed to be throwing yourself off cliffs with skis on your feet. You're supposed to be fucking a ski bunny. *Two*, if you're lucky. Not flying all over the damn planet."

"Things changed." Noah turned to Tommy, their lineman, and gestured to the Piper. "Pull her in for the night, fuel her, have maintenance do a run through. I had the landing gear replaced last night. Check that, too. She's going back out at the crack of dawn to Cabo."

"*Cabo*?" Shayne asked in shock.

"Yeah." No way was he taking Bailey there tonight. He wanted the night, damn it, wanted it with her in his bed.

He had no idea what *she* would think about that, but he figured he had a fifty-fifty shot. With Shayne on his tail, he went inside the hangar. Bailey was still in the bathroom. He would have stood there and waited for her but Shayne manhandled him into his office, then glared at him. "What are you doing?"

"Waiting for Bailey."

"Why? You flew her where she needed to go, right? Flight done. We'll bill it out."

"She needs another flight."

"To Cabo, apparently, at the crack of dawn."

"That's right," Noah said.

"I'll take her."

"I'm doing it."

Shayne looked at him for a long moment. "What exactly happened in Mammoth? Why didn't you ski?"

"She needed some help, Shayne."

"And you gave it."

"Yes."

"You sleep with her?"

"What does that matter?"

"Because you haven't slept with anyone since Sheila."

"You told me to stop feeling sorry for myself, remember?"

Shayne sighed. "Okay, I know what this is. Yeah, I told you to stop feeling sorry for yourself. But I did not mean fall for the first woman who hijacked you, Noah."

"I'm not falling . . ." He had to clamp his jaw shut because suddenly he couldn't finish the sentence. Christ. He *was* falling.

Hard.

Shayne was staring at him, horrified. "Have you lost it completely?"

Yeah, completely.

The door opened. Brody came in, brow creased, a frown marring his mouth. "You've lost your mind," he said to Noah as he shut the door.

Which immediately opened again, hitting Brody in the ass, sending him forward a good foot. "Hey," he complained as

Maddie let herself in, stalking right past Brody and up to Noah.

With Maddie, one could never be sure. She could be planning on walloping him or kissing him, so he braced himself, but she pulled him close in a fierce hug and squeezed tight.

Not the typical concierge, she sported purple hair today, tipped in black, spiky around her face in some artfully messed up style that had probably taken hours, wearing some silvery outfit on her grade A hard body guaranteed to make a man's eyes bug right out of his head. The woman seriously looked like a real-life kick-ass action heroine, only where she kicked ass was in her job.

He allowed her to continue to squeeze the life right out of him because, as he discovered with surprise, she was trembling. "Hey. Hey, I'm okay." He held her tight, and over her head met Brody's gaze, which was nothing short of glowering.

Huh. Brody and Maddie had been like oil and water from day one, but this was new. Noah hugged her closer, and Brody's frown deepened. Noah grinned. Brody took a step toward him, but then Maddie cupped Noah's face. "You're *sure* you're okay?"

"Yes."

"Okay, then." And she smacked him upside the back of the head. "Have you lost your ever-loving mind?"

"That's the general consensus," he said, and rubbed his head. "And *ouch*."

Now Brody was the one to grin.

"Don't even try to tell me it knocked some sense into you," Maddie said. "I know it damn well didn't. What the hell were you thinking? Oh, never mind." She hugged him again. "Just never mind. You're back. You're okay."

"Jeez, don't smother him," Brody muttered.

Maddie shot him a glare that matched his own. "It's called sensitivity, Brody. I know you're missing that gene, so—"

"Point," Shayne said dryly. "Let's stick to the point."

They all looked at Noah, who lifted his hands. "The point is, she's got some trouble."

"Dude, they're all trouble." For this, Shayne got his own cuff to the back of the head, courtesy of Maddie. "Well, they are," he muttered.

"The *real* point," she said, and once again everyone eyed Noah. "You just started flying again. *Yesterday*," she clarified, as if he'd forgotten. "After six months of a leave of absence from flying after the accident—"

Brody sucked in a breath.

Shayne did the same.

Because no one, absolutely no one, liked to talk about the accident.

At least no one but Bailey . . .

"And then you go off for a break, but instead hook up with trouble. Honey," she said gently, as if she were sixty-five and using a walker, instead of twenty-six and extremely hot. "What I'm trying to say is that on top of everything, Bailey is a walking/talking time bomb. These guys came looking for her, and—"

Noah's heart stopped. "What guys? When?" Jesus, were they still here? With Bailey out there, unprotected? Fear blocking his throat, he strode to the door, but Brody stepped in front of it.

"They're gone," he said. "She's safe here. You know that. The question is, safe from what?"

Noah tried to push past him, but again Brody blocked him. "They said she owed them big-time, that she was a thief. They said the fact that she was on the run proved them right."

"Bullshit," Noah said.

"Which is why we didn't tell them where she was."

Noah looked at each of them in turn, and in spite of being cornered, felt a swell of emotion. Yeah, these guys were pains in the ass, but they were *his* pains in the ass. "Look, she's *in* trouble, not trouble herself, and I'm helping her. Any of you would do the exact same thing. Now, I've got to go. Move," he said to Brody.

Instead, Brody shoved him.

Noah shoved back.

"What, are you guys like eight?" Maddie demanded, but Shayne gently set her aside and stepped between Noah and Brody. He looked into Brody's eyes. "Back off." Then he turned to Noah. "The guys are gone. We had them followed. They went to the main terminal. United. They checked on flights to . . ."

"Cabo," Noah guessed.

"Bingo. So you going to tell us what we can do to help?"

He looked over Shayne's shoulder to where Brody stood tall and fierce. Brody rolled his eyes, then nodded. Maddie scooted closer, patting his shoulder. She nodded, too.

Noah sighed. "Okay, I'll tell you what I know, which granted, isn't all that much. Alan Sinclair died in debt to some investors, who didn't take too well to the fact that all their money is gone and none of the resorts are finished."

"How much?" Maddie asked, skirting around the desk to flip open Shayne's laptop. Perching a hip on the desk, she leaned over, her fingers fast at work.

"I don't know."

"Where did the money go?"

"Don't know that either. Bailey suspects Alan has hidden a stash somewhere in one of his suites. We're down to one last suite to check."

"In Cabo," Shayne said with disgust.

"I'll take her," Brody said.

"Good luck with that," Shayne muttered.

"I'm taking her," Noah said.

"See?" Shayne said to Brody. "He's hook, line, and sinker *gone*."

Brody made a sound that left no mistake to what he thought of *that*, and Maddie rolled her eyes. "Have you not a single romantic bone in your body?" she demanded.

Brody opened his mouth, then carefully shut it again, eyes shuttered.

Disgusted, Maddie turned her back on him and looked at Noah. "After Baja, then what?"

"Not sure," Noah admitted. "If we don't find the money—"

"We," Brody muttered. "He's saying 'we.'"

"If *we* don't find the money," Noah continued, "she's more unsafe than ever."

"Then *we* find the money," Shayne said.

Brody sighed. "Now Shayne's saying *we*. Christ, this is going to get ugly."

Shayne grinned. "Just like old times, getting ourselves out of every scrape we ever found ourselves in."

"And there were many," Brody reminded him. "Always ugly, remember?"

"We never lost," Shayne said.

Maddie shook her head. "This is about Bailey, remember? Not about the thrill of the fight."

"Right." Shayne met Brody's and Noah's eyes over Maddie's head. "For Bailey."

Bailey stuck her head in the door of the office. "What's for me?"

She'd clearly dived into her duffle bag of magic tricks because she'd freshened up, including changing.

Now she wore one of those filmy, multi-layered skirts that alternately clung and flew about her legs and hips, with a pale sweater in some sort of stretchy material that under very different circumstances would have made Noah's mouth run dry. It was a scooped neck, and had a row of teeny tiny buttons down the center, with both the first few and the last few unbuttoned. She could have been going into the classroom for a day of teaching, or to a tea party. Either way, she looked every inch the wealthy, elegant, sophisticated wife of a real estate mogul that she'd once been.

Suddenly everyone who had been all up in Noah's business scattered in a wave of busywork—Maddie saying something about the phones, Shayne mentioning he had a plane to look at, Brody not explaining himself at all—and in less than two seconds, Noah and Bailey were completely alone.

"You told them everything," Bailey said flatly.

"Hard to do that, when I don't know everything." His gaze was helplessly drawn to the tiny, delicate chain of gold around her neck, which dipped into her scooped neckline and vanished from view in such a way that left him dying to reach into that sweater himself and go fishing.

"Noah . . ."

He waited, but she sighed and said nothing, and he felt as if someone had just run over his heart. "Forget it. Let's go."

"Now?" Her sandals had heels, and were the same pale, pale peach of her sweater. "Okay, good."

Her toenails were peach too, and on her big right toe was painted a tiny little daisy. Never in his life would he have imagined a thing so flipping sexy, but he couldn't stop looking at it.

"Where to?" she asked.

He knew she meant which way to the plane. "Do you trust me?"

"Yes," she said, shocking the hell out of him.

Noah opened his mouth to tell her he was taking her home to his house where they were going to spend the entire night trusting the hell out of each other—naked, hot, and sweaty—but Shayne came down the hallway at a speed faster than his usual laid-back tortoise slow.

"Problem," he said.

Noah looked into Shayne's eyes and knew. The men were back.

Shayne whipped open the supply closet.

Noah pushed Bailey inside. "Hang tight," he told her.

Shayne shut the door on her.

"What—" she asked from the inside, and Noah whipped the door back open, meaning to say something cool but calming. Only instead he kissed her hard and quick. "I'll be back, don't make a sound."

He just hoped that for once, she listened.

Chapter 18

Bailey stood there in the pitch-dark closet and tried not to hyperventilate. She'd seen Shayne's face, she'd heard "problem" and she knew.

Stephen and his men had found her. God, oh, God, if anyone got hurt because of her . . . Just thinking it, her legs went weak, and she sank to the floor, hugging her knees close to her chest.

When Alan had died and she'd found out her life had never been what she'd thought, she'd been hurt and angry but determined to change things.

Then she'd had her little run-in with Alan's thugs, and she'd expected to die. She'd expected to die many times since.

But in a last ditch effort, she'd used Noah to take her to Mammoth on the off chance she could find the money, and once again, everything had changed.

It was almost as if she'd been living in black and white, and he'd colored her world. And a secret, deep dark hope burgeoned inside her—that she'd find the money, she'd pay off Stephen and his men, and she'd go back to her life, to teaching. She loved the world her kids lived in, the sweet innocence, their precious minds that were like little sponges.

In fact, she'd always dreamed of having her own, but that dream had recently been set aside for the more pressing one—living to see her twenty-ninth birthday.

But now she had a new secret dream—Noah.

Where was he? Worry and fear knotted within her. She stood and slipped her hands into the deep pockets of her skirt and felt the comforting weight of her cell phone.

She debated for a moment, then pulled it out and turned it on. She needed to hear from Kenny, and indeed she had a waiting text message. A WHERE R U?

SAFE, she typed and sent.

To her utter shock, she got an immediate response: DID U FIND IT?

Before she could respond, the closet door handle turned. Before she could even squeak, it opened. A tall, dark shadow slipped inside, pressing her back, shutting the door, which meant she was alone with—

"It's me," came Noah's unbearably familiar voice.

Relief spilled out of her along with her breath when his arms encircled her.

"What happened?" she demanded, but his answer was to cover her mouth with his. She had no idea how he did it, but with his mouth open on hers, his hands all over her, it was hard to think past the sensual, earthy haze he created.

And that wasn't the only thing hard. With a startled little hum, she pressed even closer to his amazing body, afraid she wouldn't ever be able to get close enough.

And that thought was just deep enough, real enough, to nearly shatter her. Then he turned her, pressing her back against a wall—a shelving unit, she decided, because things fell from it to the floor. "Noah—"

He ran a hand down her spine and then back up again, beneath her sweater, his warm palm on her bare skin. "*Noah*—"

Before she could get out anything else, his mouth covered hers again, and since hers was open, his tongue slid right in and danced to hers in a slow, sinuous, sensual movement that made her knees wobble.

There were other reactions as well, and when his hand came around, up her torso to cup a breast, his thumb gliding over her hard nipple, he discovered that very thing, and a low, hungry sound escaped him. It tightened her body even more. Then he shifted angles to get even closer, deeper, which drove her wild because his kiss was hot, melting, and only a taste of what she really wanted, which was him deep inside her, sliding in and out like his tongue. This need for him shocked her because she'd never felt it before, all consuming and as necessary as air.

But Noah . . . Noah made her that way, and she climbed all over him trying to get closer, *inside* of him.

The pitch black only added to the sense of intimacy. She felt the heat of him burning into her, igniting every single erogenous zone she had, which was a hell of a lot more than she'd known about, all of it turning her on in spite of herself, when she really had no business getting turned on.

The men were here.

She had to talk to him, had to know what was happening, but he cupped her face, tilting it up, pressing her into the wall, pinning her between the plaster and his even harder body. "Noah—"

"I know. Christ, you make me hot." He slid a thigh between hers, ripping a dark, needy sound from her throat. Her head thunked hard back against the wall.

His hands slid up, into her hair, massaging where she'd hit while his mouth made its way down her throat.

"Tell me," she whispered, putting her hands on his chest to push free. "Is everyone okay?"

He slid his hands down her arms, taking her wrists, lifting them over her head so she couldn't move, leaving her stretched out on the wall for him.

"Noah—"

His mouth was busy at her jaw, her neck . . . and she lost her train of thought. "Uh . . ."

Holding her upright with his hands, his body, the thigh he'd thrust between hers, she discovered that the darkness lent a freedom all in itself. She found herself riding his thigh, wishing their clothes would fall away, so that there was no barrier between them.

His clever, clever mouth found a way beneath her sweater. Dragging her bra cup aside with his teeth, his warm breath teased her nipple, and she thought she'd die of pleasure. Then he gently rubbed his jaw over it.

Another sound escaped her throat at that, and then he leaned in and sucked her into his mouth. Her knees buckled, but with his thigh between hers, she wasn't going anywhere.

Nor she did she want to. It was a startling realization, and when he let her hands go to unbutton her sweater, she clutched at him. "Noah," she gasped. "Please tell me what happened out there."

"They're gone."

She knew he was in one piece, no bullet holes, but she ran her hands over him again just to feel him, to be sure. "I can't keep doing this to you, I won't—"

"You're not." He cupped her breasts, his fingers driving her straight to heaven. Unable to stop herself, she touched him too, ran her hands over his shoulders, his belly . . . the hard bulge behind the button fly of his jeans, loving the raw, hungry sound that escaped him when she outlined him with her fingers. Pressing her face into his neck, she just breathed him in.

"They'll be in Cabo," she whispered. "I'm going to tell them again, that I don't know where the money is, and that killing me won't change that."

"They still won't believe you. But the cops can—"

"No. They said no police or they'd hurt Kenny. And now you. They'll hurt you."

"Princess, it's not me they wanted." He scrubbed a hand over his face. "If you knew who they were, then Shayne's brother could—"

"Noah." Guilt ate at her. She did know who they were. "I, um . . ." She swallowed hard. "I haven't told you everything."

He went still.

She closed her eyes, but it didn't matter. The closet was still pitch-dark, and she was still about to really screw everything up. "I know who the men are."

Noah shifted, and she heard a click, and then the closet was flooded with light.

Noah's body still pressed hard against her, his eyes unfathomable. "You said you didn't know who they are."

"I know," she whispered. "I'm sorry." Sorrier than he could ever know. "I think . . . I think I should go to Cabo alone."

"Over my dead body." He said this so evenly it took a moment for her to process the words.

"Hey," Shayne said through the door. "You going to stay in there all night, because we're getting tired of trying to eavesdrop from out here. Can't hear a damn thing."

Noah never took his gaze off Bailey. "Go away," he called out.

"Yeah. Can't do that."

It was hard to think with his body pressed against hers, with his hands . . . oh Lord, those hands. One was still on her breast, the other cupping her bottom, pressing her against the hard ridge in his jeans. "Noah," she whispered.

"Right." He pushed away, waiting while she straightened her clothes, the ones he'd just been trying to get her out of, then opened the door.

Shayne was propping up the wall, arms casually crossed, all laid-back and easy-going stance, but nothing about his eyes was laid-back and easy-going.

"Where's the 'we'?" Noah asked him.

Shayne lifted a shoulder. "Lied. I sent Brody on my last charter; he's gone until morning. You can thank me later. Maddie needs you to sign something ASAP. She's waiting at her desk."

"Fine." Noah turned to Bailey. "I'll be right back."

Shayne waited until Noah was out of range before he looked at Bailey. "So."

"I'm so sorry about the visitors."

"Yeah. Bad-Breath and Shit-For-Brains said you were a dangerous and crazy thief."

Bailey lifted her chin. "I realize that you have no reason to believe anything I say, but I'm not a thief."

"Well then, it's a good thing I don't listen to people whose necks are wider than their brains, isn't it. Look, I make up my own mind on people. And my mind says you're in over your head, but you're not a thief. In any case, Noah believes in you, and that's good enough for us."

Bailey stared at him, a little stunned at the blind trust. Before Noah had come along, she'd have said she didn't believe such a thing even existed. And now . . . and now she only wished she could bring herself to experience it firsthand instead of simply witnessing the beauty. "Thank you," she whispered.

"Don't thank me yet."

Her heart, warmed only seconds before, chilled.

"Because while I'm not locking up the silver, I do think you're dangerous." He looked pointedly past Bailey, where beyond the reception area, Noah was bent over Maddie's desk, pen in hand.

Bailey looked at him, too. Hell, she couldn't stop looking at him. Long, built, gorgeous, he was nodding at something Maddie was saying. His hair had fallen over his forehead, and he carelessly shoved it back. Maddie reached up and squeezed his arm, and he tugged at a strand of her hair.

Easy affection.

Easy camaraderie.

God, to have people in her life like that. She had Kenny,

she knew that no matter what Noah thought, but Kenny had been gone a long time, and nothing about that was going to change.

"Bailey."

Bracing herself, she met Shayne's sharp eyes.

"Be careful with him."

Even standing as casual and at ease as he was, the worry sat heavily in every line of his face, and her immediate reaction of defensiveness softened. "Noah is in no danger from me, Shayne."

"Isn't he?"

If anyone was going to get hurt when this was over, Bailey was fairly certain it would be her. She was already nursing a broken heart. "No."

He looked at her for a long moment, then nodded.

"Thank you for what you did today," she said. "For everything. Please tell Brody, too. I can never thank any of you enough—"

"Yes, you can." He glanced at Noah, then back at her. "You can thank us by not hurting him."

And then he walked away.

Bailey watched him go, drawing in a deep breath, then slowly letting it out.

Noah was a wanderlust, a man who lived gleefully on the edge of danger and adventure, and had the scars to prove it, both inside and out.

She couldn't hurt a man like that . . .

Could she?

Or had she already, by not trusting him? The truth was, it was herself she hadn't trusted, not him. And she needed to tell him that.

"Hey."

Whipping around at the hand on her shoulder, she stared into his face.

"Let's go," he said.

In spite of what she'd done—and not done—he was taking her to Cabo. Now. Her heart squeezed. "Noah—"

"Look, I don't want to argue about this."

Male code for, *I'm done with this conversation*. "Same plane?" she asked.

"Yes." But he didn't look at her, and in fact, led her to the front door of Sky High Air, not to the tarmac. Pulling her outside, he kept a watchful eye on everything around them as he lead her to a sports car. Night had fallen, though as was typical for Southern California, the temperature had not.

"This isn't a plane," she said, eyeing the BMW.

"Nope." He unlocked the door and waited for her to get in, which she didn't.

"Aren't you going to ask me about the men?" she asked.

"I'm done asking. I want you to tell of your own free will."

Blind trust. "I'd . . . like to do that, but I also really need to get to Cabo. Are we driving there?"

He sighed, and scrubbed a hand over his jaw, making the two-day growth there rasp in the quiet air. "You need some sleep. Hell, I need some sleep."

"But—"

"Whatever we're going to face down there, we can face in the morning."

She looked into his face and saw exhaustion, and knew it was mirrored on her own as well. "I can get another pilot—"

"I said I'd fly you there, and I meant it. Just come home with me for tonight. Tomorrow, I'll take you where you need to go, I promise."

He was tense, braced for battle, but even she wasn't that selfish. He'd done everything she'd asked and more, so much more. It was her turn. She nodded, and going up on tiptoe, pressed her mouth to his jaw. "Thank you," she whispered against his skin. "Thank you for doing this."

With a low sound, he banded his arms around her and

squeezed tight, burying his face in her hair. "Cabo," she heard him whisper, and then shudder. "Jesus, it figures."

She lifted her head to look into his eyes. "What do you mean?"

He stared at her for a long moment, then shook his head. "Nothing. Let's go."

He made a quick stop at a local pizza joint for a large pizza and a six-pack of sodas, and when she looked at him, he sighed and added a salad as well.

Not used to having her mind read, or having someone even care what she thought for that matter, she found herself smiling.

He didn't smile back, but took her hand. He drove about ten minutes into the Burbank Hills, up a winding road where at the apex of every turn she caught a breathtaking view of the city below. Finally, he pulled into a long driveway and stopped outside a house with more of the breathtaking view.

He turned off the engine, let out a breath.

"Pretty house," she said.

"I rent it." He looked at the place as if still half surprised to find himself living there. "I've never lived in a house before."

"Never? Not growing up?"

"Definitely not while growing up. When I came to the States, I got shuffled around a lot. That kind of stuck with me, and I did the same once I was on my own. Shayne and Brody were my home base in LA, and when I was in town, I always just stayed with one of them."

"What changed?"

He lifted a shoulder. "We started earning money, and decided we were too old for the whole frat thing." He turned to her. "Ready?"

"Noah, you don't have to put me up tonight. I—"

He grabbed the food, got out of the car, and shut his door.

Okay, he definitely wasn't big on conversations that weren't going his way. Coming around, he opened her door, and they walked up to the house. On the porch, he put his hands on her hips and pulled her close. "Let's be clear on this one thing at least. I want you here."

She'd held him up at pen-point. She'd dragged him all over California. And what had he done? He'd protected her with his life.

She owed him. Whether he wanted to believe it or not, she did. She owed him everything, but at the very least, she owed him more of the truth. "Noah." He was close, so very close. She'd never done the trust thing while staring someone in the eyes from inches away. "The men . . . they're cohorts of Alan's. They . . . they know me. I'm sorry if I didn't tell you before, but they said if I told anyone, they'd kill my students and Kenny, and then me."

"Bailey." His voice was terrifyingly gentle. He pressed his forehead to hers. "They're not going to kill you until they get their money."

"But you—"

"They're not going to get a chance at me either." He tightened his grip on her. "Or you. I'm not going to let it happen."

It took her a moment to speak. "Still, taking me to Cabo is above and beyond the call of duty."

He just looked at her, and again she sensed something within him, something that didn't have to do with her. "Excluding what we've been through," she said carefully, "I just get the feeling something's wrong."

He let out a harsh laugh and covered his eyes, and her curiosity changed into alarm. "Noah?"

He dropped his hand and looked at her. "It's nothing."

"Now who's not trusting?"

"We're not talking about this."

"Now *there's* a male statement I've heard many times before."

His jaw tightened. "Don't lump me in with the other men

in your life." His eyes were fathomless, his big body tense, yet loose. Battle ready.

Something *was* wrong, she could feel it. Something he didn't want her to know. He was tough as hell, she knew this first-hand, but she couldn't help but wonder, Who did he go to when he needed someone?

Shocking, how much she wished it could be her.

But he'd been on his own for far too long. Maybe he let Shayne and Brody close, but they'd been together forever, and she'd bet her last dollar, if she'd had one, that he didn't easily open up with anyone else.

Still, she wished . . . "I can't lump you into the same category as the other men in my life." Going on was one of the hardest things she'd ever done, but he had to know this much about her. "They've all been clean-cut, soft-spoken, overly educated—" She let out a laugh. "The kind of man a mother dreams of for her daughter, you know? In fact, it was that whole fantasy thing that sucked me into Alan's orbit."

"Yeah. And I'm not exactly the clean-cut, soft-spoken, overly educated kind of man your mother would have wanted for you." Noah leaned back against the door and crossed his arms. His hair fell into his eyes, but even if it hadn't, those eyes were shuttered from her for the first time since she'd stabbed him in the shoulder with her pen. "I get that."

"I'm trying to explain," she said.

"You're trying to tell me that I'm not your type. Got it loud and clear, Princess, believe me." He unlocked the door. "Unfortunately, your type or not, you need my help, which means you're stuck with me until we finish this thing." Movements just a little jerky with temper, he gestured her inside.

But he'd so thoroughly misunderstood, she just stared at him, not moving inside. He actually thought she was rejecting him. She wished she could tell him that was the last thing she'd ever do, but those words, here and now, weren't fair, because they weren't going anywhere with this.

They couldn't.

And given all she'd put him through, why would he even want to?

But he pulled her inside, and with one last searching look into the night, shut the door.

She knew they hadn't been followed; he'd never have allowed her to stand outside if they had been. But on the other hand, she'd not expected Stephen to tail her as closely as he'd managed for days, and that in itself was more than a little unsettling. "Noah—"

"Look, let's just eat." He headed toward the kitchen with the pizza. "Afterward, I'll show you to the spare bedroom."

"*Noah.*"

He just kept walking away from her.

Chapter 19

He'd known, hadn't he, Noah reminded himself. He'd known he wasn't her type. What the hell had he been thinking to put himself out there, telling her how he'd crashed, how he hadn't had sex in all that time . . .

Why didn't he just rip out his heart and put it on the highway to be run over? Might have been less painful—

"Noah, please."

He kept walking. For sanity's sake—if there was even any left—he had to. He was going to feed her, get her to the spare bedroom, say good night, and walk away.

Walking away was the key here.

"*Noah.*"

Probably he'd been a pity fuck. Yeah, that sucked. Or maybe she'd been just trying to thank him. After all, she was extremely polite, even while hijacking him with a pen, she'd been extremely polite.

That sucked even worse.

Grabbing his arm, she pulled him back around with surprising strength for a little thing, and then stared up at him, hands on his arms. He could have moved away; hell, he *should* move away, but there was something so damn compelling about those baby blues he'd once thought he could happily drown in.

His mistake. "Eat," he said, and because he knew she wouldn't unless he did, he pulled out a plate and opened the pizza box. He dumped a piece on the plate. Then when she just looked at it, probably calculating the carbs and fat content in her head, he sighed and loaded it with salad as well. "There's ranch dressing."

She slid onto one of his barstools. "No thanks."

He thought of his refrigerator, which probably had beer, maybe a few apples and some questionable leftover Thai. "I don't have any other kinds."

"Plain is fine." She picked up a piece of lettuce and stuck it in her mouth. "I like it this way."

He shook his head, and forgoing a plate for himself, he grabbed a piece of pizza and took a large bite, watching her as he, against his better judgment, sat on the barstool right next to her.

She took a knife from his counter, and cut a bite from her pizza. And then ate it with the fork.

Pizza with a fork.

But then she pushed around the next bite, and he sighed. "What's the matter?"

"I was trying to talk to you."

Yeah. To tell him he wasn't her type. "And we have to talk before you eat?"

"Yes."

With another sigh, he took a plate after all and set down his pizza. Fine. She could rip his heart out now, and he'd eat afterward. "If we talk, then you'll eat?"

"Everything on my plate," she promised. "Girl Scout's honor."

"You were a Girl Scout?"

Her slight amusement vanished. "No. I was a daddy's girl."

And look how well that had turned out for her.

"Look, I really do promise to eat," she said. "Believe me, contrary to popular belief—" Her voice came a little tight now.

"I'm not a silly socialite. I know I need my strength for Mexico. Where you're not taking me, by the way."

They'd see about that. Pushing back from the counter, he gestured her to go ahead, talk.

While he braced himself for the invisible blows that would hurt a hell of a lot more than anything in recent memory, because he'd alway closed himself off to hurt.

Too bad he'd been too stupid to *keep* himself closed off, or this, too, could have been avoided. In fact, if he'd just listened to Shayne and gone out with him instead of heading to Mammoth, none of this would have happened. He'd be just fine.

Of course, Bailey wouldn't be fine. She'd have faced off with the goons that she now claimed to actually know, and would be more hurt than she already was.

Or worse.

His gut twisted good at that. Ah, hell. He was here for a reason, because he wanted to help. For that matter, she was here for a reason, too. And she'd wanted him to be the one. That would have to be enough for him. No matter what happened, he intended to see this through.

To see her safe.

"Go ahead," he said, leaning back, crossing his arms over his chest. "I'm listening."

"Well . . ." She brushed some crumbs from her fingers. Imaginary crumbs, he was certain, because her fingers hadn't touched her pizza. "Before you got all grumpy and irritated, I was trying to—"

"Grumpy?" he asked incredulously. "Irritated?"

"Yes."

"I did not get grumpy and irritated."

"Okay, then you were pouting."

He felt his eyes widen. He should have started with a beer. "*Pouting*?"

"That's right."

He laughed, but she didn't. She just looked at him with those big, gorgeous eyes, earnest now.

"You thought you knew what I was going to say before I said it," she said. "Which, actually, was presumptuous, and not very nice."

He stared at her. "I'm not nice. You should know that by now."

"But you are." She reached for his hand, slipping her much smaller, and damn it, chilled one in his. "You're one of the nicest men I've ever met."

He laughed again, utterly without humor. If she thought that, then she'd—

She'd been with worse men.

All her life.

His smile faded. "Bailey."

"You thought I was saying you weren't my type," she said. "You really thought, after all we've been through over the past few days, that I would look you in the eyes and say that."

Hell. Yeah, he'd thought that. Silently admitting it, he lifted a shoulder.

"I was trying to say that I've never been with a man like you. It'd never occurred to me, and that's my shame. Because a man like you . . . well, you're real. I can't explain it better than that. I was trying to thank you, and I wanted do that with no reflection on what we've been through personally. But you made me sec something. I can't leave the personal part out of it, because it *is* personal. Very personal."

Christ, her eyes were so soft they could break his heart without even trying.

"I mean, it feels so inadequate to say, but you have to know how much I appreciate everything you've done—"

"It's fine," he said, cutting her off. He didn't want her thanks. She wasn't trying to rip his heart out, or compare him to the other assholes in her life.

She was trying to thank him. Jesus. That was the last thing he wanted. But what he *did* want was a can of worms he intended to never open.

"Tell me about Cabo," she whispered.

"Bailey—"

"It's where you crashed, isn't it."

Like a knife to the gut. "Yeah."

"Oh, Noah."

Jaw tight, he tried to pull his hand free, but she had the grip of a bulldog. "I can fly us there," he said. "I'll be fine."

She looked down at their joined hands. "But—"

"Don't say it."

She lifted her head and killed him with those eyes, those shimmering, brilliant, shiny eyes. "I can only imagine what the flight cost you, what yet another flight there would cost you—"

"Goddamnit, I just told you I was fine."

"But you've already done so much for me, already risked so much—"

"I shouldn't have told you."

"But I'm so glad you did." Leaning in, she pressed her lips to his jaw. "So glad."

And here came another pity fuck, right on schedule. Unable to handle it, he went to pull away, but he was still seated, and she held on with that grip of steel. She slid off her barstool. Her thighs bumped his knees, and without permission from his brain, his body went on high alert.

Bad body.

Still on tiptoes, she skimmed her lips toward his mouth. "I can never thank you for everything you've done," she whispered, kissing him again, on the lips this time, softly, so achingly sweetly that he felt the iciness inside him slowly loosen. "Thank you," she whispered again, and this time deepened the kiss. "Thank you . . ."

Oh, God. It *was* the pity fuck, he knew it. He just didn't have the strength to walk away from her. Instead, he put his hands on her hips and nudged her closer, between his legs. The little sound that escaped her throat was pure acquiescence, pure arousal, and it fueled his own. His hands slid down to cup her sweet ass and rock her forward, his eyes crossing with lust.

Which pissed him off. He'd had her, several times now. How could he still want her like this, with such a strong power he shook with it?

But some things, he knew, there just were no answers for.

"In fact, there are no words to thank you enough," she murmured, her hands on his shoulders. She tipped her face up to send him a tentative smile, making it even harder to resist her—it warmed his heart. Yep, the organ he'd thought dead and buried reared its hopeful little head and made him smile back.

Stupidity at its finest.

"Wow." She traced his lips with a finger, smiling dreamily. "You're so beautiful when you smile, Noah."

"Stop."

She did, but before she could take her finger off his lower lip, he sucked it into his mouth.

Hers fell open, as if she needed it that way just to breathe, and that reaction, along with her sharp intake of breath, turned him on so fast his head spun.

Even though it'd been spinning since she'd first stepped onto his plane.

"No one else would have done all you have," she said softly. "No one else would be willing to go with me now, to relive their biggest nightmare."

Jesus, she was *still* trying to thank him. "Bailey—"

"I mean it."

It wasn't her gratitude he wanted, not even close. At the moment he wanted something far easier to swallow, and far more base. She was cradled between his thighs, making it easy to slide his hands down her hips, her smooth legs, and then back up again, this time beneath her skirt.

Her breath caught. "Noah."

He loved that husky tone that had come into her voice, but just in case she planned to keep on thanking him, he covered her mouth with his to shut her up. Or so he told himself. But what he really wanted was to lose himself in the depths of her mouth, her body.

Hell, who was he kidding? He wanted her, all of her, heart and soul, because somehow, in some way, she'd become the salvation of his. His fingers encountered—oh God—some tiny lacy panties, the operative word being tiny.

Another thong.

Oh, yeah, he thought, cupping her bare cheeks, letting his fingers meet in the middle to trace that intriguing scrap of lace up . . . and down . . . and up . . .

Bailey's breathing changed, became choppy, and her fingers fisted in his shirt over his pecs. She had a few chest hairs in the midst, but he held back his wince because no way did he want her to take her hands off him.

He needed those hands, needed them on him in the worst possible way.

When his fingers slid under the lacy strap of her thong, she sucked in a serrated breath.

"Spread your legs," he whispered, then helped her along by nudging her feet apart with one of his, which gave him access to all he sought. "Ah, yeah, you're wet." It made his own breathing go as choppy as hers. "Is this more thanks, Princess?"

"No—" she managed. "That's . . . that's how much I want you."

Lifting his head, he stared into her dazed baby blues.

"I want you," she repeated softly, and taking her hands off of him, she pulled off her sweater and let it hit the floor. Beneath she wore a white lace bra that played peek-a-boo with her nipples, which were pebbled into two hard, pouty points. She let the straps fall off her shoulders to her elbows, so that the cups slipped, barely, just barely now, still covering her.

Her gaze shimmered with heat, such heat he knew he was playing with fire, and also something else, something more and deeper, and even harder to resist—affection.

It was that which slayed him.

So he closed his eyes and dipped his head, kissing his way down her throat, down to a high curved breast, and farther, dipping his tongue beneath the lace to tease.

Her hands fumbled with the buttons on his shirt, but he didn't help her because that would mean taking his hands off her body and he couldn't do that, he just couldn't. He had her shoved hard against the buttons on his Levi's in the front, his hands up her skirt in the back, one gripping her ass, the other playing in her slippery heat. He couldn't have been any closer, and yet it still wasn't enough.

He needed to be buried inside her, needed to be milked dry as she came apart for him, needed to hear his name fall from her lips as she did.

"Please," she sighed in a pleasure-drugged voice, her head falling back as he continued to kiss her breasts. She stirred restlessly against him, rocking her hips in an age old rhythm. "I need—"

He knew. He needed it, too, and he played his fingers in and out of her, swallowing her whimper with his mouth, but it still wasn't enough. She was fumbling at his Levi's, working the buttons free, and then she slipped her hands inside. One touch of her hands encircling him, and his hips jerked upward. Then she stroked him, and he saw stars.

Christ, was it always going to be like this with them, fiery hot and unstoppable? He felt like a freight train barreling without brakes into his first stop, and there was nothing he could do. He yanked her thong down.

She tried to do the same to his jeans, but he was still sitting on the barstool. With a little growl of frustration, she sank her fingers into his hair and tugged his head up. "Help me," she demanded.

With some half-baked Neanderthal idea of carrying her over his shoulder to his bedroom, he surged to his feet, but the bedroom seemed much too far away. Hell, the couch in the living room seemed too far. So was the kitchen table, just behind him.

Turning her back to him, she surveyed the room with the same desperation he felt. As if weak-kneed, she leaned on the barstool, and the hem of her skirt rose enough to expose a hint of the panties he'd tugged to her thighs. Turbulent heat and desire whipped through him, and with a hand low on her back, he let out a breath.

Oh yeah, there was a picture, Bailey bent over his barstool. Wrapping his fingers in the hem of her skirt, he pushed it to the small of her back, then nearly staggered at the sight of her white lacy thong barely clinging to her upper thighs, at the pink glistening glory between them, at the sweet curves of her amazing ass, the twin dimples at the base of her spine.

Utterly unable to help himself, he bent and put his mouth there, then worked his way up as his arms banded around her, his hands cupping the weight of her breasts, his fingers grazing her nipples.

Her hands came behind her, grabbing his hips, yanking him flush to her. He was going to last exactly one more second like that, so he took her hands in his and brought them in front of her, stretching her out, settling them on the edge of his granite countertop, tightening his on hers in a silent plea to keep them there.

She did, arching her back, still rubbing her ass up and down on him as everything within him began to draw up tight. Even his toes began to curl.

He couldn't hold back.

With her, he could never hold back.

He'd wanted to make her come first, wanted to hear her pant out his name in that breathless, sexy-as-hell way she had when he'd put her in the throes, but he couldn't, he just couldn't, and fisting himself, he gripped her hip, bent his knees, and thrust home.

She cried out, a primal sound.

Heat, pure and simple, slid through him. He groaned with the pleasure of it and sank over her body as he gave himself up to what she made him feel, gliding a hand around her front, up her belly, over her breasts, his other holding on to her hip as he began to move.

He watched as he slid in and out of her, glistening, rock hard to her gorgeous softness, which gripped him like a velvet glove with every thrust. He was drowning in her, literally drowning. Every part of him was so primed to go off that he could no longer see past the sexual haze in his own head. He bent over her, pressing his mouth to her ear, the side of her neck, running his nose over her skin, absorbing the feel of her, her scent. On the very edge, he slid his hand down her belly and further, grazing his fingers over her center, his entire body jerking again when she let out a low gasp as he gently drew her between his thumb and finger.

When he rubbed, she cried out his name and covered his hand with hers to hold him there as she shuddered and exploded for him.

Wait, he ordered himself. Wait and get a repeat performance out of her, because listening to her pant out his name, feeling her tremble, for him, experiencing her tighten and constrict around him as she came, was the wildest, sexiest thing he could imagine, and he wanted to experience it over and over. But he just couldn't hold back, and opening his mouth on the patch of skin where her shoulder met her neck, he let himself follow her over into the abyss.

She ate, as she'd promised. Noah hadn't intended for it to be *him* she put her mouth on and nibbled, but he didn't utter a single complaint when she'd tasted and licked her way over his entire body. Nope, he lay there and let her feast, and if anything had passed his lips, it had been a groan for mercy.

Which she'd given.

Later they made it as far as the shower, where they started all over again, and then finally, they staggered to his bed, where they both collapsed.

He hadn't slept well in months, but with Bailey in his arms, he slept like a damn baby, waking only when his obnoxious alarm went off at six. For the first time in far too long, he felt a grin split his face, and more astonishingly, the muscles there didn't feel so unused.

He'd grinned a lot last night.

And he was up for plenty more, say round four—

Or was it five?

He rolled over, but the spot next to him was empty.

Ah, hell. He slid a hand to it.

Still warm.

Leaping out of bed, he ran to the bathroom.

Empty.

She wasn't in the kitchen either, nor the living room. In fact, he discovered standing in the middle of his house, she wasn't anywhere, which meant only one thing.

She'd gone without him. But the pillow had been warm. He had to be only a moment or two behind her. Whipping open the front door, he was just in time to see a taxi vanish down his driveway. He was halfway out the door after her before the slice of January wind reminded him he was butt-ass-naked.

Chapter 20

"To LAX," Bailey told the cab driver in the still dark morning, and put on her seat belt with shaking fingers. She'd made a tactical error last night, a serious one.

She'd engaged her heart.

There was no use beating herself up over it. She should have moved on that first night, separated from Noah at the Mammoth airport and gone on her own.

But you'd have faced Stephen and those men on your own, too. Twice.

Okay, she couldn't have separated from Noah then, but certainly yesterday she could have.

Should have.

Instead, she'd gone with him to Catalina, and while she hadn't had any more luck there than she had in Mammoth, once again he'd gotten her out of a situation she couldn't have managed on her own.

She owed him so much.

And last night, lying in his arms, happier than she'd ever been in her entire life, she'd realized how to repay him.

By leaving him.

She'd been over it and over it in her head, and there was no other way to protect him. God. She pressed her fingers to her eyes, as if she could rub away this huge disastrous mess that she'd made out of her life.

It was still dark outside, with only the tiniest tinges of pink in the far east.

Was Noah awake? What had he thought when he'd found her gone?

He'd be furious.

He'd worry.

God, he'd worry. She knew it. But she couldn't let him do this, couldn't let him take her to Cabo, especially not now that she knew what had happened to him there.

Plus, a small part of her knew . . . she was falling for him, hard and fast. Too fast. She was afraid for him, desperately afraid. No, there was no other way to keep him safe than to leave him.

Then she realized they were passing her street. "Excuse me," she said to the driver. "I need to make a quick detour."

"No detours."

"Please, just real quick. Can you turn right here?" In tune to his annoyed sighs, she directed him to the house where she'd lived with Alan in style—and in lies.

A lifetime ago.

The place was dark and had a For Sale sign in the driveway. It was being sold as a part of the impending bankruptcy, but hadn't gone yet despite the fact it'd had some heavy traffic. Looky-Lous, mostly, but it didn't matter to her. She wouldn't receive a penny. She didn't care, she didn't want a cent of Alan's tainted money.

She just wanted her life back.

And herself.

She really wanted herself back. Last night she'd felt a glimmer of the old Bailey, and it had been wonderful, so wonderful her heart still ached. "Thank you," she said to the driver, taking her last look at a house she never wanted to see again. "We can go straight to LAX now."

As they drove away, she wondered if her life would ever be the same. How much of herself was she going to have to give up? She thought of Noah, how it felt to give him up, and rubbed a hand over her heart.

She was truly alone now. She hated the feeling. She slipped her hands into her pockets. Her fingers closed over her cell phone.

Not completely alone.

She still had Kenny, and suddenly she needed to hear from him in the worst possible way. Pulling out the phone, she turned it on, and read a waiting text message. BAIL, WHERE R U? K

She began to type in her answer, then stopped. Every single time she responded to Kenny, Stephen had caught up with her.

Coincidence?

She might never have even thought about it, but for Noah's suspicions. He believed that Kenny was somehow using her texts to locate her. And if that was true, if he was in cahoots with the bad guys, then she was playing right into his hands by answering.

She stared at the phone as if for the first time. A little frisson of doubt of Kenny's innocence went through her.

But if she was being honest, it *wasn't* the first time. Truthfully, she'd been fighting with the doubt for days now. She turned off the phone, then stared at it with growing dread as she remembered Noah's words.

Don't give anyone a way to track you.

With a small cry of pain, betrayal, and a bone-deep despair, she lowered her window and tossed the phone out in the street.

"Hey!" the cab driver yelled back. "You can't do that!"

"Sorry." She craned her neck to watch as the phone hit the ground, only to be run over by the car behind her—

Oh, God. The car behind her.

Noah.

The sun was rising now, slanting across the low lying hills on either side of them so that she couldn't see in past the windshield of his BMW.

She didn't need to.

He was looking at her, *right* at her. She could feel the weight of his gaze as she'd felt the weight of very little else, ever.

He'd followed her.

Torn between terror and a huge, almost overwhelming relief, she nearly slipped bonelessly to the floor, but she forced herself to sit there and look at him.

Could he see her?

He'd already seen far more of her than she'd meant him to, and she didn't mean just her naked body. She'd done everything in her power to keep him at arm's length, but for the first time in her life, that had been impossible. He'd taken down her carefully constructed walls that she'd built around herself, one brick at a time.

Hell, he'd blasted through them.

But he hadn't left her to her own defense; he'd hung around, no matter what the cost to him personally. Oh, God, the implications of that alone . . .

"If I get pulled over," the crabby cab driver yelled at her, "the traffic ticket is going to come out of *your* wallet, not mine! The rules are stated very clearly on the back of the seats!" Reaching behind him, he patted his headrest, where indeed, a list of rules had been clearly laid out for any idiot to read. "There. You see?"

"Yes," she said, still staring at Noah. "I see, and I'm sorry, very sorry."

"Nothing else out of the cab, or no more ride for you."

"I promise."

The cabby sniffed in indignance, and continued driving. Bailey waited with baited breath as they pulled into the huge drop-off loop at LAX. The cabby hit the curb in front of her airline and held out his palm.

She was still pulling the cash out of her purse when the taxi door on her side was hauled open. She'd no sooner handed the cabby his money when two big, warm hands pulled her from the car.

"Hey," she said to one damn fine chest, covered in a beat-up leather aviation jacket.

"Hey," Noah said fiercely instead of friendly, then hauled her against him. "Now tell me you're in one piece because I'm not sure I can believe my eyes."

Running her hands up his arms, she felt the tension in his body. It gripped him from head to toe, and she pulled back, looking into his face. "I'm in one piece."

"Unhurt."

"Unhurt," she promised.

He stared at her for a long moment, then let out a slow, deliberate breath. Probably trying not to strangle her, she thought.

He had remarkable control that way.

"Look," he said. "Probably another guy, a normal guy, would assume you'd left this morning because you were done with him."

Her throat closed up at the thought of him thinking that.

"But I'd like to think I know better," he said. "Stop trying to protect me, Bailey. Because the truth is, you're the one who needs the protection."

What could she say to that, the utter truth? When she'd left him only a half hour ago, he'd been gloriously naked, sprawled facedown over three-quarters of the bed, looking much finer than any male had business looking at the crack of dawn.

And she'd stood there for just a moment, throat nearly closed, eyes filled, a shaking hand to her mouth to hold in any words that she might have recklessly spilled.

God, he meant so much to her. In such a short time, he'd come to mean so much.

In any case, he hadn't stayed gloriously naked, and she had a feeling he'd dressed while cursing her and running for the door. Besides the jacket, he wore a T-shirt and a pair of faded, soft-looking jeans that fit him in a way that had the other women walking past them giving him both a second and third look.

He was oblivious of course, his full attention on her. He had his sunglasses on, but she had no trouble detecting the temper in him. Just in case, he shoved the glasses to thc top of his head and glared at her, those normally warm green eyes cool as rain.

Cool, and furious. "So. Where were you going?" he asked with remarkable politeness.

"You know where."

He reached into the cab for her bag. Once he did, the cab took off, and she was left alone with him. Except for the hundreds of people at LAX, going about their day.

"I would have flown you," he said, shouldering her duffle bag.

"I know." She stepped close and put a hand on his chest. "I couldn't ask you to do that, Noah. Not after what happened to you there—"

"Don't," he said. He pulled her into the terminal.

She knew that had been to get her out of the brisk morning air, and her heart squeezed all the more. Even now, he cared. "Noah—"

"Which airline?"

"I want to explain—"

"*Which airline*?"

She pointed, and he looked over his shoulder, noting the take-off times, and the long, winding line of people waiting. He headed toward the end of it, with her in tow.

"I already have my ticket," she said to his stiff, broad shoulders.

"But I don't." He kept a tight grip on her hand, not a lover's touch, as he'd used on her last night, all night long, not even a friendly one, but a tight, don't-even-think-about-letting-go grip.

"You can't just buy a ticket because of me—"

He shot her a scathing look.

"It'll be expensive," she said. Hers certainly would have been except she'd used her dead husband's frequent-flyer miles. "And I can't—"

He ignored her. Just totally and completely ignored her, making sure to keep her hand in his as he turned his back on her and studied the people around them.

"Noah." His spine was tense when she set her hand on it. The muscles quivered beneath her touch, the only sign that he was aware of her. "*Noah.*"

He turned and looked at her. Someone jostled her from behind, and she used the excuse to slide her hands up his chest, and around his neck. She set her head down on his shoulder. "I couldn't keep leaning on you," she whispered.

He didn't touch her back, but let out a tense breath. "I just keep thinking . . . I nearly missed you."

I'd have come back. The words nearly rolled right off her tongue and into his ear, but she clamped down on them. She had no right to say such a thing, and no right to even want it.

He stepped back from her, as if needing distance. "Why did your cell phone take flying lessons on El Segundo Boulevard?"

She smiled wryly. "Saw that, huh?"

"Ran it over."

She'd left her hand on his chest. She didn't want to ever let go.

"Why, Bailey?"

"I got a text from Kenny."

The look on his face as he absorbed that defied description: amazement that she'd allowed the contact, fear for her safety, and temper that he hadn't been able to stop it. "How?" he finally asked. "I thought we agreed you would leave the thing off."

She felt the guilt flash across her face. "No, you agreed I should. I . . ." She shook her head. "I'm sorry, Noah. I had to see if he'd tried calling me."

"I understand."

"I mean, he's my only family, and I just couldn't seem to reconcile the fact that he'd—" She stopped. "You understand?"

"Do you think I'm completely cold and unfeeling?"

"No," she said softly. "I don't think you're cold and unfeeling at all."

He held her gaze for a long beat, then let out a breath. "So he called?"

"He texted. He'd done so before. Yesterday, too, when I was in the closet at Sky High. But this time he came right out and asked me where I was." She took in his knowing expression and closed her eyes.

"Ah, hell, Bailey." His sigh warmed her temple. "I'm sorry."

"I didn't want to see it . . ."

Again she was jostled from behind, and she bumped closer into Noah. Chest to chest now. His hand settled on her waist, and for a moment, she let herself pretend that they were a couple.

He brought a hand up to her hair. "I'm sorry. I didn't want to be right."

She set her forehead to his chest and absorbed the betrayal and pain. "I don't know how or why, but if he's working with the investors to recover their money, then . . ." To even say the words felt wrong. "Then he's been using our text messages to keep track of where I am. It would explain how they always seem to be right there with me, you know?"

He tipped her face up, staring down at her for a long beat. "No matter what happens, I'm there. On your side. Can you believe that?"

She wanted to. "I'm not very good at believing. But . . ."

"But . . . ?"

"But I'd like to try, with you."

He let out a long breath, then pressed a kiss to her jaw. A conciliatory kiss, a sweet connection that had her sighing as she leaned into him. She had no idea what she'd ever done to deserve him here at her side helping her, but she was ever so grateful that he was as stubborn as she. "I've always held back, you know. I think a part of me knew I couldn't reveal everything, couldn't fully trust."

He ran his hand up and then down her back, comforting. "A sucky way to live."

"It nearly killed me," she confessed. "In more ways than one." She managed to look at him, into those melting eyes and admit the truth. "I don't want to live that way anymore. I want to learn to believe. To trust."

"Then don't pull another vanishing act on me. Let's see this thing through to the end. Together."

Her breath caught. "Another weak point of mine."

"What, seeing things through to the end?"

"No, the together thing."

"Me too," he said. "But maybe it's time for us both to try. To take a risk."

"Next!" one of the airline representatives called from the counter.

For a moment, Noah didn't move, just looked at her, gaze heated. Then he shifted around and moved to the counter.

"A ticket for your next flight to Cabo," he said.

Bailey rifled through her purse and pulled out the last of her cash and slapped it on the counter.

Noah pushed it away.

Bailey pushed it back.

The airline representative divided a bemused gaze between the two of them. "I can split the cost, fifty-fifty."

"No." Noah pushed his card toward the representative while

palming Bailey's cash, which he handed directly to her. "How about the *next* time we fly commercial, you buy," he suggested.

"But you never fly commercial."

He smiled. "I know. Come on, let's do this." He looked up their gate number, then at the long, long walk they had to make, and sighed. "What do you think the chances are that they'll serve something more than peanuts on board?"

"Slim to none?" she responded and tipped back her head to look into his face.

And caught him.

He'd been talking to her with a light teasing tone, keeping his touch casual, but though his head was bent close to hers, nothing about the tense, still way he stood was light or teasing as his eyes carefully and thoroughly and continually scanned the area around them.

"Expecting trouble so soon?" she asked softly.

His gaze dipped momentarily to hers. "With you? Always."

"Noah."

He lifted a shoulder. "Did you tell Kenny where you were off to before you sentenced your phone to cell hell?"

"No, but it won't matter. We're going to the last place the money could be. They've been following me; they'll have figured it out by now. They'll be watching for me." The spot between her shoulder blades began to tingle, and she turned around, looking.

No one was paying her any mind at all, but that didn't mean they weren't out there. "You think they're here, too."

Noah didn't say anything to that as they made their way through the line to get past security. Ahead of them, security agents opened up two more lanes, calling out warnings for everyone to remove their shoes, jewelry, and keys. The crowd collectively obeyed with the usual grumbling.

Noah toed off his athletic shoes, stuck them in a bucket, and then handed her an empty bucket to use.

Bailey bent to unstrap and untie her sandals. One of these days she was going to get over her shoe fetish and just buy regular, easy to put on and easy to pull off shoes.

Okay, probably she wasn't. She carefully set her Nine West sandals in the bucket and watched them move on the conveyor belt until they vanished from sight.

"They're going to be okay," Noah said dryly.

She nodded, hoping her underwire bra didn't set off the alarm as it had the last time she'd flown commercial.

"Sir." Another uniformed security officer waved Noah to come on through.

Just as he stepped under the metal detector, and just as Bailey was dumping her purse into her gray bucket, she heard the voice calling through the crowd.

"Bailey!"

And everything within her went still.

Kenny.

Clutching her purse, she whipped around.

Her brother was weaving his way through the crowd, his gaze on her, his face creased into tense lines. "Wait!"

"Bailey," Noah said urgently from the other side of security. He made a move to come back through, but the security officer stepped in front of Noah. "I'm sorry, sir, but—"

"Bailey!" Kenny yelled again. He was wearing a white button down and trousers, not looking anything like a wanderlust carpenter.

She had no idea how he'd pinpointed her exact location, but the thought terrified her. If *he'd* found her, then the others could, too. She hadn't seen him in a few weeks, and before that it had been months, so she wasn't prepared for the changes he'd undergone.

He'd always been an athlete, albeit a bit of a pampered one. But the muscles he'd refined in basketball, track, and baseball had faded. On top of that, he'd lost weight. His face seemed too thin, almost to the point of gaunt.

Worse, his eyes were hollow, and haunted.

And leveled right on her.

"Excuse me," he said to the people in his way, pushing past them one at a time, his expression growing more and more desperate. "Excuse me—"

"Hey!" A huge guy who looked as if maybe he was a linebacker for a living, shook his head. "Dude, wait in line like the rest of us."

"I just need to talk to—"

"A hell to the no," the linebacker dude said firmly, slapping a hand to Kenny's chest. "Get in line."

"Get through security," Noah said tightly, looking as if he might leap back over the security table, the officer be damned.

"Bailey! Bailey, it's not what you think!" Kenny shouted, now being held back by a security guard who'd stepped in front of him. "Don't go!"

She stared at him, throat tight, eyes burning. "I have to. You know I have to."

"It's not there. Please. Trust me. You don't understand—"

Another security guard joined the first, and now she could no longer see Kenny at all.

He wanted her to wait. Possibly so that he could get more men in place.

More men to take her down.

Kill her.

Oh, God, Kenny.

And turning her back, she walked beneath the metal detectors toward a waiting and clearly relieved Noah.

Chapter 21

They boarded their plane without any trouble, though in Bailey's case, she half expected to be held back for being over the weight limit, since she felt so heavy and stressed she could hardly move.

She was bringing Noah back to the place of his personal hell for her own gains.

How could she do that?

Leaning in, he put his mouth to her ear. "You're thinking so loud over there that I can't hear the flight attendant's emergency spiel."

She managed a smile for him, one that turned more real when he returned it.

"Why don't you try to sleep?" he murmured. "You've got to be exhausted."

True enough. She hadn't managed to sleep more than a few minutes last night. Although, to be fair, that couldn't be blamed squarely on this. Nope, she'd burned the midnight oil in Noah's arms, letting him de-stress her.

Many times.

Yeah, as a stress reliever, Noah Fisher was pretty amazing.

Thinking it, she glanced at him, sitting next to her, his eyes watchful as they rose to altitude and the seat belt signs went off, his body prepared for whatever came his way.

He caught her staring at him and gave her a what's-up look. Everything about him was focused on her, and in his eyes was the capacity to handle whatever she dished out. Whatever life dished out. Just looking at him made her feel incredibly alive, and shockingly . . . happy.

When she didn't say anything, he cocked a brow. He was so inherently male, so unintentionally sexy, she could have laughed, could have thrown her arms around him, could have opened her mouth and told him she was falling, and falling hard, and any of those reactions, or all of them, were real. Utterly and one-hundred-percent real, as nothing else was in her life at the moment.

Oh, boy. The surprising depth of her feelings for this man after what—two days?—completely and totally unnerved her.

How am I going to let him go?

It was going to hurt, more than anything else. Suddenly she needed a moment for her own private little pity party, and she scrambled to unbuckle her seat belt.

"Bailey?"

"Bathroom," she choked out. "I need the bathroom." She stumbled over his long, folded legs to get out of the row.

In the bathroom, she stared at herself in the mirror. She was in the midst of the biggest nightmare of her life. So what did it say about her that she could fall for him?

Had fallen for him?

The knock at the door nearly startled her right out of her own skin. "Bailey," came Noah's low voice. "Open up."

Before she could tell him to go away, another voice, a female one, came through the door. "Sir, there's another bathroom—"

"Yes, thank you, but I'm with her. Bailey, let me in." This he said directly to the door, not quite as politely.

He was losing his patience.

"Sir," came the flight attendant's voice, also losing patience. "I'm afraid that's against policy. You can't both go in there."

Bailey stared at the door, stifling the shocking urge to giggle.

Giggle, in the middle of her personal hell.

But evidently, Noah was not going to give up, because he tried a different tactic. "I know it's against policy, ma'am, but my wife's had an incredibly rough day."

Wait a minute. Wife? Had he just said . . . *wife*? Bailey turned from the mirror and gaped at the locked door.

"She just lost her father," Noah was saying. "And her brother, and—"

"Oh, dear," whispered the attendant. "The poor thing!"

"She's upset—"

"Of course." This from the attendant, in a low, commiserating voice. "Does she need anything? A drink, anything?"

"Frankly?" Noah said. "Me. She needs me. In there."

The attendant apparently agreed because after a short silence, Noah's voice was back, a low whisper this time, and much closer to the door, almost as if he were kissing it. "Bailey? Let me in before she changes her mind."

Bailey once again glanced at herself. Her eyes were just a bit wild, as if she was a woman on the run for her life, as if she had a man whose mere voice made her just a little weak, trying to coax her into letting him in—"Noah—"

"Do it."

She'd no more than pulled back the occupied lever than he'd slipped inside and locked the door again.

She braced herself, but he smiled. "Hi," he said.

"Hi back." And then she couldn't help it; she let out a helpless laugh that sounded so close to a sob she had to clap her hand over her mouth again.

With a finger, he stroked a strand of hair off her face, while never taking his eyes off hers. "How's it going?"

"Terrific."

"Uh huh. You going to ever talk to me?"

His hair was falling into his eyes. His shoulders were so broad they blocked out the harsh light. All she could see was his face, a face she'd come to rely on, need, want . . .

"Bailey?"

Love. She loved him so much.

"Is this about Kenny?"

No, but as that was also on her mind, it was a fine diversion. "He said it's not what I think. I don't' know what he meant by that."

He grimaced. "He'll say whatever he needs to—"

Bailey didn't say anything to that. She realized he didn't want to add to her misery by agreeing that Kenny had to be guilty as hell.

"He said it's not there," she whispered.

"I know."

"How would he know that unless he'd been in contact with the men who've been following me?"

"It's possible he went himself," Noah said. "Maybe he already got the money, and then outran the others."

"And kept it?" She paled at that thought even as her heart started a slow, heavy beat. "If they catch him . . ." Oh, God. Didn't bear thinking about. *Kenny. God, Kenny, what have you done?*

Noah squeezed her hand. "Then there's the other possibility . . ."

"Which is?"

"That he doesn't know where the money is, that he hasn't found it yet."

"Then why warn me off?"

He looked at her, and she let out a long breath. "Because he wanted it all for himself," she whispered, and felt her eyes fill.

Noah looked at her, muttered, "Fuck it," and pulled her close.

"He won't be that far behind us," she said against his chest, voicing her fears out loud as adrenaline kicked into her system. "It won't take him, or the others, that long to find another flight."

"No," he agreed grimly, holding her tight. "We'll definitely have company. Look, it's not too late. We can get Brody to come get us, and get Shayne's brother involved. Get restraining orders, and—"

"And what?" she asked. "The fact is, Alan screwed those guys. Unscrupulous or not, he owes them that money."

"Fine. The money is theirs. Let *them* find it."

"Noah—"

"Look, you can't really believe that even if you manage to find it and hand it over, this whole thing is just going to go away? That they're going to just let you go?"

She stared at him, then squeezed her eyes shut and covered her face.

He gently lowered her hands, and when she found the courage to open her eyes, he was watching her with that deep, penetrating look that never failed to catch her breath.

"You're not alone," he said.

Was it wrong to want to melt into him at that? She was a strong woman who wanted to handle herself and her problems by herself, but . . . but she ached for him. Needed him in some fundamental way that felt right. Definitely not a concept she was used to. No, she wasn't alone. She was with a man who'd, so far at least, never let her down.

Never would.

The marvel of that was enough to drop her to her knees, but he was standing so close she couldn't have dropped anywhere.

"You're not alone," he repeated, looking tall, big, fierce. *Gorgeous*. "Say it."

Her heart kicked it up another gear. And other parts of her

body, too. She felt warm, too warm, and . . . sort of as if her skin was too tight. If he didn't touch her, she thought, she was going to die. "Noah—"

"Say it, Bailey."

"I'm not alone," she whispered, putting a hand to her chest to keep her heart from bursting right out. And then there were the other reactions going on, all erogenous-zone based.

Adrenaline, she told herself. Just sheer adrenaline.

"Now believe it," he demanded.

"I'm not alone," she repeated again. "Because I have you."

He nodded. He had his hands on the sink behind her, on either side of her hips. His arms were bent so that their faces were level, their mouths a mere breath apart.

"So now what?" she managed just a little hoarsely.

"Now . . ." Nudging her back against the counter, he invaded her space, and everything within her leapt to attention.

He kissed her jaw, sank his teeth into her earlobe, and let out a slow breath in her ear.

She shivered wildly. "We should probably go back to our seats."

"Yeah. Have you ever made love on a plane?"

"No." Already breathless, she wrapped her arms around his neck. She'd never made love on a plane. "I never really thought we could—*Oh*," she murmured as he lifted her onto the narrow counter. Her entire body went on high, hopeful, quivering alert. "Here?"

In answer, he slid his hands to her thighs and pushed them open. Then he stepped between them, slipping his hands beneath her bottom to haul her up against him.

"Okay, here," she said desperately, and almost before she got the words out, he'd shoved up her skirt, hooked his fingers in her panties, and tugged them down.

"The attendant—" she gasped, but then he'd opened his jeans and pushed inside her in one movement, and talking was beyond her. So was thinking.

He let out a low, raw sound of pure pleasure, and gripping her hips, nearly pulled all the way out.

A soft cry escaped her.

She couldn't help it, she needed him back in, needed him hot and hard and throbbing inside her, right now, now, *now*.

"Shh," he said, and covered her mouth with his to ensure it, and then, oh, God, and then he began to move. Suddenly all her fear and anxiety and nerves . . . everything . . . went away. Flew away. Her existence went from overwhelmingly complicated to amazingly, shockingly simple.

Just as it always did when she was with him.

How did he do that?

She didn't know, just held on, bringing his mouth back to hers, letting him and everything he was work its magic.

The approach to Cabo was smooth enough, but Noah found himself white knuckling the armrests regardless. The location was the stuff of his nightmares, made all the worse for being the passenger, with absolutely *no* control.

So much for being over himself.

He needed to work on that.

The pilot banked the aircraft, and Noah caught a good up-front view of the landscape, specifically where he'd fallen out of the sky and hit the desertlike hills.

"Noah?" Bailey was looking at him with concern and regret lining those gorgeous baby blues. "You okay?"

"Perfect." He felt a drop of sweat run down his temple. "Is it hot in here? I think it's hot in here."

Bailey didn't say a word, just entwined her fingers with his and held on tight.

He found himself pathetically grateful, and for the first time since . . . well, ever, he wanted to set his head on someone's shoulders and let go.

Bailey's shoulders.

Wasn't that a kick. He wanted to reach out to the woman who was causing him all this grief.

The pilot banked to the other side, just to give everyone a view of the ocean, and Noah's stomach flipped over and revolted. He'd had that view as well, thank you very much, up close and personal. He didn't need to see it again.

Jesus.

Landing anywhere close to this place was never going to be smooth enough for him.

"Excuse me, sir. Are you all right?" This from the female passenger on the other side of his aisle.

"Yes," he said as lightly as he could through his clenched teeth. Bailey was holding his hand, stroking his arm, and still, still goddamnit, he was sweating. "I'm fine," he said. "Fine."

Bailey just kept touching him, and he tried his damnedest to suck it up because he was making her feel even worse about getting him down here, but he just needed a damn moment.

Or two.

When they finally touched down, he resisted the urge to kiss the ground. They made it to the terminal without him further humiliating himself and without any other incident, but Noah had no doubt that *that* streak of luck and fortune would not be lasting long.

Not when Bailey was around.

She was sharp as hell, she made him smile, hell, she made him want to walk around *singing* for crissakes, and she was gorgeous to boot.

No doubt, he had a major thing going for her, but there was no question—she had a knack for bringing the trouble.

He'd been momentarily sidetracked while helping her to join the ranks of the Mile High Club in the airplane bathroom, but now that he was thinking with his head, at least his big one, some of the euphoria from the great sex began to fade.

That they hadn't been able to put their hands on the so-called hidden money was a bad sign.

Her brother showing up at LAX was a bad sign.

Bad signs all over the place, and it made him feel edgy. He was missing something, something big.

That much he knew.

What he didn't know for certain was if Bailey was missing it, too, or if she just hadn't shared it yet.

He hated that thought.

They got through the airport and car rental without seeing any action and were on the road in a beat-up old Blazer, old being the operative word, driving down the main drag, surrounded by the dry salty heat of Cabo, when his cell phone began vibrating. "Fisher," he answered.

"You're not skiing, you're not boinking a ski bunny, and you're not piloting Trouble-Walking to Cabo. Where the hell are you?" Shayne demanded.

"Do you really want to know?"

"You're already in Cabo."

"Bingo."

"You flew commercial."

This wasn't a question, but a statement of disbelief. Noah glanced over at Bailey, who was watching him. She had her window down. The wind was playing havoc with her hair, which she was trying unsuccessfully to hold back. With her arms lifted, attempting to corral her hair into submission, her neck was exposed.

She had a little bite mark right beneath her ear.

His.

And just beneath the bite was a patch of red skin, from his two-day-old beard.

He'd marked her.

The thought should have disgusted him, but apparently he was just Neanderthal enough for the opposite reaction.

He wanted to pull the falling-off-its-own-axis Blazer over to the side of the road and haul her into his lap and start all over again. He wanted to put his hands back on her, and while he was doing that, he wanted to be buried deep inside her body, his mouth on hers, swallowing those sexy little panting cries she made as she came—

"Noah?" Shayne said.

"Yeah." He tore his eyes off Bailey and her body. "I flew commercial."

"Oh, Christ. You're in deep." This was also said with disbelief. "You've fallen and can't get up."

"Shayne—"

"Maddie said you were in love with her, but—"

"Maddie needs to mind her own damn business."

"We are her business," Shayne said.

Noah pinched the bridge of his nose. "Is there a point to this?"

"Sure."

"Are you planning to get to it anytime soon?"

"Look, man. I know she means something to you. That's new."

Noah didn't say anything to that. Yeah, she meant something to him.

Everything.

And yeah, it was new. Not to mention a little unsettling.

"You're going to see if you can find the money and get those guys off her butt."

"Yes."

A sigh sounded through the phone. "Maddie's going to give you a whole ration of shit."

"No, she won't. She thinks it's romantic. Stupid, but romantic."

He got another long-suffering sigh. "You're making the rest of us look bad, dude."

"Got to go."

"Fine, but given the situation, you're going to get yourself in more hot water, right?"

Yeah. Of that much, at least, he was quite certain.

"Give me your location. I'll fly down there and provide the getaway."

"You don't have to—"

"No shit, Sherlock. Location."

Noah knew it wasn't just the getaway. Both he and Shayne knew that being here was a problem for him. And then there was the commercial airline factor. If he could get out of the return flight . . . "Meet us back at the Baja airport in a few hours."

"Done."

Still debating with himself over whether having Shayne come was a good idea or a bad one, Noah shut his phone.

Bailey directed him along the main drag. It was only early afternoon, but the heat beat down on them as they drove, the Pacific Ocean tumbling the shores on the right, the hotels and resorts lining the beach.

"It's up ahead," Bailey told him. "Turn right here."

Instead, he drove right by the construction site.

"Noah?"

"Hang on." He turned into the next property, which was, surprise surprise, yet another hotel. He drove along the far side of the parking lot until he found a vacant space, and pulled in.

They had a perfect view of Alan's resort. The Fun and Sun's lot was still unpaved, and opened to the hotel itself, which competed for attention with the two hotels it was sandwiched by.

The site was far messier and more disorganized than either Mammoth or Catalina, with equipment and huge piles of materials like brick and mortar lying everywhere.

But there was no doubt, the place had that same deserted feel as the others.

"I don't see anything," Bailey said. "No cars, no movement."

"Which, as we've discovered the hard way, means nothing."

Yeah, Noah was quite certain of two things as he sat there in the Blazer next to Bailey and surveyed the situation. One, the money hadn't yet been found.

And two, they weren't alone. "I'm assuming there's a suite here where Alan stayed, just like the others."

"Yes." Bailey eyed the buildings, which had been designed and built in a slow-arching half circle around a natural bay, only feet from the waves.

The hotel itself was one building, with a series of bungalows, all undoubtedly pricey and absolutely showy, and all clearly designed for the Hollywood celebrity crowd.

"One of those bungalows was built as a prototype, to show off during tours while construction went on." Her voice changed, almost indelibly so, but he knew her now, and he heard it.

A new tension.

"This way," she said before he could figure out what exactly was wrong. She got out of the Blazer.

He followed, and ignoring the sun, the heat, the salty air, hooked a hand around her elbow and pulled her back around.

She avoided looking at him.

Ah, hell. "What is it?"

She merely pulled free and turned her back on him, and a full five-alarm raced up his spine.

She was omitting again, which didn't bode well.

Chapter 22

"Bailey," Noah said quite calmly to her back. "What's wrong?"

What was wrong? *Was he kidding*? Bailey whirled around to face him. "You mean other than my life is in shreds, and that I have guys with guns after me, and oh, yes, let's not forget the fact that my brother is very likely a lying, thief bastard to match my dead husband and father."

"Yes," he said without giving in to her. "Besides all that." He caught up to her, and in a gesture she hadn't expected but should have, one that tugged hard at her poor heart, he took her hand and looked right into her eyes. "Something else is getting to you."

She turned away and studied the resort. How did he see everything?

"Have you been here before?"

Ha! If he only knew. She'd honeymooned here. "You might say so," she managed, her gaze on the bungalows lining the beach.

"Might you say exactly?"

Shrugging out of his grip, she began walking toward the beach. He followed her. Of course he followed her, but he was a smart man and didn't say a word. She had no idea where he'd learned such a useful tactic, holding his tongue so effectively, so that the silence filled the air, her head, and drove her absolutely insane with the urge to fill it, but he could teach government officials volumes on how to get information out of the bad guys. "I honeymooned here," she finally admitted, and glanced up at him. "And when I say I, I mean me, myself, and the television set. Alan got called away the moment we arrived."

"So Alan was an even bigger idiot than I gave him credit for."

They walked closer, and she had to admit, looking up as they moved into the shadow of the building, the place had a certain charm. If one was into ostentatious, over-the-top expensive beach resorts.

They bypassed the large hotel and moved toward the bungalows, specifically Alan's.

Oddly enough, the door wasn't locked. They pushed it open, and could immediately see why. The place had been pillaged and pilfered through. Tiles missing, trim gone, door handles, even whole windows . . . The finished suite was no longer "finished."

They stood in the middle of the main room, which had once held gleaming wood floors and beautiful furniture, but was now empty. "The local builders must have used this place as a freebie," Bailey said in disbelief.

Noah was looking around, quiet, alert, braced for trouble.

"I don't think it's here, Noah."

"Yeah. You know, I'm beginning to think it was never here." He shook his head. "It doesn't make sense to take it out of the States, where it wouldn't be safe."

They left the bungalow and stood on the beach. Bailey sighed and rubbed her temples. "Another dead end." Which was going to lead to a very dead her. "Let's get out of here, away from one of my most unfortunate mistakes."

He touched her cheek. "Yeah, I'm with you on the leaving

part. But about the mistake." He waited until she looked at him. "Sometimes they just have to be made. It's a part of the experience; it makes life real."

Tipping her head up, she looked directly into his warm eyes, and her heart squeezed. "I've never thought about it like that."

"Maybe you should."

"But I was—"

"What, young? In love? You were entitled, Bailey. We're all entitled to our mistakes."

"Really?" Going up on tiptoe, she cupped his face, bringing it down close enough to gently kiss him on the lips. "Even you, Noah?"

His eyes shimmered as he stared at her, silent again.

"Yeah," she whispered. "Even you."

His voice was low, and just a little bit husky. "You undo me, you know that?"

She let out a low laugh. "Is that a good thing?"

Instead of answering, he turned his gaze to the building behind them, and frowned.

"What?"

"Go back to the car," he said, and turned her in the right direction.

"What? Why—"

"Go." He added a small but inexorable push this time.

She didn't stop to question him, but before she'd taken a step, her gaze locked on the parking lot where they'd parked, and the two men there, one at either corner, watching her, watching them.

Stephen's men.

"Damn," Noah said very softly, and pulled her back to his side. "Okay, you're with me."

Good.

"Stick close."

Uh huh. "Like glue," she promised.

They ran toward the large building. She really had to stop wearing her cute little shoes. Her feet were killing her. All this running for her life was exhausting business.

Noah pulled her into the alley between Alan's resort and the hotel next to it. Now they had some cover, that being lots of overgrown bushes, some blown and scattered trash, and two stray, mangy-looking dogs who lifted their heads but didn't even bother to growl.

Noah held Bailey behind him and peeked around the corner, looking back to the lot while Bailey took the time to huff like a woman who hadn't put nearly enough time into her cardio workouts. She'd change that.

Assuming she lived, that is.

A sobering thought, so instead she concentrated on Noah's body, and what it could tell her.

And what it told her, with his broad but stiff shoulders, and tense, tight profile, was that once again, they were in deep trouble.

He didn't say a word as he pulled her through to the front of the resort. As before, at Mammoth and also Catalina, the glass doors were now broken. So they had the two goons in the parking lot, and who knew how many more within somewhere.

Waiting.

Noah swore again, quite colorfully, and in Spanish to boot, which was pretty impressive. They went back through the alley to the neighboring hotel this time. The parking lot here had plenty going on: cars, buses, taxis, people walking, talking, staggering with drinks in their hands.

Using the chaos, Noah and Bailey headed through the lot toward the beach, where every inch of sand was covered with cabanas, chairs, lounges, towels, carts with people selling sandals, hats, towels . . .

Noah kept them moving.

"As far from the guns as possible."

Her heels sank uncomfortably in the sand, and she struggled to both keep up and keep her mouth shut as the complaints racked up in her head. Hot. Toes cramped. Thirsty.

Terrified.

They moved past the hotel and came upon yet another, this one smaller, more accessible, and even *more* crowded.

They let the people sort of swallow them up. Finally Noah came to a stop in the middle of an outdoor cantina. The barstools were all filled, as were the spaces in between. Everywhere were bodies in bikinis and swim trunks, shirt and shoes optional.

Noah nodded to the bartender, and two beers appeared, the chilled bottles already weeping condensation. Bailey grabbed hers and brought it up to her lips, grateful for the cold liquid soothing its way down her parched throat. Far before she'd sated her thirst, Noah tugged her away, and damn it, they were on the move again.

"I just wanted to—" She sent a longing look back at the bottle she hadn't managed to grab fast enough, but Noah didn't wait, and then she saw why.

One of the baddies had come to the edge of the beach, between the sand and the parking lot, and was surveying the crowd intently, his hand in his pocket.

Looking for them.

Oh, God. She kicked it back into a high gear, and they ran through another cantina, and then a mini swap-meet of some kind, slipping between two aisles filled with wooden donkey statues, leather purses, woven ponchos, and sombreros. Noah stopped so abruptly, Bailey plowed right into the back of him.

Reaching behind him to steady her, he spoke in rapid-fire Spanish to the tiny, old woman sitting on a stool watching them. The next thing Bailey knew, she was standing in a dressing room—nothing more than a bright red shower curtain wrapped around a stand—with Noah crowding his way in, arms full.

"Strip," he commanded.

"Uh—"

He dropped his booty at his feet and began to strip her himself. "Lift up," he said, and yanked her sweater up to her forehead before he let go, leaving her arms caught straight up.

"You get that," he told her. Then without so much as glancing at her breasts, he bent his head and unzipped her skirt.

She fought with her sweater, but he hadn't undone that zipper. Worse, her hair had caught in the metal catch, threatening to rip out a good chunk by the roots. "Hey."

"Hang on." His long hair brushed her belly, and unbelievably given the circumstances, it quivered.

Then he shoved down her skirt.

Her panties accidentally went with it, and she was left standing there with her hands over her head, the zipper caught on her ponytail, wearing only her bra because her panties and skirt had twisted around her thighs, leaving her hanging out in the wind.

Literally.

Oblivious, Noah was fighting with her strappy sandals. "Lift up," he instructed, trying to get her skirt off without removing the heels.

She could have told him it wasn't going to happen, but it was hard to talk with her panties down and no foreplay involved. She struggled to free her hands and hair of her sweater, to no avail. "*Noah—*"

Sitting back on his heels, he glanced up, his hair brushing at her upper thighs as he did, and for the first time since he'd shoved her in there, he went absolutely still. In the charged silence, he took in the sights right at his eye level.

Her sights.

His eyes darkened, and he dragged his teeth over his lower lip. "Good Christ," he whispered.

All around them, on just the other side of the curtain, in

fact, were people everywhere; talking, bartering, going on with their day—and yet just in here, alone, together, she felt as if—there was no one else on earth except Noah. An incredibly sexy Noah, whose mouth quirked.

"Don't you dare laugh," she warned him.

Slowly he shook his head, still not lifting a finger to help her. "Not feeling like laughing," he said silkily.

Oh, God, she knew that voice. It was his aroused voice. It was the voice he used right before he took her out of herself, every single time, and while being taken out of herself right this minute would be a good thing, she was absolutely not going to have sex in a makeshift dressing room in Baja, with guns looking for them.

She wasn't. "Noah—" Again she struggled to free her arms, the movement jiggling her breasts.

Noah watched, and let out a low groan that she sensed more than heard. "Hold still," he commanded.

But then instead of freeing her, he ran a callused finger over the pushed-up curve of first one breast, then the other, making her let out a sound that shocked her in its neediness.

"You should see yourself," he whispered, and that finger snaked in beneath the lace and rasped over her bare nipple, eliciting another gasp from her.

"Noah—" This got choked off when his other hand slid down her belly, then lower, gently gliding right over ground zero.

"Ohmigod," she gasped. "Stop that—"

But he didn't. Of course he didn't, and with the intimate knowledge he had of her body, he knew exactly what to stroke and how hard to stroke it and oh, good Lord, the man pressed his mouth to her hip as he played with her, nibbling his way across her low belly to her other hip, all the while keeping his fingers very, very busy, taking her right to the edge of an orgasm, something she would have bet her own life would be impossible at this moment. "Noah—*please*."

"I will most definitely please," he promised hoarsely, and tugged on her.

"*Ack*," she said as she fell.

He caught her. She had a feeling he would always catch her, and as he did so now, he maneuvered her so that she was sprawled in his lap. With her skirt trapping her at the knees, and her sweater trapping her arms, there was little she could do to save herself.

Not that she tried.

Nope.

Not with his head bent and his mouth seeking out her breast, and then, oh, God, her nipple, sucking it into his mouth, his fingers still between her legs . . .

Beneath her, pressing into her bottom, he was hard, gloriously so. It would take nothing, she knew, for him to unzip and push inside her, and as far gone as she already felt, she knew it would take less than a minute for them both to go off.

But though he gripped her hips and rocked once against her, eyes closed, his face a mask of desire and pleasure, he then set his forehead to hers and just breathed.

Finally he lifted his head. Heat and desire had darkened his eyes to two black pools of lust, but there was also regret, and after one more rock of his hips and a low groan, he sighed and reached up to untangle her hair from the grasp of her sweater.

And then he helped her stand, handing her a Mexican white sundress, and then a poncho. When she had the dress on, he placed the hood of the poncho up over her head himself, and then pulled a poncho over his own leather jacket as well.

Together they left the sanctity of the dressing room, and after a quick exchange with the old woman, during which Noah slipped her some cash, they stepped out of the booth and back into the main aisle of the swap meet.

She could hardly walk, she was still so turned on that her legs were rubbery. But Noah pulled her along the maze of aisles as if the past few minutes had never happened, as if he knew exactly where he was going, holding on to her with one hand, speaking into his cell phone with the other. And then suddenly they were out in a parking lot a good quarter mile down from their Blazer, and a cabby was waiting for them.

"How did you—" she started in sheer amazement as he hurried her into it.

"Maddie is a goddess," he said, and then switched to Spanish to direct the cab driver.

While she just stared at him. "What are you saying?"

"That we want to be driven back via the main drag, so I can see if our favorite goons are still there." He switched back to his cell phone, speaking English again, and she realized he was talking to Brody, who she gathered was in contact with Shayne, who in turn was on his way.

They'd beaten the odds again, and better yet, were still alive. She knew it wasn't her who had kept them that way, but Noah and his unique ability to twist any situation to his advantage.

It wasn't that she kept underestimating him, but that she was continuously surprised at the depths of his resourcefulness, not to mention his ability to fit in anywhere, doing anything.

He was a chameleon, and possessed skills she could only dream of having. "You're amazing."

He'd been watching in front of them, behind them, on all sides of them, but at her words, he glanced at her in surprise.

"You are," she said.

He took her hand, pressed his mouth to her palm.

The cabby drove by Alan's resort. Noah said something to him, and he slowed. The place looked as deserted as it had before, sandwiched in between two points of hopping activity.

Goons gone.

Noah said something else to the cab driver, who then pulled into the next parking lot.

The Blazer was still there.

Tires slashed.

An undoubtable warning, one that said keep at this and more than just four tires would be slashed.

Sweat beaded on Bailey's forehead. "*Noah.*"

"Are there any more resorts?"

She knew where he was going with this line of questioning. He wanted to know where she'd be heading next, and the terrifying truth was, she had no idea. "No more resorts," she whispered, staring at the slashed tires, imagining how she was going to feel when it was Noah they caught up with next time, and slashed him.

Oh, God. When was this all going to stop? *Now*, she decided. It stopped now. "I'm out of plans," she admitted. "I've got nothing left. I have to give up. I'm going to call the police and throw myself on their mercy and hope they can help me."

"Bailey—"

"No, I mean it. I can't do this anymore, I can't keep putting other people in danger. Especially you, Noah. I have to stop the madness before I get you killed."

He said nothing to that, but his jaw tightened, and she knew he wanted to argue the point with her, or maybe . . . maybe not believe her. She couldn't blame him. "I have no more secrets from you," she promised. "I've told you everything."

"Bailey . . . are you sure Alan didn't warn you about this, about any of it?"

"No. He just went on his trip like always—Wait." She closed her eyes to remember exactly. They'd been standing in the foyer of their home, Alan holding his bag as he'd left for his fateful hunting trip. "He was different that time. More somber, lingering to talk when normally he couldn't wait to leave."

She remembered being surprised by that, and by the tight hug he gave her. He'd pulled away and looked deeply into her eyes, something he hadn't done in a very long time. And then he'd said, "Whatever you need after I'm gone. I've kept it all safe, Precious." She repeated the words.

Noah didn't say anything for a long beat, and she opened her eyes.

His were on her, dark and speculative. "He called you Precious?"

She thought about that, and suddenly, like a one-two punch to her gut, it dawned on her. "Oh, my God."

"What?"

"No," she whispered, shaking her head. "He never called me Precious." He'd never called her any affectionate pet nickname, nothing but her given name.

But he had made up pet names for all his houses, all his resorts. "Oh, my God, Noah."

"Tell me."

"When they told me about the money, I remembered he just kept safes in his various suites. I figured the house was too obvious, but . . ." She shook her head. "But he had nicknames for his places, each and every one of them. And the house, our house, he called it—"

"*Precious*," they said together.

"Yes . . ." She clutched his shirt. "We've got to get back. Kenny was right, it's not what I thought. None of it is what I thought." She gulped hard, then shook her head to clear it. "I've been on a wild goose chase. And . . ." She let out a helpless laugh. "And I've led the bad guys on a wild goose chase."

As she said that, there was movement on the top floor of the hotel. A sliding glass door of the supposedly deserted penthouse suite opened.

A figure stepped out.

Stephen.

He looked down at them, right at them, and even from this distance Bailey had no trouble reading the malice and hate directed toward her. "*Noah.*"

"I see him." She felt his hand settle on her arm as he leaned forward and spoke to the cab driver.

The cab driver nodded and pulled away. They were going, and she'd never been so glad to leave any place in her life.

Chapter 23

Maddie sat behind her desk at Sky High Air, working her keyboard, her cell phone, and her radio all at the same time, twisting in her chair to work a second keyboard as well. She was lining up her chicks: Noah was in a cab on the way to the Cabo airport, Shayne was due to land there any second, where they would hook up with each other, get Bailey out of Baja, and presumably all would be well.

A job well done.

But *all* her jobs were well done. She always saw to that. Perfection was incredibly important to her. Some called her anal, some called her obsessive, some just called her a cold-hearted bitch.

She could be all of the above, she knew, but that was fine with her. She didn't care what people thought.

Brody came out of his office, and she had to revise that, because she did care what *he* thought.

Of her.

Too bad he was a stubborn ass and never let a thing slip.

He walked as though he didn't give a shit what people thought either, and she knew he didn't. His stride was long-legged, easy, confident; all tall, dark and completely one hundred percent attitude-ridden as he headed directly toward the vending machine at the end of the hallway.

That he was doing so didn't tell her a thing about his mood because he headed to the vending machine several times a day, always for a soda and something with milk chocolate, though in a pinch, dark chocolate would do.

Sometimes, in the deep, dark of the night, she had dreams about that, about covering herself in chocolate, just to see what he would do.

In her dreams, he licked it off.

All of it.

Every inch . . .

He was facing the vending machine, feet spread, hands on either side of the machine as he studied his choices. His shirt was stretched taut across his shoulders, his jeans soft and faded, fitted to his extremely nice butt. Then he unexpectedly glanced at her over his shoulder and caught her staring. "What?" he said.

"Nothing."

He frowned. "You're all flushed."

"Just a little hot." *For you.*

"Well, take a damn break. We're not slave drivers here."

"Right." She slipped out of her sweater, which left her in an admittedly fabulous silky little tank that clung to her curves. She knew this because she'd picked it for this very reason. Plus, it was the same pale, pale blue as her eyes.

Also on purpose.

She had great eyes, and she lowered them now, then peeked at Brody from beneath her lashes.

He was staring at her, a slight scowl on his lips. When he realized she was still looking at him, he didn't quickly turn away, or show any sign of being embarrassed to be caught staring.

That was probably because the man was never embarrassed about anything.

To have *half* that confidence and not have to fake the other half. "Oh," she said casually, running a hand over her breast and down her belly. "Do I have something on me?"

"No." He jammed his money into the vending machine. "I tried calling you last night. I couldn't log onto the computer here. You weren't home."

"No, I wasn't."

"Figured you were on a date."

If that was a fishing expedition, he was going to come up empty-handed. "You didn't call my cell."

"Didn't want to bother you." That said, he went back to studying his selection choices, as if he hadn't done the same exact thing twice already today.

Damn stubborn mule. She tossed her earphones to the desk. A break. He was right, she needed a break.

She needed to break something right over his clueless head.

To keep from doing just that, she drew a deep breath, picked the earphones back up and tried to call Noah for his ETA, but got nothing. "Damn it."

Brody stopped dealing with the vending machine and came close, his gaze on her face. "What is it?"

"Probably nothing."

"But maybe something. Tell me."

"Noah isn't answering his cell."

"*Shit.*"

The Baja landscape didn't exactly whirl past them as the cab driver made his way toward the airport.

"*Andale*," Noah said. *Faster*.

The cabby nodded but didn't speed up, and Noah resisted the urge to tear his hair out one strand at a time. He looked at Bailey, who was sitting with her hands clenched, mouth tight, eyes worried. "We'll get there," he promised.

She nodded.

With a sigh, he slipped an arm around her and pulled her closer, pressing his mouth to her temple. "We will."

"I know." In his arms, she relaxed some, and the marvel of that was never going to get old.

"*Nos estan siguiendo*."

Noah looked up and met the cab driver's eyes in the rearview mirror. They were being followed. Well, that was just perfect. He whipped around and indeed saw a dark SUV working its way around traffic to keep up with them. "*Rapidamente.*" He couldn't stress enough the need to hurry, but neither did he want to risk having the cab driver pull over and kick them out. "*Mas rapidamente.*"

Again, the cabby nodded but didn't speed up. In all fairness, he couldn't. They were on a two-lane highway, with a huge rickety old truck weaving down the road in front of them, the back loaded to the brim with goats, all bleating mournfully in the afternoon air.

Coming the other way was a steady stream of traffic as well.

The cabby caught Noah's eye in the rearview mirror again and helplessly shrugged.

"What?" Bailey asked, gripping Noah's arm. "What's the matter?"

The goat truck veered off to the right, and the cabby took his turn, revving the engine.

But nothing happened.

The cab was simply going top speed at approximately forty-eight miles an hour.

"What's going on?" Bailey asked, searching his face. Clearly she could read him better than anyone else ever could because she looked scared. Hell. What had happened to his poker face? He was famous for it, but she seemed oblivious to the fact that no one was supposed to be able to read his thoughts and emotions like a damn book.

"*El ir de la subsistencia*," he told the cabby. *Keep going.* They'd get to the airport, and he'd figure it out when they did.

Bailey looked behind them and gasped at the dark-windowed SUV behind them.

Finally they began passing some other streets, a residential area. Noah directed the driver into a series of turns, and at the end, miracle of all miracles, they'd lost their tail.

Finally, something going their way.

Then the cab driver met Noah's gaze in the mirror, his filled with apology. "*Gasolina de la necesidad.*"

Need gasoline.

Hell. Before Noah could open his mouth to say . . . what, he had no freaking clue, the cab sputtered, coughed, and then stalled.

"Ohmigod, what just happened?" Bailey asked.

"A little car issue."

"It broke down?"

"Out of gas."

She stared at him in horror. "That's some bad timing."

"Princess, I couldn't agree more." He took in their surroundings, even as he opened his cell phone to call Maddie. No reception.

Oh, this just got better and better.

They were in front of a church, which had its doors flung open. There was a huge courtyard filled with people dressed to the hilt, laughing and clapping and dancing to a band.

It was a wedding, and everyone there was on the floor, partying hard. As far as diversions went, it wasn't a bad one. Reaching into his pocket, Noah grabbed some cash, handed it to the cab driver, and pulled Bailey from the car.

"What are we doing?"

"Mingling."

She looked down at their clothing. "At least we're semi-dressed for it."

No hysterics. His heart squeezed with pride and affection and something much, much harder to define.

Or maybe not so hard at all. He pulled her into the courtyard with one eye on the road—still no SUV. Thc wedding music was louder than his thoughts, and so was the crowd. No one so much as glanced at them. "Try to look like you belong," Noah said. Bailey shot him a look that said she had no idea how to do that, so he tugged her onto the dance floor, spun her away from the street and hauled her close.

"What are we doing?" she hissed, stiff in his arms.

"Dancing." He slid a hand down her spine. "Do it with me." He rocked his hips into hers, moving with the music while she just stared up at him.

"You know how to dance?" she asked, clearly shocked.

"Yeah." He shifted with her in tune to the beat, which was louder and more manic than he was used to, but then again, he didn't spend a lot of time listening to Mexican carnival music. In either case, he had to figure it out because he was doing the dancing for the both of them.

Unbelievably, the music got louder. Bailey had to go up on tiptoe and put her mouth to his ear to speak. Since it plastered her body to his, he didn't mind in the least.

"Do you know how to do absolutely everything?" she asked.

No, he didn't know how to do everything. He didn't, for example, know how to tell her he loved her.

And he did.

So much he ached.

He also didn't know how to make her love him.

And he wanted that, he wanted that with everything he was, because when he was with her he felt alive. He felt happy. Hell, even running for their very lives, he felt those things, and he wanted to tell her. Instead, he just pulled her in closer and kept an eye on the street, sure that he could at least do as he'd promised and keep her safe.

No, that was a lie. He was pulling her closer because he couldn't help himself. He moved with her across the floor, feeling the press and heat of the other bodies, the humid salty air, absorbing the music and the slight weight of her head against his shoulder, her body snuggling into his.

It would have been a moment to treasure for always, if it

hadn't been for the bad guys, or the ear-splitting music, or the fact that they were still in Cabo . . .

Damn, they had to get out of here.

"What if they see the cab and pull over?" she asked. "They can find us here." Her fingers dug into his poncho. "We can't bring trouble to these people, Noah. It's a wedding."

"I know. We won't." Over her shoulder, he kept checking his cell phone for reception. He needed to know exactly how far they were from the airport, and how fast they could get there.

At least if he didn't check in with Maddie soon, Shayne would come find them. His only comfort at the moment.

Around them, guests were as loud as the music, and half of them looked plastered, with the other half well on their way. Now they were doing some sort of dance that involved hugging their partner real close and shaking everything they had.

"Let's sneak into the back," he said. "Maybe there's a working phone."

"And if there's not?"

"I'll liberate someone's car and drive us."

"Liberate? As in steal?"

"You have a better idea?"

"No." She let out a soft laugh in his ear. "You really are a superhero."

He was incredibly aware of her fingers, gliding up the back of his neck, sliding into his hair. Of her body, curvy and warm, pressed to his. "Not a hero. Just a man."

Pulling back, she smiled into his face. His heart caught, and he fell even harder, if that was possible. "A man," he said. "Who loves you."

At that, her eyes widened, her mouth curved into a perfect little "Oh" of surprise.

"I do. I love you, Bailey."

Her eyes went soft with what he sincerely hoped was wonder and hope, and not terror. "Noah—"

But then her mouth snapped closed, her body went stiff, and she didn't finish her sentence.

Frowning, he went to pull her tighter to him, but she resisted.

That's when he realized the problem. Someone had moved up behind her. Several someones.

And several more behind Noah.

He turned his head and looked out at the street. The cab was still there.

And just behind it? A black SUV.

Whipping his head back to Bailey, he could only look into her eyes as the asshole holding a gun to her back pulled her from his very grasp.

Yeah. Some superhero he'd turned out to be.

Chapter 24

"So, you lost contact with Noah?" Brody asked Maddie in a voice that had, over the past year, sent three previous assistants running for the hills.

Brody didn't scare her. Not one little bit. Sure, by turns he frustrated her, angered her, worried her, and turned her on more than any other man ever had, but he never scared her.

"Working on it," she said. She was working on a thousand things at once actually, checking the GPS, dialing her cell, radioing Shayne . . . It was her particular forte, multi-tasking, and she could do it at work, at home, in bed . . .

Oh, yes, she was extremely good, even with the big, bad, sexy Brody hunched over her, scowling fiercely.

He'd never say it out loud, but she knew he'd been worried sick about Noah, with good reason. Noah had been to hell and stayed there a good long time. So long, in fact, that none of them had been sure he'd find his way back.

But he had.

Maddie had taken one look at his face after he'd been with Bailey, and she'd known. Bailey had brought him back.

She'd love the woman for that alone.

"Where is he?" Brody asked tightly.

"Still working on it." She didn't let her own concern show. One of her little chicks was in trouble, and she'd fix it.

She knew it amused Shayne, Brody, and Noah to no end that she thought of them as "hers," especially given that she was younger than all of them, but the three men had saved her life.

She intended to return the favor, however needed. Dramatic, she knew, but fact was fact. She owed them her life, and she always repaid her debts.

Now Noah was in trouble. She knew it with every ounce of her being, and not just because he'd fallen off the face of the earth, but because he hadn't checked in when he'd arrived at the airport after taking the cab she'd arranged for him on the fly, and also because that cab hadn't yet arrived at the airport.

And worst of all, because he wasn't answering his cell phone.

"When did you last have him?"

She turned and faced Brody, who stood watching her with that eagle eye he had. It still unnerved her that he, and only he, could tell when she was upset, disturbed, or hot.

He constantly made her all three.

But that was another problem, a private problem. "At the Cabo resort. He was taking Bailey to the cab I got them."

"Okay. Okay, he's a big boy. He'll be all right."

She knew he was saying this to ease his own mind as well as hers.

"Where's Shayne?" Without waiting for her, he leaned over her shoulder and grabbed the phone, punching in Shayne's cell number.

Maddie didn't move, and because she didn't, Brody's broad chest brushed her arm and shoulder. Nobody invaded her personal space, nobody, and yet all she could think was, if she shifted even a fraction of an inch, his arm would brush against her breast.

Twenty-six years old, and the thought made her knees wobble.

Stupid. But she could smell him, some absolutely heart-stopping scent of soap and all man that damn it, made her nostrils quiver. "Excuse me," she said in the haughtiest voice she could muster. "Personal space bubble being invaded."

His eyes cut to hers, and he very carefully, very carefully, didn't move a thing except for the brow that arched in question. "Space bubble?"

She would have scooted back, but that would have given him the edge. "*Move.*"

Eyeing her with some amusement, he straightened away from her. "Shayne," he said into the phone, eyes still on Maddie's. "Where are you?" He listened while Maddie tried not to squirm. Damn it, she couldn't keep her mental distance when he was this close.

"Yeah, but Noah isn't picking up." He listened again. "Good. Do it."

"Do what?"

Brody put the phone back into its base. "He's going to find the cab."

"Great. Go away, I'll call you when I hear something."

He slid his hands in his pockets and stood there, brooding and gorgeous. "Huh."

"Huh what?"

"Interesting, how eager you are for me to leave."

"I'm busy."

"Busy?" he asked. "Or unnerved?"

"Unnerved? By you? *Ha.*"

He smiled, but he did not, as she'd half hoped, stay and argue the point. Instead he did as she'd asked and left, moving toward his office.

"You're watching my ass as I walk away," he said without looking at her.

She jerked her gaze off the ass in question, blew out a breath and whirled her chair around. "Am not."

His laughter rung in her ears long after he'd shut his office door.

Damn it. Damn him.

Bailey felt the gun against her spine and went utterly still in a world that was in total motion around her: the wedding partiers, the wild, loud music, the hot, humid air.

Utterly. Still.

And looked straight into Noah's eyes. They'd been dancing, she'd been pressed as close to him as she could get, and she'd absorbed his lovely, oh-so-amazing words to her—*he loved her*. She loved him, too. It sang through her like her breath, her blood, but now she might never get to tell him.

"*Vamanos*," said a rough voice in her ear as a hand closed tightly over her arm.

After that, everything seemed to happen in freeze-frame motion, all in tune to the loud, over-the-top Mexican carnival music.

First, they yanked her clear of Noah.

Noah tried to close that distance, but then he froze, too, and Bailey saw why.

There was a man behind him as well, undoubtedly making his presence known with yet another gun in the back.

A real gun, nothing as silly and stupid as a Bic pen.

Oh, God.

This was it. Her number was up. They wanted her to take them to the money.

This was her last moment with Noah, her last chance to tell him what it had meant to have him in her life, however briefly. How much his support and belief and unimaginably sharp, quick wit had done for her. How she couldn't imagine being without him.

How she loved him.

She had to tell him that much, she had to.

His eyes had filled with blazing fury and disbelief, and torturous misery that she was going to be taken now, like this, right in front of him, and there was nothing he could do about it.

Her vision blurred with the tears she refused to shed. "I love you," she mouthed, hoping he'd understand, *needing* him to understand.

He did. His eyes flamed, went shiny with the knowledge, and he reached out for her in spite of the gun, in spite of everything, but the men on either side of her simply turned and took her with them.

They made it to the gate, and no one stopped them. Hell, no one but Noah probably even noticed, just as no one had noticed them joining the wild wedding party in the first place.

Then she was shoved into the black SUV and sandwiched by two stern-looking, armed-to-the-teeth men.

Twisting in her seat as they took off, she looked out the rear window in time to see Noah come running out of the church yard. He barreled over the gate and then skidded to a stop in the middle of the street, staring after her with a look of deadly intent on his face.

But then they screeched around a corner and he was gone from view.

Good, she told herself. He was out of danger.

"Now," said the man in the front seat, and her blood froze because she knew that voice. When he turned to face her, she gasped. It was the face of a man who'd smiled at her at any number of banal cocktail parties, the face of the man who'd worked closely with Alan, and yet had been able to attack her in her own home.

With a hard swallow, she looked into Stephen's cold, dark eyes.

"Now, you tell us where the money is, Mrs. Sinclair."

"Where's Kenny?" She hated that her voice shook. "I want

to talk to Kenny." He might be involved, but there was no way *he* could look into her eyes and hurt her. She knew this.

Was banking on it.

"Kenny?" Stephen smiled, and a chill ran down Bailey's spine. "You want to bargain with Kenny?"

"Yes."

"When was the last time you spoke to your brother?"

"Why?"

"You really don't know."

"*Don't know what*?"

"That Kenny didn't do as I asked, which was a bad decision on his part."

Oh, God. "Where is he?" she whispered.

"Soon to be dead, actually."

"*Why*?"

"He didn't bring me you, for one. But it turned out he had a better-paying gig all along—the feds."

Kenny worked for the good guys? Relief, and an almost giddy sense of love, welled up and choked her so that she had to press her hand to her mouth to keep a sob in. Kenny *had* been trying to warn her at the airport. No wonder he'd looked so terrified when she'd run from him. He'd known what was going to happen if they caught her.

"Now," Stephen said. "Your turn. Where's the money?"

Her thoughts raced. If she told them the truth, that she had no idea where the money was, then she was dead.

She had to stall. "Little problem with the whole money thing."

"Wrong answer," he said, and then there was a prickly pain in her arm, and her world faded to black.

"We'll get her back," Shayne promised Noah, who didn't say anything as he slipped his headphones on and waited for air traffic control to give Shayne the okay for take-off.

He didn't say anything because he couldn't speak past the

lump of fear the size of a regulation football jammed in his throat.

He'd lost her.

Shayne had moved in with a welcome swiftness, but not swift enough.

The black SUV had vanished into thin air.

But he knew where they'd gone. Straight to the airport to haul Bailey back to Burbank, to the house that had been beneath their noses all this time.

Precious.

Jesus, he couldn't believe it.

Now they were in a race to save Bailey's life. They'd run up against resistance at the Cabo airport, unable to stall two private jets from getting airborne.

If Bailey was on one of them, which his gut said she was, then every moment that ticked by counted. They sat on the strip waiting for their go, Noah grating his teeth, his gut tight with fear. Because once they got Bailey to the Burbank house, once she located the money—or not—her life was as good as over, and he could scarcely breathe at the thought of not getting there in time to help her.

Finally they were approved for take-off, and when they got to altitude, Shayne glanced over. "I wish you'd say something."

"Fly faster."

Shayne smiled grimly and did just that while Noah contacted Maddie. "What have you got for me?"

"You were right, two jets got through ahead of you," she said. "They've both been air bound for approximately thirty minutes. Nothing else, and nothing after you, so one of those two is her."

"Where are they heading?"

"Working on that."

"If it's Burbank—"

"If it's Burbank, we can bring the local authorities into it."

"Do it."

"Okay, I'll report back with where and when they land."

That had to be good enough, but it sure didn't feel like it. For the second time in a year, he'd failed someone who'd trusted him.

He didn't know if he could live with that. Or how to.

But he knew how to live with the knowledge that she loved him. She'd looked him in the eyes, her own shimmering brilliantly with emotion, as she said it, too.

I love you.

He hadn't heard a single one of those three words out loud because of the music—which was going to headline his nightmares for years to come—but he'd caught every single one in his heart. He rubbed the organ right now because it ached like hell, and had been since she'd been ripped out of his arms.

Bailey loving him was his very own miracle. Now he had to make another miracle happen; he had to get her back.

"She's going to be okay," Shayne promised. "They won't do anything to her until they figure out she can't deliver, and by then we'll be there."

Maybe they wouldn't kill her, but they sure as hell could hurt her, and everything within him tightened as he wondered where she was right this moment, if she was holding up.

If they touched one single hair on her head, he'd tear them apart.

Slowly. "Thing is, I think she *can* deliver."

Shayne looked at him in surprise. "What?"

"She figured out where the money is."

"No shit?"

"She knows where it is, and if they get there with enough lead time—"

"What about the brother? Kenny, right? You said you thought he was in on it. Was he there today? Did you see him?"

"At the Burbank airport. He was trying to get to her." Noah

chewed on that for a while, then radioed Maddie. "Can you locate Kenny?"

"Hang on."

Noah pressed his lips together and waited until she came back.

"Got him," she said. "Apparently he tracked you down, but you haven't been answering your cell."

"I've been out of range."

"Yeah, well, he's unhappy that you managed to lose Bailey's protective tail for her. I guess some of those guys you've been ditching were the good guys. He's frantic to talk to you."

Noah's gut couldn't possibly clench any tighter. "Does he have Bailey?"

"No, and he wasn't happy to realize you don't either. He says, and I quote, 'if anything happens to her, I'm coming after you and kicking your ass.' He's fed, Noah. He's working to nail Alan's investment partners. They're trying to get them for fraud, extortion, and a whole long list of other stuff."

"Why didn't he say so sooner?"

"He was under cover and trying to protect Bailey at the same time, without tipping off the bad guys."

"Well, he did a hell of a job of that, didn't he?" Noah looked at Shayne. "I think I underestimated the brother."

"I hate it when that happens."

Noah's head hurt. "Can you work your magic and patch him through to me?" he asked Maddie.

"Stand by."

What else could he do. "*Shit.*"

"You know, we probably don't pay her enough," Shayne said.

"Brody says we pay her a fortune already."

"Brody can kiss my ass," Maddie said. "But you're damn-A straight I'm worth every penny. Oh, and I've got him. Kenny? Go ahead."

"Noah?" Kenny sounded extremely uptight and extremely unhappy. "*Where is she*?"

Noah's gut tightened at the unmistakable sound of fear and worry in Kenny's voice. "That was my question for you."

"She was with you at the airport. I saw you."

"They came for her in Baja. At the time, I thought it was you."

"No. Jesus, I'm on her side. I'm her brother!"

"But your text messages—"

"*Shit*. Are you the one who made her suddenly stop trusting me and suspect me instead?"

Noah opened his mouth, then shut it, because yes, that had been him.

"I thought she was safe with you, man. Or I'd have—"

"What?" Noah said. "Come clean and told her the truth? You should have done that anyway!"

"Yes, but they had to know for sure . . ."

When he trailed off, Noah's blood ran cold. "Wait a minute. Wait a fucking minute. You thought . . . you actually thought she might be *in on it*?"

"*I* didn't, but *they* needed proof—"

"Okay, you listen very carefully," Noah said, feeling extremely violent. "You screwed this up by not trusting her and telling her the truth at any time since Alan's death. You could have protected her better. You could have believed in her. If you had, none of this would have happened."

Kenny let out a breath. "I know."

"Here's how to repay her. You meet that plane with every single resource you have, making damn well and sure she's not harmed in the process—"

"Yeah, except we can't. We need her to lead us to the money—"

"Jesus. Jesus Christ," Noah breathed. "You're using her as *bait*."

"Not me," Kenny said tightly. "Believe me, this is *not* what

I wanted, but we need to catch these guys in the act. So just tell me exactly where they're taking her, and I'll make sure this thing has a happy ending."

"What? How can you be sure of that? You haven't managed to protect her so far."

"I was doing a damn fine job until you turned her on me."

Yeah. *Shit.*

Noah looked at Shayne, who paused in the middle of his landing preparation and nodded. Trust him. Do this.

Noah didn't want to. *He* wanted to be the one to haul her into his arms and know she was safe, damn it.

He let out a tight breath. "They're going to the Burbank house."

"But that place was already searched, way back after Alan's death."

"For hidden safes?"

"No, but that house is on the market, people have been in and out of there—"

"It's still furnished, isn't it? With artwork included?"

Kenny swore softly. "I can be there in thirty minutes, with backup."

Noah looked at Shayne, who nodded grimly. They could be there in thirty minutes as well. "Meet you there," Noah said, and hung up. "I really didn't see that coming. He's on the good side. Jesus, Shayne, we're going to run out of fuel at this speed."

"You wanted to haul ass, I'm hauling ass."

"At least it's not Brody. He flies like a woman."

Shayne looked pained. "Don't let him hear you say that. He'll kick your ass."

Chapter 25

Bailey woke up with a monster headache and a horrible groggy sensation that reminded her of a bad hangover. Worse, she'd believed she couldn't get any more terrified, but despite the fact that they'd left her alone on the plane, she knew that wasn't going to last long.

They took her from the private jet to yet another dark SUV, and though she'd thought she'd scream real loud and gain some unwanted attention for her captors, she never saw another soul. Even if she had, she felt so weak and discombobulated, she couldn't have worked up enough strength to scream.

They drove to the Burbank house. How ironic, she thought as they brought her inside, to be back here where it'd all begun. It seemed like years ago since she'd packed a bag and walked away from this life. In fact, it'd only been barely a week.

And only three days since she'd brought Noah into the mix. At the thought of him, her heart clenched hard.

She was shoved into the living room, and with her legs so weak, she went flying, falling against a bookshelf. At the impact, books rained down over the top of her. She sat there on the floor, dazed, taking in the design that Alan had picked out, and the cool, modern furniture he'd loved so much but was so damned uncomfortable it was all like sitting on a cactus. He'd loved this place, and for the fortune he'd spent having it decorated, he should.

Precious.

I've kept it all safe, Precious.

The words mocked her now, bouncing around in her brain. Or maybe that was the drugs . . .

The money was here. She knew that with a certainty.

"Now." Stephen walked up to her, his toes nearly touching hers, looked down his long, straight nose at her. "*Where*?"

"I don't know."

"Ding, ding, wrong answer."

His two goons bent and dragged her to her feet, then stood on either side of her, holding her up. They had no choice; her legs were noodles. One of her arms hurt from the needle they'd jammed into it. Her belly was quivering from the first time they'd done this whole talk-to-me thing, and now that she'd had a taste, she shook with fear and the need to throw up. "If I knew exactly where," she said, "I'd have found it by now."

"So you lied before, when you said you knew."

Oh, God. Not good. "I said I could find it, and I will." This was another lie, and her voice quavered just a little bit. *Please don't notice . . .*

The man nodded thoughtfully, then stepped forward and without warning slid his fingers in her hair and yanked her head back hard enough to bring tears to her eyes. "Tell me the truth," he said softly, almost kindly. "Or I will have both your brother and the man who's been flying you around hunted and killed." He looked directly into her eyes and smiled. "Like Alan."

Then he stepped back, and nodded to the men to release her.

She slid to the floor.

They all looked down at her, waiting.

I've kept it all safe, precious. Precious. The name of this house. *Safe.*

It would be in the safe in the bedroom behind the large framed print over their bed upstairs. She knew that now.

She realized she should have known it sooner, as in soon enough to save her own ass. Because now she had no doubt that if she handed over the money, the need to keep her alive became slim and none. In fact, she'd become an instant detriment.

Stall. Noah is moving hell and high water to get here. She knew it.

"Mrs. Sinclair, you've kept us waiting long enough."

On legs that shook, she managed to stand, then realized her head was clearing. But playing it up a little, she staggered a few feet. Immediately, the two goons moved in to help her.

"Where to?" Stephen asked.

"Upstairs."

She'd no sooner said the words than they assisted her up the stairs.

In the hallway, she considered her next move.

"Mrs. Sinclair," Stephen said smoothly. "You're trying my patience." He flicked his wrist, and a blade flashed before her eyes, settling against her throat.

"Master bedroom," she said tightly.

They dragged her there. Over the bed was the large print. She walked to the mattress, and one of the men snickered. "Look, she wants us."

"Shut up," Stephen said. "Mrs. Sinclair?"

"There's a safe. Beneath that picture. Maybe . . ."

He moved past her, pulled the picture down and smiled at the wall safe. "Nicely done. Combination?"

She hesitated.

Once again the goons moved in to her sides. "Sixty-nine, sixty-nine."

More snickers from the goons. Stephen just looked at Bailey, then without a word turned to the safe.

Bailey held her breath.

The safe clicked open, revealing the inside, which was loaded with cash. Bailey stared at the unbelievable sight of the stacks and stacks of bills.

Stephen clicked his fingers, and one of the goons produced a large duffle bag, which they filled while Bailey just stood there, shocked.

Alan had really had the money.

He'd really stolen from his own investors, never mind that they were all thieves, too. "Okay then," she said with forced joviality. "So you guys can go now."

Stephen looked at his men, jerked his head in her direction, and walked out of the room.

The two goons looked at her and smiled. Leered, really.

Her insides shriveled.

Once again they moved in close, one on either side, and took her arms.

"Don't worry about me," she said, trying to pull free. "Really. I'm good."

They laughed, then headed out of the room, toward the stairs, taking her with them. Her heart was racing, and so was her brain. She figured all she had to do was push one of them down the stairs, grab the other's gun, and then shoot them.

No problem.

Ahead, Stephen was on the phone. Once again he jerked his head in their direction. Apparently this was yet another wordless command because they immediately halted while Stephen ran down the stairs to take his call in privacy.

Both goons were breathing like a St. Bernard, and drooling like one, too, as they stared at her. She realized in the various scuffles since getting out of the SUV, her dress had slipped off one shoulder. She quickly scooped it back into place.

One of them nudged it back off with the tip of his gun, which pretty much made breathing impossible.

"Still dizzy, Hot Thing?" he asked.

What if his gun went off by accident?

The other thug took out his gun, too, and played with the collar of her dress. An involuntary squeak of terror left her lips.

They liked that.

She crossed her arms over her chest and tried not to make eye contact with either of them.

"She's scared," one of them whispered, and trailed the tip of his gun over her breast, lingering at her nipple.

"Yeah. Think she's scared enough to do whatever we say?" The other slipped the tip of his gun along Bailey's waist.

The steel was icy even through her garment.

"Hey. Boss is still busy. Let's take her into one of the downstairs bedrooms. She's still pretty loopy—"

The other goon grinned. "Yeah."

Stephen was still gone. She didn't know where, but she was completely on her own. They were going to rape her, and then kill her. They'd each gripped an arm when she heard an odd thunk from below, and with it came the softest sound, almost . . . a sigh. Out of the corner of her eye she caught a flash of—a beat-up leather jacket?

Noah?

Her head spun, making her realize she *was* still dealing with the effects of the drugs they'd given her. Then she saw another movement, in the doorway to the kitchen, and she'd have sworn on her life it was Kenny.

Noah and Kenny together . . . But if she was hallucinating, then maybe she could dream up some superhuman strength to go with it. Drugs did that to people; she saw it on *Cops* all the time, stupid people fighting the police officers without a care.

She'd fight.

Thug Number One, the guy just above her on the stairs,

was looking at his cell phone. Big mistake for him because she'd just morphed into the Bionic Woman. Whirling to the other, she jammed her knee right into his crotch. She'd seen this done in the movies, and truthfully, had never really believed a woman could drop a guy to the floor, but that was exactly what happened.

He dropped like a stone, tumbling down the stairs, hitting each one with a thud and an "oomph." The duffle bag went with him, breaking open at the halfway point. Money flew through the air like confetti, floating slowly to the ground as the man landed, then slid into the foyer—just as the shadow that she'd seen, the one with her brother's face, pointed a gun at the guy's chest and said, "Don't move."

Bailey turned to the other thug, and once again saw that flash of beat-up old leather jacket, now at the top of the stairs, above them.

Huh?

Her hallucination-in-leather executed an impressive roundhouse kick to the goon's chest, who went sailing. He hit the stair railing, which cracked and shattered. With a scream, he continued his sail through the air, landing on the hardwood floor ten feet below with a groan.

Kenny . . . my God, it really was Kenny . . . stood down there between the two thugs with a rather shockingly serious looking gun. "Got 'em," he called up just as Bailey felt two strong, warm, almost unbearably familiar arms encircle her.

"And I've got you," Noah said fiercely, hugging her close. He sank to the stairs with her in his arms. "I've got you."

"There's still Stephen—"

"Got him, too. He's unconscious in the foyer."

She cupped his face to make sure he was real. "I thought I dreamed you." She said this without letting go of him, because she was never going to let go of him again. "I thought . . ."

"Me, too." His voice was thick, hoarse with emotion, and he squeezed her tight. "You're not hurt?"

"No. You—"

"They never touched me. God, Bailey, when they took you—"

"When we were on the dance floor, just before they came," she said. "You heard me, right? You heard me say—"

"Say it again."

"I love you." She fisted her hands in his shirt, feeling his heart pounding sure and steady beneath his ribs. "I love you, Noah Fisher."

Two uniformed officers ran inside, guns drawn. From the kitchen came two more. "Drop your weapons!" they yelled to everyone.

More uniforms poured into the house. While chaos ruled, Bailey tipped her head up. Unbelievably, money was *still* dancing through the air, coming down like green rain. "So it's over?" she whispered to Noah.

"No." He buried his face in her hair, as if he could inhale her. "It's just beginning."

Epilogue

It was Friday afternoon, the last day of school before summer vacation kicked in. Bailey was back in the place she knew she was meant to be—at the head of a classroom.

She had no more fears from her past. Alan's resorts had been sold and were being completed by a different resort company. The men he'd invested with were in jail. If Alan hadn't been killed, he'd be there as well.

Kenny was gone, on another case. She still marveled that he was FBI. . . .

Her life was good, and she knew she owed that to her smart, sexy adventurer . . . Noah Fisher. They couldn't be more different; he the world traveler, never settling down, never wanting to. And she wanting nothing more than to do just that, to make a real home.

They'd been together plenty in the past few weeks since that long weekend where he'd saved her life. They'd laughed, talked, danced, made love. They'd spent enough time together for her to know what they had was rare, and real, and exactly what had been missing in her life.

And yet she couldn't tie him down; she would never want to tie him down . . . "Everyone take out their crayons." She stood at the front of her second grade class and smiled at the bent heads, as each of the kids hustled to do her bidding, pawing through their desks for their crayons.

Her life was back, just as she'd wanted. "We're going to color your folders to fill them with your schoolwork," she said. "That way you can look at it over the summer." They all got busy, and she filled her heart with joy just watching them. She paused as the door to her classroom opened.

When Noah stepped in, her heart squeezed tight.

Tall, tanned, and smiling—God, she loved his smile—he waved at the class, then walked to Bailey and handed her a cluster of wildflowers.

The class whooped and hollered.

Noah grinned.

And she felt her own tug at her mouth. "Excuse us, Mr. Fisher, but school is still in session."

"Yes, but I wanted to say good-bye to the kids before I left."

Her heart, which had stopped at the sight of him, kicked hard. "You going somewhere?"

"Yes," he said with a smile she recognized. It held excitement and daring.

He was going on a trip. Though the thought made her ache, she smiled, because she knew how much he needed to wander, explore.

Be.

The bell rang, and he stood by her side as she hugged the kids good-bye, smiling and laughing and joking with each kid in turn, and when they were all gone, her heart felt heavy and uncomfortably full as she turned to him. It was always bittersweet to say good-bye to the kids, but she had a feeling it was going to be nothing compared to *this* good-bye. "So."

"So." He smiled.

She tried to return it but failed. "You going on a new adventure, then?"

He stepped closer. "As a matter of fact, I am. My biggest one yet."

"I see," she said, though in truth she didn't. She'd hoped, she'd dreamed, that she would be enough for him. "What's your plan?"

He stroked a strand of hair from her cheek and tucked it behind her ear. "I've left most of it unplanned actually, wide open for the unexpected, because I'm thinking there's going to be a lot of the unexpected going on in this one."

His eyes were bright and shining. He couldn't wait to go. "Is it dangerous?" she managed in an even voice.

"Physically? No." He drew a deep breath. "But to my heart and soul? Possibly lethal. I'm buying the house I've been leasing. I want to make it my home."

"Really? But you've never wanted—"

"Things change. People change." He took her hand, then pulled something out of his pocket and set it in her palm.

She stared at the diamond ring sparkling against her skin. Her heart threatened to pop out of her chest as it sank in, as it all sank in.

"I love you, Bailey Sinclair," he said. "I don't know what's ahead of us, but I know it's going to be an amazing adventure. Say you're up for it."

She laughed through a few tears, slipped the ring on her finger, and threw her arms around his neck. "Oh, I'm up for it." She pressed close, then closer still, very happy to feel that Noah was *up* for it, too. . . .

Please turn the page for a first look
at Karen Kelley's
CLOSE ENCOUNTERS OF
THE SEXY KIND.
Available now from Brava!

"Would you like something to eat?"

Eat? Mala had two food capsules prior to leaving her planet, which was enough nutrition for one rotation, but she was curious about the food on Earth. Her grandmother had mentioned it was almost as good as sex. She just couldn't imagine that.

"Yes, food would be nice."

"Why don't you sit on the sofa and rest while I throw us something together." Mason picked up a black object. "Here's the remote. I have a satellite dish so you should be able to find something to entertain you while I rustle us up some food."

She nodded and took the remote, then watched him leave the room and go into another. The remote felt warm in her hand. A transferral of body heat? Tingles spread up and down her arm. The light above her head flickered.

She glanced up. Now that was odd. But then, she *was* on Earth.

Her attention returned to the remote.

Very primitive. The history books on her planet had spoken about remote controls in the old days. You pointed it at the object it was programmed to work with so you wouldn't have to leave your seat.

She pointed it toward the door and pushed the power button. The door didn't open. She tried different objects around the room without success. Finally, she pointed toward a black box.

The screen immediately became a picture. Of course, television. She made herself comfortable on the lounging sofa and began clicking different channels. Everything interested her, but what she found most fascinating was a channel called Sensual Heat.

She tossed the remote to a small table and curled her feet under her, hugging the sofa pillow, her gaze glued to the screen. A naked man walked across the set, his tanned butt clenching and unclenching with every step he took. When he faced her, the man's erection stood tall, hypnotizing her. It was so large she couldn't take her gaze off it.

A naked woman appeared behind him. She slipped her arms around him, her hands splayed over his chest. Slowly, she began to move her hands over his body, inching them downward, ever closer.

Mala held her breath.

"I want you," the woman whispered. "I want to take you into my mouth, my tongue swirling around your hard cock."

The man groaned.

Mala leaned forward, biting her bottom lip as the man's hands snaked behind him and grabbed the woman's butt. In one swift movement, he turned around. "Damn, you make me hard with just your words."

"And I love when you talk dirty to me."

"So, you want me to tell you what I want to do to your body?"

The woman nodded.

He grinned, then began talking again. "I want to squeeze your breasts and rub my thumbs over your hard nipples." His actions followed his words. "You like that?"

"Yes!" She flung her head back, arching toward the man.

Mala leaned forward, her mouth dry, her body tingling with excitement. Yes! She wanted this, too!

"Do you like French bread, or white bread?" Mason asked, walking into the room.

She dragged her gaze from the television. Bred. That was what humans called copulating. Getting bred. Her nipples ached. "Yes, can we breed now?" She stood and began slipping her clothes off.

"No! That's not what I meant." He hurried forward and grabbed her dress as it slipped off one shoulder, quickly putting it back in place. Damn, what did Doc give her? This was one hell of a side effect.

"You don't want to copulate?" Her forehead wrinkled, causing her to wince and raise her hand to the bump on her head. "Do you find that I'm not to your liking?"

"Yes, I like you."

"But you do not wish to . . ." She bit her bottom lip as if searching for the right words. "To have sex?"

His hand rested lightly on her shoulder as he met her gaze. "Of course I'd like to . . . uh . . ." He marveled at how soft the fabric felt. His fingers brushed her skin, thinking it felt just as soft. What would she taste like? His gaze moved to her lips. Soft . . . full lips. Kissable.

He jerked his hand away from her shoulder. Anyone watching would think he'd been burned . . . and maybe he had because he certainly felt hot.

He cleared his throat, his gaze not able to meet those innocent, sensuous turquoise eyes. He felt like such a heel. He'd invited her to his home and all he could think about was having hot sex.

Here's a look at Alison Kent's
THE PERFECT STRANGER.
Available now from Brava!

"You're not pregnant." The dress hung blade straight to her ankles, not an inch of rounded belly between shoulders and knees. Jack couldn't even think to move.

"Your shorts." She held out one hand.

"Uh-uh. No way. You drag me out here, posing as a pregnant woman, no, a pregnant *wife* needing my help, and you want me to give you my drawers? I don't think so. In fact, I'm outta here."

Jack started walking.

"You've been in the back of the cart three days, *Señor* Briggs."

Jack stopped walking.

"We followed a road that leaves no trail. I'm the only one who knows where you are, the only one who knows how to get you safely out of here. You give me the shorts or we both die."

She'd walked toward him as she talked. A step for every two or three words. She stood close enough that all he had to do was reach up and push the hood off her head to see her whole face.

The machete tip inches from his nose dissuaded him.

One day, lady. One day, Jack thought, stomping to the far side of the cart where he shimmied out of his shorts. She caught them, and Jack grimaced as they went up in flames.

He unrolled the canvas knapsack, shook out the paper-thin tunic and trousers and draped both over the edge of the cart. They looked as bad as his fatigues. Butt naked, he stifled his complaints and dressed.

The fit of the shirt left much to be desired. The frayed sleeves barely hung to his elbows. And she'd been right about the length. The hem only hit his waist.

He struggled into the pants; the legs ended a good six inches above his ankles. The flax chafed every part of his skin that wasn't already raw. Hands out in surrender, he walked around the end of the cart and headed toward the fire.

"You've got me. I'm who knows how many miles from who knows where. These clothes would scare away a scarecrow. And even if I were to try and walk out of here, I'd no doubt lose my toes to jungle rot.

"Don't you think it's about time you let me in on the conspiracy? It's not like I'm the father of your *baby.* In fact, I'm beginning to wonder whether or not I'm your husband."

Heedless of her blade, Jack grabbed her wrist and drew her close. "How about it, *Señora* Briggs? Married or not?"

"Yes, I'm married." Eyes burning bright, she jerked away and lifted the machete. The tip of the blade caught the tie at her throat and nicked open the ragged neckline. Grabbing both sides, she jerked and pulled. The hooded dress fell to her feet.

She kicked the pile of cloth away, then bent to scoop it up. Dropping the burlap squarely on the flames, she defiantly faced him down covered head to toe in a black habit and veil.

"But not to you."

Jesus H. Christ! He was married to a pregnant nun.

Wrong, Jack. You're not married, and she's not pregnant.

But she was a nun.

She was also china doll exquisite, a testosterone fantasy that sucker-punched Jack in his near empty gut. This woman had kidnapped him, taken ten years off his life with the wife and child routine, burned his clothes, refused him a bath and still he wanted to see her naked.

She was centerfold material, as close to perfect as a female got. Except for the tiny scar that bisected the arch of her right brow. And now that he looked closer, he wasn't too sure about her eyes.

It wasn't the exotic almond slant, or even the seductive get-me-drunk-Jack Daniels gold. No. It was the way she'd seen a lifetime of too much, the way she saw too much now. Those eyes scared him.

No soft-voiced china doll should be so tough, so world-weary, or so wise. She was all three. She was also a nun. And she was as Caucasian as he was.

Ignoring the machete she wielded like a sharp tongue, Jack glared down. "So, *Sister Señora* Briggs. Guess the marriage certificate was a fake."

She glared back, the fire in her eyes a one-hundred proof whiskey burn. "Yes. But it was necessary."

And now a peek at
SATISFACTION GUARANTEED
by Lucy Monroe.
Coming next month from Brava!

Beth was shaking with nerves by the time that Ethan buzzed her condo that night.

She'd told herself over and over again that this was not a real date. It was an opportunity to solidify their cover. Right. And the fact that they would be sitting across an intimate table for two should not be sending her libido into overdrive. She'd read somewhere that women were at the sexual peak in their thirties. Well, she was only twenty-nine and she'd been peaking for Ethan for almost two years.

Which meant it wasn't some kind of hormonal joke her body was playing on her. She wanted the man. So much that she'd stopped calling herself depraved and learned to deal with the urges. Only now she was faced with more temptation than she'd ever had where he was concerned. She didn't know if she could deal with *that*.

Darn him anyway for being the one man she was sure would not only not balk at her sexual fantasies, but who would know what to do with them.

She bit her lip as she took a final look in her full length mirror. She had not morphed into a cover model for *Vogue* in the last ten seconds, more was the pity. Because while she was sure Ethan would get her sexual fantasies, she was equally certain he would have no interest in sharing them. She was not his type.

At five-foot-six, she was at least three inches too short, a cup size too small in the curves department and several lovers shy of the experience a man like him was no doubt used to.

None of that had stopped her from trying on six different outfits, doing her makeup three times, and trying her hair four different ways before settling for a sloppy topknot with tendrils framing her face that went well with the simple black dress she'd settled on. It left a good portion of her legs and back bare . . . all in the effort to look as sexy as she could for him. For this non-date. Sheesh.

She needed to get a life.

The problem was that she didn't want a life . . . she wanted *him*. Every sexy, tantalizing, irresistible inch of his six-foot-three frame.

The buzzer went again and she jumped, grimacing. Showtime.

She rushed to release the entrance lock for downstairs. Ethan was knocking on her door less than a minute later.

She opened it, keeping the kittens back with one wary foot. "Hi."

"Hi, Sunshine. Is there a reason you're blocking the door?"

"The kittens." She scooted back, keeping the cats away from the opening as she widened it to let him in. "Come on in and I'll get my jacket."

Ethan moved swiftly, grabbing Beethoven as the black and white kitten tried to make a break for the hall and shutting the door immediately upon stepping inside her apartment.

"Thanks. They want to go exploring, but with my luck they'd end up at the manager's apartment. She's allergic to feline fur and was very dubious about letting me get the cats."

Ethan grinned. "I can imagine." He whistled as he looked around. "Nice place. Exotic."

That's what she'd been going for. She'd decorated with

Byzantine colors and rich textures like silks and velvets as well as faux fur throws on her sofa and chaise lounge. It fit her, but usually surprised people that did not know her well. Even some who did.

Ethan didn't look surprised, only intrigued.

She grabbed her vintage velvet dress coat from the back of the chair where she'd left it in preparation. "I'm ready to go, if you are."

"Dinner's not for another hour." He took the coat and laid it back over the chair.

Then he shrugged off his own leather jacket and put it on top of hers. And she let him. Without a protest. Weird. This man brought out more than one unexpected reaction in her. Even odder . . . she then just stood there staring at him and trying really hard to remember . . . *this was not a real date.*

But his dark sweater clung to his muscular chest in a mouth watering way. He looked so hot . . . in every way.

He cocked his brow at her and her stomach dipped. "Um . . . if not dinner yet, then what?"

"I thought we could have a drink and talk a while before we go." He looked around her living room again. "I want a chance to soak in who you are away from the office so I can relate to that person in front of Preston."

It sounded reasonable, but Ethan Crane was the last person she wanted to invite into her life on a more personal basis.